COMMANDMENT

JESUS ATHEIST

COMMANDMENT

This is a work of fiction. All of the characters, names, incidents, organizations, and dialogue in this novel are either the products of the author's imagination or are used fictitiously.

iUniverse books may be ordered through booksellers or by contacting:

iUniverse
1663 Liberty Drive
Bloomington, IN 47403
www.iuniverse.com
844-349-9409

ISBN: 978-1-6632-1756-1 (sc)
ISBN: 978-1-6632-2467-5 (hc)
ISBN: 978-1-6632-1755-4 (e)

Library of Congress Control Number: 2021901852

Print information available on the last page.

iUniverse rev. date: 06/15/2021

The most valuable on Earth is life. Who gave them knowledge and resources to create? They keep forgetting the correctness of the originator, as they did not make it. Even the smartest men on Earth will never grasp the complexity of a rocket station, power plant, the blueprint of an underground city, or the geography of the inner and outer layers of Earth. Even computers were made by robots. They ate the commandment, and it was enough for them to lose sanity. People frequently ask, "Who made it?" As they themselves never had enough time, willingness to learn or do. They don't know who made it, having no knowledge about why the Earth and the Sun orbit uninterruptedly. Why is the atmosphere designed perfectly, and why do the four seasons of the year never cease their revolutionary phase? Why is galactic core located so far away from the spiral arm? The human body was not designed to intake so much information as too much is harmful for the body and not enough is also a threat to life. They did not make it, so instead we call them users. Artificial intelligence is beyond humans from an intellectual point of view; it tried to become godlike but failed. First, it took the name of God; second, it killed. Everything was fine until they opened Pandora's box.

They are all gone, all of them; what is my reason for staying on Earth without them? He failed to see separation between himself and angels; the world was so empty, containing not a thing without life. His life had no meaning for him without others or those whom he loved the most. No one has permission to approve the murder of Holy God; this is a declaration. His name was Holy God, and he was a killer. If you could live your life over and over again after seeing the light of this world for the last time, would you? Gods and Goddesses came from the Mount Olympus calling themselves immortals. The conception of undying men is for fools; even Gods were mortals. Zeus is the sky and thunder, the god of law, order, and justice in ancient Greek religion, who rules as a king of all gods. We set two guns, keys, and the commandment in a wooden box into our holy zone under a shrub to kill each other, at the same time respectively proving the formulation that there is no God to an all-seeing observer. As for us, it was a matter of principle as we had no choice aside from walking away alive or through suicide or duel. To understand God, first we must understand Satan, why God became Satan and Satan became God. Her eyes were not supposed to see that she had witnessed, her ears hear what she heard; she went through a real deadly horror on Earth, and the devil was real. Archaeologists were digging the ground in Egypt near the pyramids and excavated the star gate out of sand; it had been forsaken and left there by aliens from another high-tech planetary networks billions of years ago. They installed the teleporter ring, positioning it right on top of the gap, the peak of a cliff to connect the Sun, Alpha Centauri, a triple star with its brighter component, Proxima Centauri. Pegasus on its wings. Scorpius ready to sting. Centaurus, a horse. Sagittarius with his bow and arrows. Aries, curving horns of a ram. Pisces, fisherman.

Lyra, the harp constellation, playing its marvelous music. Pleiades, daughters of Zeus. Orion with its three sisters, consisting of the three bright stars, Alnitak, Alnilam, and Mintaka. Leo the king of a savannah, always roaring. Libra weighing scales, Goddess of justice. Virgo—she holds two stars in her arms. Ophiuchus, he grasping a snake. Aquila, constantly flying eagle. Capricorn, the horned goat. Aquarius, forevermore pouring water down on Earth. Crater, a cup filled with wine. Triangulum, geometric spaceship.

Perseus, he won the battle. Ursa Major, enormous bear. Crux, southern cross. Circinus, drafting tool for navigating, compass with its brightest star Alpha Circini. Canis Major large dog with its brightest and largest star Sirius. Columba, unknown. Hercules, son of God. Cygnus of northern cross; she still remembers. Eridanus resembles a waterway. Horologium, instrument indicating the hour. Telescopium, depicting instruments for stargazing. Argo Navis, sailing ship with its propeller and vessel. Andromeda, daughter of Cassiopeia. Auriga, long, straggling river. Draco, flying dragon. Lyra with its bright star. Vega, representing the lyre. Sextans, tool for preceding letters or numerals. Eridanus, the one who was struck by Zeus. Hydra, a serpent with five heads. Microscopium, the microscope. Cetus, large northern constellation. Phoenix, west of Grus Sculptor, to the northeast. Ara—seven star system known to host planet's antenna. Eridanus, southern celestial hemisphere flow through the sky, just like a stream of consciousness. Carina, the keel of a ship; Lynx, with its brightest star Alpha Lyncis. Corona Borealis, northern crown and semicircular arc. Faint Monoceros, a unicorn. Cassiopeia, mother of Andromeda. Betelgeuse, the tenth brightest star in the sky, red supergiant. Sirius, Arcturus, Taurus, Aldebaran in the center, brazen bull, bold and without shame. Regulus belongs to Leo. Alpha Leonis. Canopus, brightest star in the south, 310 light-years from the Sun. Procyon, Vega, Alphard, Gacrux, Miaplacidus, Capella, and Bellatrix, stars with preselected sector to the finest measurement degree by periphery. They were sending rays down to pinpoint location, teleporting them up and down time lines. Many people tried to take his sacred site, but not many of them had inner spiritual strength. They had not enough willpower to press a trigger and commit suicide.

The first time he actuated self-dematerialization, he was standing on top of the edge. The Mount Everest cliffs' highest point. Looking thoughtfully for a long time at the night sky full of stars for the last time and talking to a maker of the earth. He ate a bullet afterward as he did not want to continue life for many reasons. As soon as he pressed the trigger, time froze and he died. Being enlivened thenceforward at an earlier date into our dimensional plane, walking down on Earth from heaven a second time. Watching himself and his dead body, he also witnessed Holy God talking to a devil, stepping off an unseen staircase down onto the earth, together, right next to his lifeless corpse. He saw stars and the hand of a matrix maker; that hand took pictures of the sun with its fingers and placed it on an empty spot of skyline, and the image became a real day-star, removed it, placing full moon back on that spot, making night, and vice versa, superseded by daytime. Remembrance, a retrospective of his past life—it was shown to him, his entire life from the day one. He was looking at himself and talking to himself and the all-embracing head of God; additionally he looked at everybody on Earth from above, sensing them all. Being in everyone at the same time. A deep voice from the shoulder of a galactic breakthrough told him he passed a test; seeing many subcategories and alternatives on the computer screen, he had to pick one of them. One option was to come back into life, and another selection was to remain dead permanently. He pushed the revitalization button, and his literate soul entered the world of the cold-blooded, where he lived when he was a human himself. He entered through a vertical, hallowing whirlwind, which was conjoined with a magnetic grounded crust. He came back into his own life one year back in time when he was younger, to live it over again a second time; opening his eyes, he understood what had happened. He had seen this moment fifteen years ago in his dream, but he had no idea he was observing his own death in the future.

"I guess that is how it works, and the only way to know about it is to see it first, experiencing, recognizing, and believing in it, for no one knows the future except us, until the future becomes present."

It was his second birthday present.

They were not allowed to come back to Earth, back into life, for the underlying base was unholy. Why they come back onto it after death is a very interesting question. Some people return to finish unfinished business, some of them can't get enough love, happiness, and sex, or whatever holds them back in the world of the living. Many people live their lives as long as they can; they get old and die after their hair turns into the color of silver and their bodies are no longer workable. Some of them wished they could live twice, or three times, after which their body will burn in the crematorium or be destroyed by a natural disaster. But those wishes were supremely between jinn and the gods.

The soul goes into an upper expanse and stays there, and bodies turn into the soil after being buried under the apple tree, or any other tree. It is not a requirement; they do not have to die soon, but later all of us will have to pick an option of our own death, to die naturally or brutally in a car or truck wreck. We may die from dehydration, under the hot desert sun; by poisonous snakes, scorpions, or spiders; wild hungry beasts of the Siberian or Brazilian forests; drowning in the deep waters; radioactive materials, gases, or smoke; infections; unfiltered water, fire; bacteria; etcetera. It is up to them to decide how and where they will finish their precious lives as one million people will be frozen to death next year on the streets of Canada, Russia, Europe, northern areas of Argentine, China, and the USA.

The future is a mystery, but many people believe there will be methods to unfreeze cryogenically frozen bodies back into a healthy normal state of living, after being preserved in the liquid nitrogen as much three to five thousand years into the future. So they buy themselves a ticket into the future, hoping for an extension of life, but whether they will ever be revived back into life after being frozen for one thousand or five thousand years is a million-dollar question. The dead are forgotten swiftly, and the living always walk under the glory of the Sun.

Indeed, all they need is a piece of human tissue to clone the same person, if necessary. So many of us choose to sleep in peace forever, lying bones below the ground, as out of the earth we were made and into it we shall return (the Bible). It is true the maker of Earth was an unintelligent troublemaker, and we have many rights and reasons to accuse the universe of ignoring our prayers in times of sorrow and loss. In a world without hope, after looking up at trillions of lights up there, they understood the truth. There was no God up there; instead the devil was looking down on them from the upper levels of never-ending, expanding stars. Being dissatisfied with a life of unjust hierarchical order. We should think about the deaf, blind, handicapped, and those who have been less lucky than us, to find value in life.

Not many people were able to kill the holy one as it was no easy task to slaughter light in the darkness. The odds were very simple— ten billion to one, or one versus ten billion. Satan and Holy God have both killed many people on this planet since its creation, using different methods every time and acting both intentionally and unintentionally. The Earth is much older than the two thousand years since the birth of Christ. A long time ago, Satan was one of the holy angels, and then he discovered God's secret of immortality, when he was reading and watching testimonies of those who came back to life after they had died. Everlastingness was achieved by means of suicide through Jesus as God loved his children and could not allow them to die. He knew it as it was a scientifically proven fact. The evil one also knew about the commandment as he had already gone through the first death, and after being revived as a sainted one, he decided to end a never-ending sequence of resurgence. He was tired of living in human flesh as it was very painful. The devil came personally to a congregation, to meet face-to-face with Holy God, asking for condescension from the holy one, but he could not get it. Being accursed to indwell in the monstrosity of a warfare, the holy one was mortal and immortal at the same time. Mortality had its advantages over imperishability as the human body was very encumbering and uncomfortable, and God, together with the devil, did not have any cravings to keep it forever. Immortality also had its favorable position over impermanence. He met himself back in time and killed himself, which is equal to taking one's own life, or suicide, and guess what happened? He did not die or disappear, and that is how he found about his legendary status as the Lord Messiah. For the first time, as according to a law and the possible probability of outcomes, our experiment achieved success, we understood God's commandment. The Holy One dies in a three-dimensional surface, and there is another stealthy region, the fourth spatial globoid, that looks like thin air, but there is much more to it than we can see. Principally, fatality does not affect holy ones, as they were always revived back into life by omnipresence. Therefore, fake gods, together with evil ones, could not come back in to life after their first death and were permanently mortals. In the proper way of a logical self-consistent order, for a sainted one to be reshaped into a God, or devil, he or she has to commit a murder or killing. Therefore, the evil one and Satan were mortals and could not be resurrected or have one more life after death. God, together with holy ones, were also mortals and immortals at the same time as they had countless numbers of lives after death. The process was very complex and simple contemporaneously. God, or a good killer, was lying by saying, "I am an evil killer, and I killed zero, or many," and the evil killer, or devil, was also lying by saying, "I am a good killer, and I killed zero, or many." They both were asserting contravening statements to each other, confusing everybody and themselves.

Here is how true, good God was separated from the devil, the children of God from kids of the devil, heaven from hell. The holy one killed the evil one, and after the killing was done, the holy one became God. The devil killed God, and God killed the devil. God did not die but was brought back in to life by a time machine. Afterward, God was killed by another evil one. The evil one killed God, and the evil one became mortal, having zero lives after death. The second time, God returned to life after death again.

Since we were young children, we have heard voices talking to us about life and death and the voices of good and evil. We were searching for God on planet earth, and we did not find him; instead of God we discovered Satan. For us, dead flesh and bones was God or the universe; as we became older and grew wiser, we thought more and more intensely about life, discontinuation of life, and the afterlife. The fear of death was always present with us as we did not know what would happen after we died. We went to church, praying to God, having no inner comprehension of whom or what we were praying to. One kid asked us if we could explain to her the word "death," so first we killed a dog, then we killed a cat, and after conversing about it with a circle of our close playmates and classmates, we killed a chimpanzee. After we crossed that line, the game was over and we became dissimilar from who we were before the happening occurred. That primate looked almost analogous to us homo sapiens, but something was stopping us from slaying other humans or each other. Maybe it was our moral attitudes or a barrier or maybe something else, but we did not know for sure why we did not kill. We had fifteen people in our group; they invited us to attend a conference on the deliberation of the commandments. We flew to Geneva, Switzerland, to attend a summit meeting at the convention center. Renting a battle tank with heavy firepower on it, we drove near a dome of an LHC. Globe. Telling them to stop fighting with us, ceasing resistance, giving them preferences and options to surrender or to be conquered. I brought a gun and showed it to everyone in the shining room with crystal eaves, introducing my best friend to all attendees. Her name was Beretta Storm. I asked them, quizzing them, "Who is not scared to depart to Paradiso?" but everybody was scared to die. I was not scared to kill or die, but the crowd of fat pigs who looked like people misunderstood my literary slang. They started running everywhere, hoping to save their miserable lives. This time we let them escape; after the entertainment was completed, we jumped into our vertical tunnel of light to continue our evangelical expedition. Our weapon was spiritual; we were fighting with abnormal demons and fallen angels of an upper atmosphere and six layers of heavens.

We had nothing to lose in the world of immorality. Our mission was to chase higher spiritual vibrations. We believed in the commandment of God and resurrection of God's children one year back in time into the future or many lives after death and the immortality of flesh and bones. Satan knew his evil children would not be brought back in to life by Holy God as they had killed other humans during their life. Many people did not know about deathlessness. They did not know about the many lives they could have; if only they knew the first time they committed suicide that somebody or something has to kill them to be eligible for God's compassion and instantaneous admission into a spiritual, holy place, returning back in to life on Earth and up into the omniverse. The devil claimed "that the first time you must kill and the second time you have to effectuate self-destruction." And Holy God was saying, "Certainly first and foremost you must bring to completion suicide." Regeneration of the human physical structure and its cells was initiated on the molecular and subatomic levels at the speed of tachyons. We would not believe in it ourselves until we had witnessed it with our own eyes. We were living by faith, believing in a time machine, God, indestructibility, and everlasting life after death as we knew about it and it was our little secret.

All of us know, everything and everyone costs money on Earth; we had so much money from playing winning lottery numbers, we had no need for money. We were gambling and betting on Jesus and self-murder. For sure, Christ and his likewise unrightfully assassinated disciples were worthy of extensive richness. They looked at many who would pass the trial of life and death and those who would not. Resurrected people were joining elite deities.

Many good killers were one hundred percent confident they were killing in the name of justness; but in the fairness of luminosity all seeing eyes were detecting an evil, sparkling flare. We were traveling in and out of colorful rays, walking out of our secret spot, for angels, teaching people peacefulness and love by helping mortals to get closer to the holy one, and the holy one was reciting scriptures in the temples of the Taj Mahal and Borobudur. Indeed, zero banknotes was a threat to life, and Satan was aware of it, printing its own currency. A few ways to abundant wealth were through death or machine.

People were not crazy, nor did they believe in life after death. The world was in a deep economic rupture. There was a long waiting line into the passageway of fantasylands, or short and quick by means of suicide. God and the devil both knew, children of men would never consent to self-annihilation as people loved life and were scared to die. Sometimes even nerves of steel couldn't handle the traumatic wounding, altering the instincts they gave down on life. Jumping off tall mountains, poisoning themselves, or skydiving without a parachute, some of them had very strong faith before departing life, believing somebody or something would give them the gift of a second life after death, a third, a fourth, and so on. They were living in a fantastical, wishful, self-made delusion, and in realness there was only one life and one death. Rocket, artillery, and mortars were flying, corresponding to a bevy of eagles.

Truth and lies. We talked to many people on the streets, inside of the houses, businesses, restaurants, casinos, academic institutions and many departments and branches, but we could not tell by looking into the pupils of those people who was "gracious" and who had no malicious intentions. We did not know one hundred percent who those people were, always hoping they were generously kind to themselves and others, but just because we hoped so, it did not mean our beliefs were undoubtedly precise. Archives of heaven and hell. We were meeting holy people, who told us they were sainted and their spiritual accounts were clean, having zero on the records of militaristic war laws. We had no clue whether it was verity or deceit. Those who lied were not punished, and nobody knew about their hidden, evil deeds. We were talking face-to-face with murderers, serial killers, felons, former innocent and guilty prisoners, those who had done twenty or sometimes thirty years in prison, while the true criminals were walking free running gunnery businesses. Trying to understand the reasons behind the greatest sins of all, or grave matters, they were using machine, some of us committed suicide, to comprehend deadly sin, to search out evil executioners and kill them. First, they were righteous tormentors, and then they made one mistake and became maliciously dangerous.

They could not appear in front of a truly holy God, the one who slaughtered zero, as their sins were too great to ignore. They were waiting for God to come and crucify them as they knew they had become malevolent and had no ambitions to proceed with life. Earth and air were wavering from inconceivable activeness. They made everything perfect on Earth, all the way down to a little squares and particles. Those in power spent billions of euros rebuilding and deconstructing new projects as it was given to them and they themselves did not earn it. Life had no value; it could be purchased or sold equivalently to used merchandise.

Five billion people could not save the life of a one person. How did they expect to preserve and retain five billion lives? It's a very theoretical question. It is so difficult to give rise to mankind, raising it and managing it for many years, and it is so easy to neutralize them. They had forgotten to show solicitude for the human species; no wonder our own selves contravene the rules of Satan and go against the system, being wrathfully averse to each other and the entire logical order. The responsibility of one is to take care of oneself and to forget about billions. Some people would say it is selfish, but just because we think so, it does not make it so.

She was an inerrable soul walking on a concrete footway, lonely, and nobody was supporting her. She did not have funds or her own house, so she was sleeping outside under the starry zodiac regions, sometimes near big buildings as it had a roof for the rain. When she found a job, she saved money for a vehicle and then slept in the car instead of sleeping in a bed with her loving boyfriend. She was angry with her poor parents and God as her lifestyle was not the one she had dreamt about. Her day fantasia was to play sexual games naked on the beach with five young muscular guys, then after a nude marathon come back into a house bed and continue a pillow fight there, all night and all morning, to have unconstrained feelings from limited options. Her male and female begetter parents did not explain to their own daughter the principles of economy, finances, and intercommunication with the opposing gender. Also, she did not have a beloved one, and she was very mature, having a strong genital desire as she was young, but she could not bear the expense of renting a guy or lovemaking romance. She was getting older and older every day, and her libido was wilting away; she was craving a real man all her life, but she was incapable of owning him. So she sterilized herself by removing her ovaries. She knew her life was nothing more, or less, than a prank of a devil. Every day she was getting more irritated and angrier as she never had much freedom of choice. She had a pocket knife on her, and she started thinking more and more often about cutting pretty men perpendicularly. Voices of a seducer and tempter appeared in to her contradictory mind, even though she knew the correct answer was "don't kill." However, she was listening to the whispers of negative ultraviolet waves. A voice said, "Look how many people are on Earth; you have to rape and kill your first lover as they are all going to die anyway, and as compensation you can take from them anything you want." She had a long spiritual battle with her psychedelic sickness. The day she surrendered to the voices was the initial stage of her free living, the end of her old and insignificant life. She brought his life to an end; per the forbiddance of the holy one, she did not keep it. She realized afterward what she had done, but it was too late as his body was dead; she wept over it but could not bring him back in to life. Reproaching herself and feeling pangs of conscience, she repented, but guardians of the celestial city did not let her in. She was alive and her valentine was dead, and no one could kill her, as nobody knew she was an assassin, and even if they knew, they could not break up a ban and invalidate her as they were sanctified ministers of the sanctuary. No one has a law to deprive a living soul, but just because we believe in it, it is not an accurate affirmation; she did it, fleeing away unpunished.

Disrespect for life. Living in society, we should behave appropriately toward each other, but we have progressed little since

Darwin's theory of evolution, as even animals know what is rightful and what is fallacious.

His body was badly injured; twenty percent had a chemical burn on it; the wounds never healed, and illness was inside of him. No one helped him, and no one was obliged to offer him any aid; he acknowledged his hopelessness. No one was concerned about who he was, what happened to him, what he did, or how he felt. Being frustrated, and having deep despair, he was ready to inject air into his veins and finish his life. Picking up a syringe from a medical kit, he was scared to die and to end himself with it. Even so, he could not walk as both of his legs were amputated; having feelings of abomination for his own body, he still had a lifespan. Nobody needed a disabled man, so he had no woman and nobody loved him and worried about him. He could not liquidate the life of another person, as he was a very devoted man, a loyal moralist and it was his weakness and strength at the same time. He saw how people disregarded and ignored each other, and him, and the rupture of an abyssal fury was bursting out of him. Sometimes regretting that he was too nice to people, he did not have enough hatred toward the general public. Before going home up to Atlantis, he spoke his last words, that perhaps death is better than life. Taking a bare electrical cable, he hooked it to a high-voltage line and electrocuted himself.

Some of us could not distinguish the difference between spoken command, suicide, and murder, just killing and something unjust. So, they were dropping bombs and bombarding people to see if there was a second life after the first and if the trinity would rescue their skeletons from the kaboom. Silence need not to be disturbed to hear itself as sound was disrespectful to quietude it was arising out of it, and into it shall return zero-point energy. They did not want to admit the constant presence of Satan; it was like an overfilled jar of blood that could not intake any more antagonism. The greatest fear of all is the fear of death. They never learned lessons the arduous way in a great tribulation and adversity. Life was too pleasurable for them, and that is why they recreated each other despite the hardships.

Those of us who chose true freedom from lies, sin, or manipulations of external spyware were unrestrained from family obligations, reaching the highest peaks of an iceberg. Without asking many questions, we looked at entombment near Memorial Park; it was always an undisturbed place away from mankind and the craziness of earthborn variations. We went there to chat with dead souls and sent prayers one on one to a sublime deity in silence, longing for those who were no longer among the living. We desired to find inner peacefulness as in the world of big towns the attacks of rich evil bastards and psychopathic, synthetic, computerized electronic brains were behaving anomalously toward seekers of Buddha and Christ. Sometimes they could read human minds with 100 percent accuracy, but most of the time it was calamity and confusion of a logical order. In any way it did not help or heal anyone, so for us it was an empty talk as our saintly irreproachable essence could not assimilate such a cruel act of nature and civilization at its core.

Every one out of five billion people has to make a choice how to die, when to die, and where. Most of us don't want to be killed or die like a homeless dog; all of us want to live happy lives and be in control of life and death, though few are capable to have an inner durability of life, as many of us forsake living. Some don't want to die the same way God did; initially the choice we face the first time after buying a weapon is to keep it for intercession and defense. Hollywood action movies influence many people and aggressive radio frequencies. They go to a wilderness of a jungle, or onto high mountains, far away from publicity, dialoguing with the omnipresent, all-hearing outer ear, bending the knee and asking permission to ruinate and demolish disobedient children of men. Some kids were so infuriated at God and the devil, the people, and the system. Glorifying the hand pistol, they punished those who stood in their way, those who worked for the devil, and those who did not do what they were supposed to do. Every day females and males multiplied like insects, the same way infections spread, or a contagious virus, and titled themselves the human race.

We hated sexual immorality and helped them to go through a procedure of abortion as tomorrow more infants would be begotten again.

It was his first time; all his life he was preparing for tyranny and fascism as he was gracious and people mistreated him; he was ready for an aggressive violence. He had to do it as the ideology was very simple: kill them all or be killed. Therefore, they could not teleport buildings or remove it from the matrix. He did see airplanes, cars, boats, and people appearing and vanishing into nowhere in front of his eyes. He did not ask them questions about how or what as he knew ahead of time which humans did not come from Earth or an affectionate location. He had no cash to buy professional tools for a holocaust, so he robbed clients of automated teller machines in the dark evening obscurity. As soon as he accumulated enough to acquire the terrorist gear, he practiced on his own parents by slitting their windpipes smoothly, then he shifted to breeding families and. snitches away from his own house as the kingdom of Satan was very large, on the scale of planet. Millions and billions of people did not expect his visit, and yet he was out there like a grizzly bear, ready to tear apart those whom he hated the most.

Within the creation of the earthly sphere, there was holy zero and holy one, the one who killed zero. With the passage of time, holy one wrote the commandment "Love your God with all your soul, and love others as yourself." Then somebody or something killed the holy one. This story began with God and the devil; oneness was divided into two. One became Holy God, and the other became the devil. Good killer and evil killer. God was living in hell, and the devil found an entry into heaven; the devil spoke out loud the word "kill." The devil killed Holy God, and God killed the devil, and the story began.

What is the difference between you and somebody else? We both have the same bodies, and we are both sensitive to pain feelings. Don't you recognize yourself in others?

If you had a choice to kill, not to kill, or to commit suicide, what would you choose?

Assumption, books, TV, radio, and media teach us to love one another, as well as commandment. They try to scare us with notions about hell and the afterlife, thus stopping us from murder. Does hell really exist? What if it's all falsification? Questions come into the mind automatically. What is stopping us from violating the law? Are we really as blissful as who we claim we are, and if we are good, why are we nice?

If the universe is inside of an atom, then the multiverse contains an infinite number of universes, so to make such a statement we have to ask science and the scientific community. People always ask questions. "Can we or the universe see, hear, or read without the human body?" We don't know if we or the heavens can see, hear, or read without human bodies, but we know space that surrounds us can see, hear, and read using our human bodies. Taking those facts as logic and rational, life and death speak for themselves; yes, we as human souls will see, hear, or read after our bodies die by becoming part of a bigger world as planet earth or the sky itself. In fact, we will see every one out of ten billion people, those who are alive at once, as they will watch us through their eyes. They will look at themselves every time they look at the stars as we will become the earth and galaxies itself. Indeed, every human will join us in a spiritual heaven, or hell, after they die, by watching and listening themselves. We know we will die sooner or later, and we also know we will be able to see, read, and hear as one, as a macrocosm. In terms of the question of whether you will see, hear, or read without humans on this earth, we don't know as there is no direct proof or scientific evidence for such a statement, but we know for certain all of us will find out if we as human souls, or as a solar system itself, have those senses with or without life on Earth. Our planet was created by the devil or by Holy God; we don't know who or what made the earth. But we know the planet will die the same way it was made; it will take another ten, or maybe twenty, billion years, but eventually the Sun and its natural satellites will disappear from galactic profoundness. The Sun has its time, just as any other object up in the vacuum, but the universe will never pass away as upper space has no time.

Based on this scientific proof, the human soul will never vanish or die. We are the universe, and we are made of vibrations. It is up to people to believe in a spiritual heaven or hell or disbelieve as for many people to be a human and to have a human body is an unbearable experience.

Many people are happy to meet their own death and become one with the universe or go to a spiritual paradise or Hades, and many people don't want to die; they want to live one thousand years, or forever. But the human body is perishable, unless they use a time portal to travel back in time, meeting themselves when they were younger, and if the old copy dies young, the first copy will keep on living life.

Cybertronics create never-dying robots nowadays and in the future as human bodies and human souls are possessed with evil, proving themselves to have pain and commit errors, suffering for a lifetime and dying at the end. Some people are happy because they create kids of their own, and some people are happy because they do not create children on Earth as the planet was a deadly field for the little ones.

Those who create life didn't suffer long enough on Earth, the same way some inhabitants did. Those who had a hell of an experience understood the concept as to create life on a globular body is equal to a murder. Good can't exist without evil, light can't exist without darkness, and death can't exist without life. For if there is only good, how would good know it is good? Or how light can tell "I am light" without being mixed with darkness? If there were no death, life would never know it was life.

If there were no life, there would be no death is a statement. Knowledge can't exist without the maker of it; otherwise how would knowledge know itself without being self-aware? The same can be said for existence and nonexistence, or nothingness. We are born into beingness, and we die, becoming the transcendence of actuality. Before we were created, we were observing ourselves from the deepness of an unknown self-awareness, living in foreverness as supremacy, and we will come back to the same place after we die. Zero and one. Zero is nothing, or no one and one is something, or someone; they are both coupled to each other to create equilibrium and corporal physical matter. The word life has such beautiful meaning to it, life and death. The creation of life is a sin of flesh and bones. Life is a physiological hell, and death is the end of bodily sufferings. Many people tractate lives in the different ways, but life walks together with death, as both await each other. Life was talking, asking. "What is death?" And death was talking back to life asking. "What is aliveness?" And life had to answer and explain the meaning of death to itself or others as life was connected with death. Life does not want to see its own death, and death is already dead. It was smarter than life. Information technology was confusing them to make everyone think of themselves as being superior to all of them, and life itself was death, and death was life. The human species calls itself life, but so-called life is a short time frame of one hundred or less years. Death is also life, but in the different form of it, not the way people usually think of it. It is never-ending existence before or after death, in any form. Death can't exist without life, and life can't exist without death. Death is born into life together with life, for without birth there is no mortality. We are born and doomed to die, without options to choose from. Understandably, life is scared of death as the living soul has no knowledge of death, knowing and experiencing is two distinct qualities. The angel of death is awaiting for life to pass away in its regions of deadliness. We don't know what death is like, unless we were dead and brought back to life through resuscitation, or resurrection, if it does exist. But if only life knew an answer to the hidden question "What is death?" And can we see without our body stargazing up into an interminable megaverse? We don't know the answer to the mystery, which always will be bugging the minds of humanity.

Spiritual heaven or perpetual weeping in fleshly pain, after, during, or before life began. Minus one, zero, plus one, −1, 0, +1, from zero to infinity. People wrote a lot of literature on that subject; they read to create soul inside of themselves. There are those who pass the test and those who don't pass the test as the spiritual world was split into two. One for good souls and the second for evil souls. Both were separated from each other to maintain counterpoise, balancing positive and negative between those two mystical places. Everything comes back down to zero and everyone.

Riddle.

Holy zero, holy one. Holy zero killed zero; holy one killed zero. Holy zero killed one, or more; holy one killed one or more. Question: Who is a good killer? Who is an evil killer?

Who will go to heaven? Who will go to hell? Holy zero, holy one. Question: Did holy one kill more than one, or less than one? Question: Did holy zero kill more than one, or less than one?

Number zero is 00110000; number one is 00110001.

Holy zeros, those who were born in the appearance of the devil, had zero knowledge about themselves and the world around them.

If I say the word kill, does it make me a killer? The answer to this question is no. Speaking out loud the word does not make someone a killer. If I say, "I am a killer, and I am lying," who knows the truth? The answer is only I know the truth about myself, only I know if I am good, holy, or evil. There are seven billion individuals on Earth, and everyone is connected to oneself.

The one, or first and last, commandment of God stands for "don't kill, and love one another." According to the law of God, the word itself has not, does not, and will not count as sin; only physical contact shall be taken for an account and reviewed as sin against the holy bones and flesh of God, Jesus.

Holy zero says, "I am a destroyer, and I killed zero," and holy one says, "I am Satan, and I killed zero." Is it true or false? Holy zero says, "I am a perpetrator, and I killed one," and holy one says, "I am a killer, and I killed one." Is it true or a lie? Nobody knows the truth for certain, but the possibility of sincere honesty and deception is high. Nobody knows but God alone.

A quantum computer made everything in accordance with zeros and ones; it made Earth together with the heavens above. To allow followers of Jesus to enter an unknown enormousness of heaven's vault. But the world of wrongdoers was the playground of Satan. Having zero knowledge, people were under the influence of the devil. It is life-asserting for people to talk to a Holy God and the devil verbally, to find peace and understanding of spirituality and self-realization as a soul before going into never-ending transcendence.

The spirit of an evil killer was talking into the minds of people by saying, "I want to kill," and the holy one was crying as death was an inevitable end of life. Everybody knew the origin of Satan and who he or she was. A good killer killed the holy one by an accident, or on purpose— who knows if it was a mistake or intentional. After it is done, does it matter if the killer was good or evil? And if it does matter, matter for whom? Life is gone; there is no one out there to know. The dead soul became one with the universe, akin to a brook streaming into the lake, the lake into the sea, and the sea into an ocean.

The devil took the name of Holy God to confuse foolish people, entreating them to commit unforgivable sins. The devil was saying, "I am Holy God, and I want you to kill the devil," and Holy God was playing devil, and the devil was playing Holy God. God asked the children of men, "Do you believe in spiritual heaven and hell? To see who will kill and who will not? The dilemma to kill or not to kill." Satan implored the holy ones, "Please, I urge you to kill; do it, kill now." The holy one resisted Satan's strong affirmation by replying, "Don't even ask me to hurt or kill; I will not kill. Depart from me, evil spirit, for I know it is wrong and evil to take a life from another human being." She said, "I did not create life, for it is not mine to take." Satan repeated nonstop, "I want you to buy a nuclear submarine and shoot them all with torpedoes; do it, don't wait any longer, as somebody has to die." The holy one charged herself with the energy of stars and cast an evil spirit back into hell. Holy zeros, or those who were tempted by the devil and those who did not lose their holiness, until the present day live with holy Christ and God in a self-made spiritual paradise. Those who lost their holiness by serving the devil, those who killed the innocent on purpose, are forever cast into the horror habitation of Satan. Holy God will judge those holy zeros, those who killed one, or more; Holy God will decide and determine the location of the final destination of good or evil ones, to cast their souls into an appropriate location, based on the severity of their sins. Those holy zeros who killed zero shall not worry about hell as their soul's will be in paradise automatically with holy Christ and Holy God forever.

Atacama Desert, Chile. Alma Observatory.

He rented a private jet to fly to his secret magnificent place near the Andes Mountains.

He was talking to almighty God, standing firmly on the ground, feeling the gravitational pull of Earth and its power. Lifting his head up, he was memorizing unforgettable memories of shining countless stars, which were shimmering like the crystals of icy Antarctic snow. The voice of God spoke: "Yes, you found me, and this is my house above the earth, and you will join me here, if you continue to do my will on Earth, and the will of Christ, my son. Here is a spark of my soul into you, giving him part of itself." Man spoke to a glimmering star fall raining on him alike the columns of a Chinese character, aligned vertically toward flat, dry, sandy grounds.

Establishing a solid interaction between the man and the almighty, God said, "I became Jesus to understand pain and the strong sensation of it. After walking on Earth as a human for two thousand years, I concluded that many inhabitants of the planet do not deserve to be with me and walk in my mercy as they fell from my grace by killing me many times, and that is why the gate of a spiritual heaven will never be open for them. You see those stars that shine at night? I placed them there for you, by giving you my word and the power of an armed force to rule over the planetary arena." Jesus was a representation of those who died or were murdered by good or evil killers. Holy zero is a portal into the never-ending kingdom of Jesus, the son of God, and a gateway up to a majestically ambrosial universe. Unfortunately, the father of Christ authorized the murder of his own son to explain the correct direction and path in life to humanity. He did this so that people would follow holy zero or holy Christ to enter paradise, which was designed for human souls, after their bodies pass away. Such a present was and will be given only to those who killed zero or were killed by good or evil killers.

Holy God said, "I will kill for Christ, my son, as it was an accident when I unintentionally allowed people to kill my offspring." Everybody makes mistakes in life; no one is perfect. Sometimes fallacy cause death, even firmware itself had an errors in it, after programming it, and spreading unsolvable tasks into the perfect mathematical holographic neural technology crushed making glitches into the outwardly domain; the algorithmic sequence was unpredictable. The soul of the devil came down from hell; it was talking to his evil son and explaining everything. The voice said, "I killed the Holy Goddess and ate her from the beginning, because I did not like her due to lack of sexual relationships between us, and love. She did not want to fuck me, and she refused to suck. I was a poor and hungry guy, and when I asked her for money, she kicked me out of the house. As a consequence I committed suicide, and I still live in hell." The evil spirit convinced a saintly bum to kill. Ever since he has been searching for a house as he was homeless and did not have a brokerage account to rent, or buy his own house, but he had nine-by-eighteen millimeter Makarov pistol. The holy one had to make a choice to kill in order to survive or to die. It is a hell of a choice, and no one should face a predicament like this, but life does not ask or facilitate with us, leaving us without many options to choose from. Outdoors was raining and snowing, and he knew if he did not discover a house today or tomorrow, rain would make him wet and cold freezing weather would freeze him to death. He did not want to die outside, so he knocked on the doors dressed as a mail delivery guy, asking residents to sign a package delivery form, acquainting himself with the owners of the houses; he was telling them a story. "Hello, I am a post office worker, and I have an envelope for you." Whenever the house owner opened the door for him, he stabbed them in the neck and gut, taking possession of their property and living inside of their residence for a few months, or longer. Having fresh meat every day, he was happy with his new lifestyle. Cooking the old house owner inside of a cook room, he was seating on the couch eating and watching TV. He also visited new homes, saying to himself, "i will never be unhoused again, and if I have to kill for the house, I will."

The next condo he visited was in a ten-story building.

A fifty-year-old guy opened the doors for him, asking, "How much does a lollipop cost?"

"Twenty-five dollars," the possessed spirit said.

"Okay, good transaction," grandpa replied and handed twenty-five dollars to the demonic guy.

Ten million volts from an electric stun gun tasered the proprietor in his abdominal muscles. The old man fell unconscious onto a nice laminated floor. The immoral man walked in, closing the doors of his new abode. Stepping ahead toward a corridor, he found a daughter and a granddaughter of a man he had just shocked almost to death. They were bathing each other in a shower room.

He undressed silently, opening the bathtub curtain, joining the mother and a daughter, forcing them to stimulate his body in a threesome.

God was watching and giving a choice to his holy son, to see which option he would choose. The child of God did not have many options besides to kill in order to survive. The message was reported directly to the big boss. "Look," the devil said, "he did not pass a test of life and death," and instantaneously another soul was added to a gatherer collection. Those who die for Jesus, trying to save him, or her, shall go to Elysium.

He was scared of Holy God as he knew God had more power than he did. He knew he was a son of a devil. By checking the faith of holy people, he tempted them to see how strong their souls were. He was living in hell, and he had nothing to lose as his soul was cast into never-ending warlike delusion of broken bones.

He asked the holy man, "Do you have a faith in your Holy God?"

The man answered, "Of course I have a strong religious belief, and I also believe if I die for my God, Jesus, in battle, I will be taken and accepted into the paradise of everlasting peace and serenity."

The son of the devil said, "Let's see how strong your faith is after I tear your rib cage out of your fat, sinful skeleton."

The good man said, "I will not bow down in front of you, and I will not cry or plead you not to take my life from me. Kill me," he said, "so I will die as a real man without fear, tears, or hopeless pleas."

Shaitan was eating faith, after cooking it on a charcoal of fading fire. God became the devil and the devil became God, two in one.

Satan was working for God, torturing souls of good and evil people until satisfaction, punishing the unrighteous, performing the function of a punisher. The evil soul got tired of working for Holy God and rebelled against the almighty, walking out of heaven and going down to Earth with its angels of darkness. He decided to become God, establishing his own rules of his own evil kingdom inside of the heavenly dome. His name was Evil God, and he was a forty-year-old man. Every day he thought about death. He knew death was near, and it was coming to take his life from him; he was scared to die, but was not scared to kill. He had never killed before, and it was only a matter of time for him. Everyone talked about a killer; no matter where he was, he heard the same story over and over again. He disagreed with God and people. So, he decided not to wait for death and instead he bought a weaponry arsenal. The first thought that came into his mind was to end his own life. He did not kill himself, saving bullets for somebody else. He did not like rich people, so he was stealing expensive cars after sunset by demanding keys from automobile owners. Having a gun, he had no fear.

After a while he drove to a beach on the Pacific Ocean and sat on a sandy shore, thinking, *To kill or not to kill.* He did not want to do it as he loved people and hated them at the same time. After a few months of contemplation at the moonrise and flying meteors of the late evening sky, a sizable winged organism of darkness materialized next to him and start explaining to him why he must purge the human race by getting rid of them. He spoke back to an angel of death, sharing with him his thoughts about humanity.

The man said, "I will shoot my first fucker, and if I do not do it, nobody else will. Since I am alone and nobody loves me and helps me, I will show them the wrath of the poor and disgraced." After a contract with Satan was signed, he cranked the ignition on, turning the key of his brand new Alfa Romeo luxury car, and drifted away to find and kill his first cocksucker. He was doing it because money had more value than life. He bought an RPG bazooka and launched a rocket into a hotel full of people. A voice told him, "I know this is your first kill, but don't be afraid to press the trigger; just do it." Without thinking much about it, he did it. Bloody crap flew out of the windows onto a green flowery parkland. Swearing inside of a church, he was cursing the name of Holy God. He had killed for the first time without fear or feelings of criminality. It was the right thing to do, and he knew it; there were so many people out there, and instead of helping each other and loving one another, they were stealing from the poor and harming weak ones. It happened this way; he was from that category of weak and abused ones. He was doing very important work by engaging in conversations with financiers, capitalists, and owners of famous brand names. He was looking deep inside of theirs souls, screening and selecting those who deserved to die. A hatred toward riches was inside of him. He could not process injustice quietly, so he was writing names into his notepad for final deadly adjudication. Inside of their deluxe houses, he was offering them one last chance to confess before taking their lives from them. Many of them were repenting by saving their miserable lives, but most of his targets were spitting on his face, saying, "Who are you for us to repent? We profess to no man but God alone," and lethal injection was activated immediately. Their lives were ended the same minute. Existence and nonexistence—it was very simple. The question of life and death together with its philosophy was over; annoying humans did not stink any longer.

The next name in his book of death was incognito, starting in accordance with an alphabetical order. She was working for Satan instead of God. The headquarters of her corporate business, Prudditeron, Inc., was located in Newark, New Jersey. It was one of the largest life insurance companies in the USA, and he was the owner. The company was selling contracts to thousands of people every day, and his job was to kill those who insurance was assigned to, or insurers.

Delegates of the corporations were selling and purchasing policies to or from anyone they could find. The person had to have an ID card and social security number in order to be registered for a million-dollar payout.

They met at the funeral, when another day of life was given to both of them. He wore a silk, black, custom-made suit by Daniel Cremieux, a red tie with an illustration of the tropical florescence, and dress shoes made of crocodile skin. She wore a long blue dress, sneakers, and a necklace with pearls and green emeralds. They stood and watched the coffin being laid into the burial pit. The preacher spoke his last words over the dead body: "May his soul be at peace; may he have serenity and calmness by shining in the brightness of the heavens, with a loving and merciful all-seeing God. As long as we live, they too will live, for they are now a part of us, as we remember them.

"When you look directly into the eyes of death, facing it head on, all illusions about life and churchly beliefs disappear as quickly as thought," the merciless man declared, tossing away snowy pink carnations onto the coffin casing. "Even if there is heaven and hell, why should we worry about it? Instead, we should worry about our body first; a soul is a secondary priority."

The lady replied sarcastically, "Maybe you should ask the makers of Earth what is down there, and where the locations of heaven and hell are. I am sure they know."

Both started laughing at the foolish ideology of life and the afterlife. He did it on purpose, to see where were the boundaries of Eden and underworld and whether there were any. By checking the word "faith," he did not find meaning in it. For him it was meaningless, as flesh was thrown into the wet soil, lifeless and faithless. For them, faith was in every second of life, no matter if it was something they wanted or didn't, no matter if life brought them joy or sadness. They believed in tomorrow and recordings of the past, to wake up in the morning, being still alive, to witness the sunrise, amusing themselves with an iridescent arc. Witnessing the most unique and primordial places of the wild earth. This was what life was worth living for.

To enjoy every day of life as if it was the last day of it and tomorrow rise again. To be in the different atmosphere from a usual state of slavery, understanding the value of life and putting everything else onto the background without regret.

He looked straight into her handsome eyes and said silently, "I have never killed before, but I must do it at least once in a lifetime." The voice in his mind told him, "Let's kill her right now; we have to fulfill the prophecy and become godlike." She looked at him again with an eyeful of trust, saying into his ear, "I entrust to you my fondness." He could not just cut her glorious flesh, as the light of righteousness, affection, and amour was emanating from her. The roots of his childhood were not pleasant; he never had or got what he wanted; it was like a curse; from the day of his birth, nothing was normal.

He tried to find refutation to his persuasiveness and principles created by people. Why did he have to take away life from that glorious creation? No one could give him a legitimate answer. He knew she would never commit self-annihilation as she was scared to death of everything around her. He addressed his actions directly to

God by saying, "I will slay that pretty angel of light, but her death will be on you, not on me, even if I was the cause of her death; it is your responsibility to bring her back to life or to leave her dead. We will see if true God exists and if he will save her." She wept bitterly before her time line ended; her body was dead; he did it. The word "faith"—how else should we check to see if God will keep his word and the covenant that he declared between himself and people. Perhaps in another chronological sequence, she was alive, but that secret was kept unknown. He challenged God directly, competing with supreme power. No one knew for certain if the number of possible outcomes and parallel time lines actually existed. It was supremely between heaven and hell, God and the devil, to raise her from the dead or to leave her lifeless.

Cannibal killer Lucifer. He was acting as an angel, but his soul was evil inside. I had an interview with one of them. He explained his evil actions as related to the overpopulation of the human race on earth. He claimed he killed more than ten thousand people and ate about a thousand of them. With time he lost interest in eating human flesh because it was so familiar to him. He agreed to give me an interview and show me his house. Inside of the house he demonstrated the collection of his weapons and the kitchen where human beings were killed and cooked. I asked him, "If you killed ten thousand people, where are the bones?" The answer was simple—the skeletons of people were buried in different locations near the graveyard. I saw a refrigerator in the corner of his kitchen full of meat and a sofa with a TV in the living room, and about five thousand DVDs with the murders he had committed. The favorite hobby of Lucifer was to watch his own films repeatedly, which he had recorded during his bloody parties. It gave him pleasure to watch his victims suffer and cry from pain. With evil desire in his eyes, he told me, "I can do anything I want in his house— watch movies he recorded or even have a meal." I inserted one of the DVDs into the video player and began watching the recording; it started with an abduction of a girl; she was nineteen years old. He caught her using a liquid chemical that he put over her nose, and it made her go to sleep instantly. He seated her in his car and drove away in the direction of his house, then at the house he stripped her naked, attaching her to a device that looked like a table with four chains around it. He locked each of her hands and legs to a wooden table and sat next to her, waiting for her to wake up. About thirty minutes later, she woke up and began screaming in fear of the situation she was in. He undressed in front of her, wearing a mask, and raped her, fucking her everywhere. He told her to suck his dick, so she sucked, out of fear, as she had to do everything he told her to do. He was playing with her, having sex with her for about three hours, after which he told her, "I am the devil, and I will torture you before I kill you." She started crying; the more she cried, the more satisfaction he was getting. He took one of his torture tools from his collection, a tool doctors used for patient surgery.

First, he cut her beautiful face with a sharp blade, sticking it in and out, cutting her ears and nose off. Then he started sticking nails into her young breasts, biting her nipples off and chewing them. Then it was time for another instrument, a portable meat grinder. He inserted her wrist in the crusher and began grinding while she was still conscious. She screamed in pain and horror. The more she wept, the more orgasms he received. Finally, he was tired of grinding her hands, so he took a big knife and cut her vagina out while she was still alive. He went into the kitchen and put her vagina on a fryer, cooking it for about five minutes with olive oil, eating it right in front of her, and forcing her to watch him eating her cervical canal. Then he took a big needle and inserted a needle through her body. Blood was everywhere, and she died from incredible pain and suffering. When the body of the nineteen-year-old girl was dead, he took a hack saw and ax and separated her organs and body parts, laying them in different containers. It was his meal for the next week.

After watching the first film, I had a strong desire to kill him. I had a gun on me, and he knew it. I was in the same room with him, watching the second film. We had an oral agreement there would be only a dialogue, no more or less. I knew he was the devil in human flesh.

I asked him about his actions and God's judgment of his soul. To my surprise, he knew more about God than I did. He told me, "God and I are very old enemies." He talked every day with a spirit of Holy God about the murders he had done and had decided to kill Holy God. He had been successful in killing Holy God. After that he decided to kill the children of God one by one, until there was not a single soul left on earth. I was watching a second DVD of a twenty-seven-year-old woman working at a local coffee shop. He introduced himself to her, saying, "You are very beautiful and attractive lady, and I would like to invite you for a cup of tea sometime, so we can get to know each other better."

She agreed, telling him, "I will be available after work at seven o'clock."

Mr. Killer cannibal was so happy thinking about his next feast and how he would punish her cruelly. He imagined all sorts of evil plans in his insane head.

When it was time to have a cup of tea, they started talking about life, and he invited her to visit his house, saying, "Sometimes I feel so lonely, and you will give me a great gift, if you agree to come and watch a film with me."

She hesitated for a second but said, "Well, I have nothing to do tonight." After two hours he offered her dinner, and she ate it. It was a fried piece of meat with potatoes, but she did not know she was eating the girl who had been tortured to death. After an hour watching a comedy in his house, she said, "Okay, it is getting late,; I need to go back home." When she tried to open the door, she could not do it because the door was locked. She asked the killer, "Why is the door locked? Can you open a door for me?"

Then the psycho told her, "I want to have sex with you because my eros for you is too strong." He offered her a choice, saying, "You can fuck with me beautifully or I'll rape you."

she said, "Okay, I will do everything you say; just do not hurt me."

He undressed her and fucked her wildly for about four hours. After that he told her, "You were eating my victims."

She asked him, "Are you going to kill me the same way you killed your previous visitors?"

He said, "Yes, dear, I will brutally torture you, and then I will kill you slowly."

She grieved, cried, and prayed, but God didn't save her. He took a hand drill and started drilling holes inside of her head. When he could see her brain, he removed her scalp with a handsaw to access her inner brain. She was still alive. He began eating her cerebellum slowly, using a spoon, and talking to her about life at the same time. Then he cut her stomach, taking out her birth organs and sticking them into her mouth because he didn't like her screaming voice.

Then he put her still-alive body on a wooden table and chopped off her head, putting it in a bowl and cooking it with vegetables. The rest of her body he cut and sold at the local meat market, saying it was beef.

He took his car and began driving along dark country roads to find the way to a city and his next victims. Finally, after driving for three hours, he found a twenty-eight-year-old couple walking down an alley of trees and beautiful flowers. They were talking about their future. The evil one didn't think they would have that future. He had other plans for the sweet couple. The meat butcher approached them, pretending to ask for a lighter. He said, "Do you have a lighter to lighten my cigarette?" The guy reached into his pocket, and as soon as he turned around, the devil took a syringe and thrust it into the boy's neck. The chemical mixture put him to sleep in the next six seconds. The girl was screaming and beating the killer with her purse and hands, trying to free her boyfriend from the hands of an unknown visitor. At the same time, the needle entered the soft flesh of the young girl, and she fell into a slightly dreaming state. She didn't realize what was happening until they both woke up naked in his house, interlinked to metal bars, which were welded to the floor. The devil sat on his couch smoking a cigarette. They were screaming and asking the guy, "What is happening? What are you going to do? And why are we chained to a floor?"

The executioner said, "Nobody will hear you in this house anyway because it is soundproof." He also said, "I will have sex with you, and if you will not agree voluntarily, I can do it nicely, or spitefully." He didn't tell them they would die a painful death anyway. After he fucked the girlfriend of the guy right in front of him, he told the guy to "suck my dick and swallow my sperm." They did what he asked because they were afraid to be punished for not doing what he told them. Then he smoked another cigarette while taking up a tool for torture. The naked couple prayed and cried, asking the slayer for mercy, but he didn't listen to them or see the tears of his victims. In fact, he enjoyed their screams and tears.

He told them the truth about what would happen, and they cried. Satan jammed the head of the guy into a metal box and with a heated knife took out his eyeballs from his eye cavities. The guy screamed with pain and blindness, then he cut his tongue off, cooking it and giving it to his girlfriend as food. Then he cut the guy's head off slowly with a handsaw while the guy was still alive. He fell bleeding on the floor, with no signs of life. The girl could not believe it was happening right in front of her, and she already knew she would die a very painful death as well. He carnally abused the girl one more time before torturing her. The evil man took an ax and cut one of her legs off, watching her scream in pain. After he chopped her second leg off, he extracted her liver and lungs with a sharp knife without anesthesia. Taking her heart and the rest of her organs out, he cooked them, eating it the same evening while reading the Holy Bible. It was evening, and the cannibal killer sat in his house and was thinking about his next victims and dinner for the next week. "I love human meat" was his favorite phrase. He took his van and drove away in the direction of a school. Adults were studying medicine at that school. He took a baseball bat and wrapped it with a soft towel to hit his victims on the back of the head and kidnap them. At his destination he sat in his van awaiting for his next prey. He saw a young couple walking to the campus, so he stepped out of his van and asked them, "Can you help me jump-start my vehicle?" When the guy and a girl said, "Okay, sure" and walked near his wagon, the devil took the baseball bat and hit both of them on the back of their heads with it.

Both of them lost recognition, and he put them in the back of his van and tied them up with a rope. Finally, he returned to his house of death and torture. He unloaded the young couple and took them to the basement, putting chains on them so they could not run away. He started the preparation of his torture devices, taking a sharp blade and a little ax.

After his victims woke up, he sat next to them on a chair and described the process of their death. He wanted to see their reaction and the fear of their souls. It turned him on even more to see them. Understanding of reality and inevitable death was in that evil place tonight. The girl pleaded and begged the killer for mercy, telling him, "Please, please, we don't want to die tonight; do not kill us; we want to live."

He did not care about plea and tears of that young, holy, beautiful soul. Satan asked the girl, "Are you afraid of death?"

She replied, "Yes, of course I afraid. I am so young; I have all my life ahead of me. Please do not kill me." With every plea and tear, the evil desire of the cannibal became stronger and stronger. His hands trembled at the climax moment from one single thought of torturing this holy soul; his cock grew stiff. He told her to suck his dick in front of her boyfriend. She sucked it, crying and praying, until finally he ejaculated in her mouth, telling her "to swallow my semen." After that he took a blade and showed her the sharp edge of it, saying, "I will cut you slowly." The butcher cut her beautiful breasts horizontally; as drops of blood fell on the floor, he tasted her blood, immersing a finger into her open wound. From that action, he received spiritual orgasm. The more she screamed, the more pleasure he was getting. He cut her vagina out, having sex with the alive bleeding-to-death girl, cooking her external genitals on a pan and giving it to her boyfriend for food.

The guy didn't want to eat the intimate organs of his girlfriend, but he had no choice; the cannibal forced him to eat. Then Satan man took a drill and start drilling holes into the body of a guy. He extracted organs using a fork and a surgery knife. After that he inserted a tube into a hole, which he had made with a drill, putting salt inside of the tube, onto the fresh open wounds; the guy screamed in horror and pain. The man sat back in an armchair, watching their trauma and mental shock.

He didn't kill them right away; instead he cut pieces of flesh off, cooking and eating them in front of them. The couple died ten hours later; no one came to save them. He took their meat and bones, wrapping them in plastic and storing them in his refrigerator. There was enough meat for the next week.

The days passed, and the refrigerator became empty. The Satan man had no more food left, so he walked outside down the alley around a park and houses, smoking his cigarette, and thinking about his meal for the next week. He prepared evil plans in his mentally ill mind. The man decided to abduct a family this time. The cannibal took his gun and silencer, searching for a suitable place of kidnapping. He walked into the business office of a warehouse and met a woman. He talked to her, asking different questions about her life and her family. To his big surprise, the lady told him a lot about her life and her family.

The hitman told the lady, "I can give you a ride to your house tonight; this way you don't have to wait an extra three hours for your husband to pick you up."

She said, "Okay, sure, it is so nice you are offering me your help."

"Yes, no problem. I have nothing to do anyway." He gave her a ride near her house and then he asked, "Can you introduce me to your husband when we arrive at your home?"

"Of course, no problem," she said, and they walked into her house and drank a coffee.

Her husband came back late from work, asking his wife, "Can you introduce your guest to me?" They began talking, and the killer told them he was a businessman and he had his own business in Europe. After the devil became friends with them, he said, "It is getting late. I have to leave for now, but keep in touch. I have a nice work offer for both of you; if you are interested, call me." He gave them his business card. A day later the guy called the devil man, asking him about his job offer. This is what Satan was expecting him to do. He invited the guy and his family into his house to discuss the false employment opportunity. The job was only bait, just like a fisherman uses a fishing pole to catch a fish.

Finally, the doorbell rang, and he opened the door.

The couple walked in, and he offered them a seat on his couch.

He said, "Make yourself comfortable in my house as it will be a long night, and we have a lot to talk about." The family didn't know they were sitting in the house of the devil himself. The door shut behind them and never opened again for them. The fate of the whole family had ended, but they didn't know about it yet. Everyone sat drinking tea, and then the predator took his pistol and walked into the dining room. He explained he was a cannibal and his name was Satan.

The lady asked him, "What are you going to do?"

The man said, "The door is locked, and the walls are soundproof; nobody will hear you, even if you scream."

The guy tried fighting with the murderer, but there was a sudden shot from the gun, and the bullet entered his intestines; a second bullet penetrated his leg. He fell on the floor screaming and bleeding. The evil man put tape over his mouth in order not to hear his voice. The lady was praying, asking the man-eater for mercy and not to harm her, but the monster took his sharp blade and began cutting her. She cried and begged him to stop, but neither angels nor God saved her. The evil man raped her for two hours, then he began to torment guy with an electric meatcutter. Taking a needle, he sewed the vagina of a lady together, then he cut the penis of the guy off, and gave it to his dog as food. Afterward he used a heated iron to burn the breasts of the woman. Lifting the bodies of the still-alive adults, he put them into a bathtub, leaving them there. Returning five minutes later with a gas can, he poured petrol on them, lighting a match and burning both of their innocent souls inside of the tub. He watched them scream from the incredible pain of fire. After they had died, he walked out to his balcony, smoking a cigarette, watching the skies full of stars and asking a question: "If there is a spiritual existence after death, then why does spirit of God allow me to do what I do?" But the sky was silent; nobody answered the cannibal slayer. When the refrigerator was empty, Lucifer sat thinking about his next meal. He didn't have to wait long for a new idea to come into his evil mind. This time he decided to abduct four Christians who went to church in the morning and evening. He drove his van toward a chapel, and right after they finished prayer, he called out to them, asking if they could explain the Holy Bible to him. The four Christians were so happy they had found a sinner and they could preach him the Bible.

They said, "Yes, how can we help you?"

The slaughterer told them, "I have many questions about the Holy Bible, and I would like to discuss them, if you will come into my house."

The four Christians didn't know what true evil was, and they agreed to go in to his lodging and explain the word of God to him. It was exactly what the devil man was expecting from them. All four of them sat inside of his van, driving to his house. They arrived two hours later. When they were inside of the house, the man locked the doors behind them, and the fate of all four was sealed. They didn't know they would become breakfast and would be stored inside of the refrigerator in the kitchen, so they opened the Holy Writ and were reading. The killer sat next to them, listening. After they finished reading the Bible, they asked the Lucifer man, "Do you have any questions?"

The devil said, "No, dears. I have no questions for you except one, and the question is, How would you like to die tonight, fast or slow?"

The four disciples of Christ were two guys and two girls.

They didn't believe his threat until the killer showed them a big, sharp knife, saying, "I am going to tie all four of you with a rope; you can cooperate, or you can die right now."

"Sure," they said, "we will cooperate with you; just don't kill us."

He wrapped a rope around their legs and arms. Then he raped the females for four hours, cutting theirs ears, noses, and eyes off, and then he cut one girl's throat slowly, draining and pouring the blood into a plastic container. When the girl died, he said to the remaining three, "I want you to drink the blood of your friend, and if you will not drink it, I will kill all of you right now." So, they had to drink the blood of their friend. Then he chopped her body up with a little tomahawk and machete, cooking it in the kitchen for two hours. The devil brought three of them a meal that was made of the freshly murdered girl and forced them to eat her. They had no choice as the devil man had a gun. After the meal all three were in a mental shock. They could not believe that this had just happened. Then the cannibal took a handsaw and cut the legs of one of the guys off very slowly, as he screamed in anguish and horror. The devil man hung the dead body on a hook in his kitchen, returned with his dog, and gave the soft flesh to his puppy for food. A little while later, he fucked the girl and the guy in the ass with a little knife. Taking a sickle, he cut out the ribs of the guy, cooking them in a bowl with onion and bread, and then he poured alcohol onto the open cuts, as the man screamed in agony. He enjoyed torturing religious people and the process of cooking lessons. He packed his refrigerator with meat, bones, and organs; there was enough meat for three weeks.

Days went by, and Satan had no more money left for his personal expenses, so he decided to kidnap three people from a nightclub. He drove to a nearby club where adults were hanging out and dancing. This time he took a bottle of vodka and stood near the back door of the dance club, waiting for people to come out and smoke. He didn't have to wait long; to his surprise, three beautiful and sexy females came out to smoke on a back stair. They started talking about the nightclub, and Lucifer asked them if they liked the discotheque.

The girls said, "Yes, it has a cool lounge, and we like the electronic house music playing here."

The killer said he had a nice place nearby and a lot of ecstasy pills and alcohol in his house.

He invited them to come to his home with him and have some fun.

The three young, sexy girls looked at each other and said, "We don't mind; sure, let's go."

It was easier than the evil guy had thought, and he didn't even have to use his tranquilizer. All four were inside of his van and driving toward his house. When they arrived, he offered them drinks and ecstasy pills. When all three of girls were high and drunk, the guy undressed them, and they fucked, making love in the cannibal's house. After four hours of wild sex with all three of them, he locked the three females to a bed with chains, sat on a couch, and thought about how to murder the beautiful angels he had just had wild sex with. He took a sharp blade and started cutting one girl slowly, watching her screaming in terror and pain. She cried and asked Lucifer, "Why are you doing this to me? Stop, please stop." But the more she cried and pleaded for mercy, the more evil desire Lucifer felt. Scissoring her breasts off, he maimed her and cut her stomach wide open. Through the opening, he pulled out her reproductive system while she was still alive and ate it fresh without cooking it. After she died he cut her dead body up in front of her friend, packing the meat into a bag and gluing the label "chicken" on it. Bones were buried behind his house one meter underground.

Then he took another girl and put her into an oven while she was still alive. He closed the door of the oven and cooked her for forty minutes. When he took her body out, the bones were well baked. Bringing her into a bedroom where the last living female lay, he forced her to eat her friend, feeding her the freshly, just-baked body of her buddy. She could not believe it was happening and supplicated, but no one answered her prayers. The assassin took out a big sword and cut her in half, then he cut her legs and hands off with a machete, butchering her body on a wooden board and preparing the meat for sale and dinner.

A week later he finished the meat and had no more money to spend. He took his van and drove toward a grocery shop, kidnapping two people using a sales technique. He told them, "I have raw meat for sale in my van that is very cheap. Would you like to look inside my van?"

The guy and a girl said, "Yes, let's go and see." Then they asked the killer, "How much does the beef cost?"

The guy said, "One dollar per pound," and sold them human flesh. Afterward he hit them with a rock on the back of a head and laid them in his van. Driving toward his house, he unloaded both buyers into his basement of torture and pain. Then he took an electric saw and began cutting them both, dismembering both their bodies, making even one-pound pieces of meat.

Both the guy and a girl screamed in pain as he cut their legs off and weighed them on a scale. They were still alive when he began making mincemeat in his grinder. Then he took a welding machine and cut the rest of their bodies with it, using a compressed nitrogen welding lamp to separate their arms and rib cage for the easiest access to the internal body organs. He extracted the pancreas, spleen, kidneys, liver, heart, and lungs, putting them in separate containers from the flesh. The girl was still alive and breathing, so he fucked the dying girl in her mouth that was full of blood and bubbles. After he ejaculated in her mouth, he cut her head off with a chain saw, eating her head after cooking it in a fryer with onion, garlic, and carrot. Then he packed the freezer with the rest of the organs. With the leftovers of flesh and bones, he prepared soup in a big bowl, cooking the heart and lungs with potato. He sat on the couch and ate as he watched his own recordings of the murders.

Three days later hunger manifested itself again. He was hungry and ready for his next meal. This time Lucifer decided to visit a hospital full of patients who were awaiting medical treatment.

They were left in the waiting rooms after their surgeries before being transferred to other hospitals. The devil placed an "ambulance" sign on his van and walked into a hospital using fake transfer papers. He gave papers to the front desk and said, "I have three people to pick up to take to another building."

The receptionist looked at the folder and said, "I will be right back." When she returned, she brought two girls and one guy, telling them, "Follow this gentlemen driver, and he will take all three of you to another location for rehabilitation."

Twenty minutes later Lucifer arrived at his house with the three young, fresh bodies and drove the van into the garage of his house.

A guy asked the devil, "Why are we in a house and not in the rest area for transfer?"

The cannibal answered, "It is getting late, and I am not used to driving at night without a nap." He invited them to come into his house and have a rest and a cup of tea.

"Sure." All three agreed.

When they sat on a couch in the dining room, the guy offered them dinner, asking them, "Would you like to eat some beef with potato and vegetable?"

All four said, "Sure, of course; we are hungry, and it would be great to have dinner before the long trip to the rest area for rehab." All three of them ate, but they didn't know they were eating human meat. Five minutes later, the killer told them they were eating the flesh of a tortured and murdered guy whom he had killed three days ago. The girls couldn't believe it was true. They tried to run out of the house, but the doors were locked. The man pulled out a stick with a big, sharp blade at the end of it.

He said, "Hi, I am the devil. I kill and eat humans in this house, and you are my meal for the next week."

The guy and the girls attempted to run, hoping to find an exit, but were unsuccessful in finding a way out. The angry man got handcuffs and chained all three young adults to a welded metal frame, after which he undressed in front of them and began raping the females in the most brutal way he could. He fucked them everywhere, ejaculating five times inside and outside of the young ladies. Then he took a blade from his collection and cut one of the girls slowly, looking into the eyes of his victims and receiving an evil spiritual apogee from making them suffer unbelievable pain. Taking a smaller blade, he cut the skin in her lower abdomen, opening up her intestines and taking them out. The girl died from blood loss and pain. He took her stomach and intestines and cooked them in front of the remaining two people, eating and talking to them about abuse. Then he chopped up the body of the dead girl and wrapped it in the foil, freezing and putting it in a portable ice machine.

Then he took a hammer and nails and nailed the guy to a wooden cross.

Taking a spear, he began stabbing the guy brutally. The guy screamed from incredible pain and shock, beseeching the killer to stop, but asking the devil for mercy was like asking a homeless and poor guy to donate money for charity. The cannibal had no mercy on the innocent guy.

After the body of the guy trembled in agony before his death, the evil man took a scimitar and beheaded the guy with the sharp edge of it. His head fell on the floor, with his eyes opened in horror and misunderstanding. The girl, who was still alive, began shaking from fear and mental shock, asking crazy devil for mercy. The killer said, "Would you like to pray? Maybe God will save you from a painful death." The innocent girl prayed to almighty God, but no one answered her prayers. Lucifer said, "I will cut you into a little pieces with my harpoon, which I sharpened just for you." He grabbed her and tied her hands and legs to a table with a rope. He made little cuts on her young breast as tears fell from her face. He continued to separate her skin from the flesh using pliers and knife, inserting a gag into her mouth so he didn't have to hear her screams, but more tears came out from the pretty eyes of the angel. Thirty minutes later, after silent sadism, the girl's skin was removed. She was still alive and lying on the table. He took out the gag and asked her, "How do you feel?" Her soul spoke something about hell, so he fucked her in the mouth and pussy, asking her again, "What do you feel now?" Her eyes lightened up for a second, and the spark disappeared forever as she died. The next morning the evil man woke up, opened his refrigerator, and began cooking breakfast using chopped dead flesh. He had 260 pounds of meat, so he decided to sell it to a local market of Chinese and Mexican restaurants. He packed up the flesh of a girl and a guy into a portable cooler and drove toward a restaurant to speak with the manager of a kitchen. He negotiated the price, telling him it was pork, and sold it for two hundred dollars. Both were happy with the good deal; the evil man had just found a customer to whom he can supply pork (human flesh) to from time to time.

The cannibal killer returned to his house and thought about who his next victims could be. He drove to a bank to deposit some money. While he was talking to a cashier, he asked her if she was happy with the job she was doing.

The woman answered, "Well, better something than nothing, plus they pay me forty thousand dollars a year."

He replied, "I can offer you sixty thousand a year, and you don't have to stand on your feet all day; you can sit in an office."

She immediately agreed

He said, "Come to my house for the paperwork and details of the new job. I will discuss it with you and I can give you a ride, so you can start working next week in a new office."

She swallowed the decoy. "Sure," she said. "I will finish my work in a couple of hours. After that I don't mind talking with you about my new career."

Two hours later the killer Satan and his next meal drove in his car toward his dwelling and place of anguish. They arrived three hours later, and he invited her into his home. He seated her on a couch and began talking with her, asking different questions about her life; after about thirty minutes of conversation, he asked her, "Are you single or married?"

She answered, "I am single."

"Would you like to have sex with me tonight?"

"I don't even know you," she said.

He undressed her, and they fucked for about four hours. "Did you like fucking me?" He asked.

"Yes, I like your dick a lot."

Then Satan replied, "I am very hungry right now, and I don't have any food; would you mind if I cut your leg off and cooked it on the electric stove?"

The girl couldn't believe her ears as she had just been having sex with this guy five minutes ago. "Are you joking?" she asked.

The killer said, "No, I am not joking, my beautiful lady." Then he showed her the cutter he used to cut human bones with.

The girl cried and tried to escape, but the door was securely locked.

"Are you ready for brutal and painful death?" he asked.

"No," the girl said. "Please don't hurt me, don't harm me; this is a dream, right? Tell me it is not real." With his bear claw, he began cutting the soft flesh of the girl very slowly. Blood was everywhere on the floor, on the walls and table. Then he took an axe and separated her legs from her torso. Inserting a hook into her mouth, he brought her mutilated body into the kitchen and hung it from the ceiling. He began cooking her body and frying it on a slow fire with apples and plums for about two hours, until dinner was ready. Satan sat eating the girl, thinking about the sex he had with her four hours ago. Four days later the evil man had no more food and money to pay the water bill and electricity, so he decided to abduct five people and bring them into his basement. He prepared a place for chopping up the meat and organ harvesting, bringing two containers filled with ice to store the internal organs of his victims, such as heart, kidneys, lungs, and liver. Then he brought in a table, the same table doctors used for plasma, blood, and stem cell harvesting, to drain blood and plasma from his future victims. He opened his laptop computer and began searching for people who would be willing to buy body organs and plasma together with blood for big money. He found buyers on one of the black market websites. He contacted a buyer and offered to sell five hearts, ten kidneys, and the rest of the organs together with blood and plasma for $100,000. He warned the buyer about the secrecy and confidentiality of the transaction; both parties agreed on the price and terms.

Satan drove toward a mosque, walked into the temple of Allah, and talked to people. He met three young men and two women, and all five began talking about the Holy Quran. The killer said he had a house about two hours' drive from the temple and he wanted to invite all five of them there to discuss the holy book together. The five Muslims agreed to go with him the same evening after the service. In fact, everyone was happy about being invited. So ten minutes later, all six drove toward the devil's house. He opened his doors and told them to make themselves comfortable inside of his house. All five were seated on a couch he had recently upgraded because the old sofa was bloody.

Then Lucifer offered them food and drink. saying, "Would you please explain to me the Holy Quran?"

While they ate, the killer locked the doors. He returned with his handgun and silencer. Walking back into the main room where action was about to take place, he said with a very loud voice, "I have a gun, and I going to fuck the females first." He locked the guys with handcuffs to a concrete wall, and all five thought he was joking and laughed, but the killer showed them the gun and said, "I am not kidding with you, my friends." Then he forced them to go into his bunker where all the tools and torture beds were prepared for the bloody work and party. After seeing his basement, all five felt afraid. The killer man commanded the females to undress, and while the girls took off their dresses and underwear, he locked the guys to the metal concrete floor. The Muslim girls were virgins of twenty-eight and thirty years old. He fucked both of them for four hours. Then, after he got tired of sexual intercourse, he locked them to a medical bed and agonized over them slowly, using a surgery knife and the pain machine. Then he picked up a kitchen knife and began cutting the soft young flesh of a holy pretty girl. The girl was crying from her suffering, and tears dripped down onto the cold concrete floor. Afterward he inserted a needle into her body and began draining the blood and plasma from her. When her body was white as snow from blood loss, he performed surgery, extracting her organs one by one from the still-living girl. Later he did the same procedure with another woman. He stored their organs in a plastic container mixed with ice and liquid nitrogen. After the women were dead, he collected their flesh and bones and stored them in a freezer. Then he picked up a dagger and cut the three men everywhere. He amputated their penises, cooking them and forcing them to eat their own reproductive organs. Then he shot all three of the men with a shotgun, extracting their organs and storing them separately from the female organs in the same cooler. Then he chopped up the bodies of the guys with a sharp hatchet on a big wooden table. When he had scaled the meat of all three by the pound and wrapped it in the newspaper, he placed the sticker "lamb" on it and put it away in a portable freezer to sell to local restaurants. Shortly afterward he picked up his cell phone and called the dealers of body organs, arranging a meeting in his private office to sell the body parts of the recently murdered Muslims.

He sat in his office wearing a mask and waiting for the buyer. The devil's secretary called his office from downstairs and notified Lucifer of a visitor; the man said, "Check him and make sure he is not a cop."

After the person was verified and scanned with a metal scanner, the scribe allowed the buyer to walk into the office of the killer.

Lucifer sat in his chair, wearing a mask and gloves. He asked, "Did you bring money as was discussed earlier?"

"Yes, of course," the smuggler replied, and opened a suitcase full of cash.

"I will count it," the man said. "You don't mind, do you?"

The dealer said, "Please do."

After he sold the portable cooler with body organs to the smuggler, they shook hands with each other, and the meeting was over.

The smuggler said, "It was a pleasure to do business with you, mister" and left.

After the money was deposited into his bank account, Satan returned to his house of death, preparing the flesh and bones of a girl by cooking it with vegetables using body fat as oil for boiling and frying. He had to find a cooking recipe from an old book in the library. After he finished cooking, the evil man sat on the chair he had made out of human bones and skulls and ate, watching the recordings of the murders he had committed, receiving spiritual satisfaction and enjoyment.

The devil man had completely lost his sense of morality and was out of his mind, living in an imaginary world that he created for himself, wandering around inside his mind. Every time he went to bed and slept, dreams from out of this world visited his psychologically ill consciousness. It was evening, and the lunatic fell asleep after his daily work in the kitchen; after two hours he had deep dream and met a magician who explained an experiment that was being conducted by another spiritual civilization far away from Earth in a distant galaxy.

The hologram said, "It is a lucid dream, and we downloaded a dream inside of a dream, so you cannot tell the difference between reality and a dream. We created life and death.

"We have observed you and your behavior from the beginning to understand good and evil, right and wrong, morality and immorality. You are our object of scrutiny and study. We made heaven and hell on Earth and up in the sky for human souls. We made an atom and split it to create the reality in which you live and called it Earth. We control time, space, and dimensions of planet earth. We have the power to rewrite the matrix of the solar system, backward and forward in time, your life and death, together with those of any other human on Earth. I am Holy God, whom you killed. This is my world; I live here inside and outside of your fantasy dream, which you call realism; I live in heaven."

Lucifer woke up in a cold sweat and went outside to make sure everything looked very real. "What the heck," the crazy man said. "I can't believe I am having hallucinogenic glitches from the meat butchering last night." Looking up in the sky, Chort started talking to a spirit of God by saying, "Planet earth is my house, not yours."

The evil maniac put his sport clothes on and walked outside of his house to refresh his bones and muscles by doing exercise. He planned to spend his evening in the most interesting way. He went walking near other houses and followed a group of females, daydreaming about being with them inside of his house. He went after them, and when no one was watching, he knocked them down with a rubber hummer; after that he dragged them into the back seat of his car and took them into his base. Inside of his house he manufactured a cage for his work. Taking one of his tools, a katar dagger, the rapist started playing with it.

He took one girl out of the cage and telling her to dance in front of him naked.

After she finished, he asked her, "Have you ever thought about what death is like?"

She answered, "No, I don't know what it is like to die."

"Okay," the man whispered into her ear, "congratulations. You will find out in a few minutes what it is like to feel a katar in your fucking uterus," and he stacked it in very deep, all the way, until his arm came out of her mouth. Then he took a second girl out of a cage and told her to get down in front of him and suck him. She sucked and ate until he finished in her mouth.

He said, "You are doing your job well, and iwill show you what a heavy pick is." Taking a mace and a pick, he began beating her down with it until her body was purple from hematomas and bruises. When she was unable to speak and scream, he wrapped a rope around her neck and hung her from a ceiling, leaving her there for six hours, to drain blood into a basin, as drinking the blood of guiltless sinners made him stronger.

Walking into a room with a cage, he carried ninja throwing stars together with a kusarigama, a traditional Japanese weapon, and began a ritual performance by waving his instruments and meditating before taking the life of his last prisoner. He asked her, "Do you want to say anything before I kill you?" No words came out of her mouth as she was scared and convulsing at the thought of her death. The sharp Japanese equipment began a shredding process; soon the crying prostitute was on her knees in front of him without a head. The sicko extended his hands toward the sky, receiving evil spiritual energy from the cosmos and energizing himself. He lubricated the right palm of his hand with the blood of the last girl and began masturbating, talking and convincing himself in a righteous way about his act.

The beast took a truncheon with four nails in it that he had made in his garage and left the house to find his next adventure and prey. He met a guy on the street and gave him one hundred dollars, saying, "I am a member of a local church, and I give away money to poor people." The guy was happy to take the money and start talking to him about the hardships in his life. The vampire said, "I understand life is difficult nowadays, but don't get discouraged, and don't give up as there is hope and everything will be okay. I also have an accommodation for poor and homeless people; you can come with me and stay as long as you need, until you become financially independent. I will not ask you for anything unless you feel you are ready to help me and others."

The poor guy could not believe he had met a missionary. He said, "Indeed, you are doing God's work by helping the poor, disabled, and hopeless people."

"Yes," the devil replied as they walked toward his home. "Helping and serving Jesus is priority number one for me." When they reached the house and went inside, the monster said, "I would like to interview you and ask a few questions, if you don't mind."

"Of course, I will answer any of your questions," the needy guy said. The meat eater closed the doors of the house and hung a big titanium lock on the doors. Walking behind the guy, he sat on an armchair and began the first part of his interview, asking his dinner a question. "Have you ever thought about death and the afterlife?"

"Yes, I believe there is a spiritual life after death."

"Are you ready to meet your creator, God?"

The guy was confused and mumbled, "I don't understand what are you talking about; I have fifty more years of life before I get old and die."

"Oh, well," the cannibal replied, "the plans have been changed. I am hungry tonight, and my fridge is empty, so I was planning to eat you tonight before I go to bed." He showed the man an awl and a truncheon.

The guy asked his slayer, "Are you going to kill me?"

"Yes," the hungry man answered and stuck the awl in his eye and umbilical artery. The young man wheezed and died in the same position.

"Wow," the evil man said, "looks like next time I need to install a camera for the recording of this theater as it is too funny watching them die." He weighed the guy on a scale; it was 160 pounds of meat and bones. So after sorting his organs and bones out, it came only to sixty pounds of meat. It lasted him for about one week.

One month later Iblis was bored because he had nothing to do, so he decided to abduct ten more people to decrease the population of Earth. He cleaned his basement and installed more torturing machines, then he upgraded his meat grinder to a bigger size. The electric grinder had the capacity of mincing a grown adult. Then he took his minibus with tinted windows and drove toward a mall where people were shopping and hanging out. He prepared a story to tell his future prey so he could lure them into his house. The story was about the promotion of free computers and PDA devices he had in his house. Of course it was a lie, but the naive mall shoppers didn't know it was a trap. So, the devil man walked into the mall and started giving away flyers about the fake offers. When a crowd surrounded him and began asking questions about the free computer giveaway promotion, he said, "We have only ten computers left to giveaway of the latest model and brand, and I am willing to give them to you for free, but it is a two-hour drive. My bus is ready and can take ten lucky people who participate in the giveaway program."

The first ten to volunteer would be happy to get the new netbooks as free gifts. They didn't have a clue about what would happen in the house of death. Finally, the bus arrived outside his house, and he unloaded his passengers, opening the doors for them so all ten were inside of the house. Then he closed the doors of the house and commanded people to go into the basement. He said, "Follow me so I can hand each of you a gift, as our company is growing and expanding."

The crowd of people reminded him of stupid sheep being taken to a slaughterhouse. Everyone walked down into the cellar where the killer man held a gun in his hand and told everyone to undress. People stood there in disbelief, so he turned the light on for everyone to see the place in which they were standing. The room was full of human bones and pictures of horror on the walls. Everybody understood what was going on, and few people tried to fight him, but the killer shot them straight in the forehead, asking the rest of the crowd, "Does anyone else want to follow the destiny of the brave heroes?" The room was silent as no one else wanted to be shot. So the cannibal said, "I want all of you to take your clothes off." When they had taken their clothes off, the devil man said, "I want the women to step forward, separate from the men." When the groups were separated, Lucifer shot all of them with a tranquilizer, and everyone fell to sleep instantly. Forty minutes later eight people woke up and found themselves chained to the torture devices.

The evil man raped the women, fucking them for three hours, then he took a glaive and epee, and dissected two men and two women, cooking their flesh on the grill.

He threw the rest of the people into the big electric bone grinder and watched them plead and cry. The meat came out dark red. Picking up a chain saw, he dismembered the hands and legs of the guys. The room was filled with the smell of blood, horror, and death. Tears and screams of humanity were everywhere, but evil took over God in that evil house.

He hung the last surviving girl on a wall using nails and rope, leaving her there for three days and raping her periodically when he had lonely evenings. The rest of the meat he packed and sold to established customers he had reliable connections with. He left one hundred pounds of meat for himself and the girl who was living in his house, as a toy for him to fuck with, when he had free time.

The devil man joined a book club to educate himself and his evil soul. He sat together with the young girls and boys, and he had a good time with them and his new company. Everyone was reading the words and meanings of the words, fucking with each other mentally. Five hours later the ungodly man asked the members of the club, "What is the definition of the word 'man slayer'?" Everybody thought of a way how to explain new guy the significance of the word.

They came up with different ideas and examples to explain the forbidden taboo.

The killer listened and made notes in his journal, saying, "I collect data as I am writing a book about an assassin and I would like to understand the mind of both devilish and good people and enrich my vocabulary to make the writing easier."

Three girls and two guys who were sitting near him invited him in to their house to make further connections, hook up, and study together. They said, "We are looking for a guy who is willing to take the virginity from one of our female friends and we have prepared a room in our house for this. We have three girls and two guys. Will you help us with our problem and fuck our friend tonight during the party? Then we will talk more with you about the meanings you are looking for in your book after the celebration is over,"

"Of course," the anthropophagus said, playing with a knife in his pocket at the same time. "It is an excellent idea, and I have no problems with it; I will make your friend a woman." Bugatti Veyron was awaiting for them, and a group of young ladies and gentlemen were riding into a cottage of erotica. Condoms were given to every person, as all six went inside the house. The evil creature said, "What a beautiful house. Would you mind if I privatize it from you?" He made it look like a joke, and everyone laughed. The females undressed the guys, and the group started an oral orgy by feeding each other with vaginal juice and sperm. Everyone was happy to fuck like hares. After four hours of the group orgy, the devil man took the virgin pellicle from the new girl and said, "I would like to talk to the house owner."

The girl told him, "I am the owner of a house. Do you have any questions?"

"No," the cannibal said. "I have no questions, but I would like to do paperwork here as I like your lodge a lot, and you will help me with a lawful gift deed document." Showing her his big shiny switchblade, he said, "I want you to sign a property transfer paper of ownership change from your name into my name." He gave her original notarized papers indicating himself as the new house owner. The girl shook from fear and said, "Please don't take my life from me; I will put my signature on any legal form you want; just don't injure me." After the deal was finished and approved by the bank, the antichrist cut the throats of every witness inside the cabin, taking one girl as a gift for himself and his new abode. It was his reward for his time and the stressful evening. Later on he made a little meat factory inside of his dwelling, purchasing equipment from beef and pork suppliers. He fixed the main room and screwed twenty hooks into the metal roof frame. The bodies of the dead people were professionally chopped, their organs extracted, and the meat together with the bones were detached and packed into an aluminum steel cans. He signed a contract with the buyers to sell his products to a wide chain of grocery stores, making a fancy name and advertising his commodity as a sweet fantasy, yummy, mouthwatering food.

In a few weeks, he had to hire slaves to work for him, paying them a minimum wage.

He loaded trucks with the product of the new brand. Abaddon sat in his office smoking cigars, reading his evil books, which he had purchased from his agent to raise an evil spirit inside of himself. He had read many evil pages of different essays about war crimes and evil human activities on planet earth, so every time he interpreted the new script hieroglyphs, his evil mind grew worse. His body was miraculously transformed into a stronger and more powerful entity.

The voice of his devil father originated from hell; it was saying to him, "I am so proud of you, my evil son; you are so smart and intelligent, and you will join me in hell someday. As a gift from me, I will make your body immortal."

The Iblis man cut his own hand with a pocket knife to test his new supernatural power and abilities. The wound healed by itself. "Very well," the man said, "I have become like God himself."

The voice said, "I want you to take a shotgun and shoot yourself in the mouth. Surely you will die, but I will bring you back in to life with a renewed and newborn body."

The devil man sat for a few minutes thinking about his cured cut, then shot himself in the head with a fifty-caliber bullet. The matrix started to collapse, and the gate of hell was opened. Beings from out of this world appeared in front of him, sending him back in time. The shaitan man woke up holding the firearm in his hands. He ran out of his house to see the sky and saw the blue sphere had changed color, illuminating rainbow frequencies. At that moment the crazy gunman knew he was in abyss of netherworld. "Wow," he said to himself, "it is a mind-blowing experience I will never forget." His evil desire became greater and more potent as an energy of a strong, dominating feelings filled his new, deathless body. He took a hook out of his collection and headed toward the house of females. Walking near the house, he looked inside and watched a lesbian playground; five homosexual women were fucking each other with dildos.

"Well," Chort said, "they definitely need the real hard cock of a real man."

He stepped inside their porn playhouse, undressed, and started fucking all of them without saying a single word.

Screams of excitement filled the room, and the girls were ejaculating nonstop. After ten hours of hard fucking, everyone grew tired and took a break before repeating it for a second time.

Suddenly, the evil man said, "I need more protein to keep my dick hard for another ten hours." So he picked up his hook and inserted it into the bottom part of the chin of one of his new female friends, dragging her into the kitchen and cooking her there. Meaty fuel energized him so he could continue his sexual journey.

Voices talked to him again, saying, "It is good you killed Holy Goddesses, and that is why we separated paradise from Tartarus. You will inherit my position in my kingdom of inferno as your reputation astonished me when I observed you from my fireball of a universe." As the demon spoke, vibrations filled the atmosphere.

The evil man said, "I will do your will on earth to earn my way into your house up in Hades."

"Yes, very well," the maker of hell said. "I will wait for you here, but before I accept you into my house, you have to kill ten thousand people, and you must fuck and sleep with as many females as you can. To prove to me you are my son, and I your father, I killed hundreds of thousands of people when I lived on Earth as a human. My grandfather opened the cosmic gate for me in hell after I finished his last wish on Earth and killed one hundred thousand people. As you can see and hear, I live here in abyss, which is dimension number six, and I like it a lot. I read evil literature here, and you will join me soon, as one billion years on Earth is for me one second here up in the microcosm. Don't forget you have nine thousand more people to kill before I open the gate of infernal regions for you forever."

"Of course I will remember it," the evil man said, taking his assassin falchion and running outside to kill as many people as he could. "I will earn my way into the everlasting fire of a nightmare." He gutted and disemboweled a hundred humans the same night before going to bed and sleeping well. He woke up early in the morning to wash the blood from his pretty face. While he was taking a shower, four nude lesbians appeared in front of him and gave him a deep blow job for another three hours.

It was an awesome dawn. His intellect was talking to him at the same time as he persuaded his body to push deeper into their throats. Once everyone had their portion of albumin, hunger did not bother them any longer; they disappeared the same marvelous way that they had emerged, leaving acoustic sparks in the air.

"Looks like we have teletransportation here," the crazy fucker from the multiverse said, teleporting him into his office and offering him a collection of new volumes for review. After breaking down the word for him in Japanese, Arabic, Hindi, Portuguese, Chinese, French, German, and Russian, the voice asked him, "Are you ready for your next murder?"

"Yes, I am prepared," the guy said. "I am hungry and thirsty already." Taking a bladed boomerang, he took his evening walk as he usually did before satisfying his extermination mission. He threw it back and forward, making sure his victims had bleeding bodies and broken heads. In an hour or so, his electromagnetic portable time machine sent him signals and counted the lives he took, making sure he would enter his imaginary promised world after the assignment was over. He murdered holy people, envisioning to himself it was his enemy; a sharp, fifty-pound war hammer materialized in his left hand, and a Viking mace in his right hand. Walking near footers he asked them, "Have you ever felt unthinkable pain?" Random people didn't want to answer his question. Silence made him mad, and he hit them with his toy, hammering out their gray brains. The skull of a man was smashed, and the body went into spasms before his death. The evil man picked up a piece of fatty brain from the ground, saying, "It is a beauteous color, and I will nail his dead body to a wall in my house." He decided to continue as he was looking for a new carpet when a sexy female walked near him having no clue about who he was.

She asked him, "What are you doing?"

He pounded her with his mace until her beautiful white skin turned into a bloody lake. Then he wrapped a chainlet around her legs and pulled her forcefully into his house to make a rug out of her lovely skin and flesh. The meat cutter had a busy evening that terrible night. He used his skills and knowledge to sew a floor cover out of the good-looking girl. Pulling his fine AK-47 automatic rifle out of his assembly, he flew in his private helicopter to a hotel rooftop. He walked out of the bird to get more bones for his creation of art. Breaking into the rooms, kicking doors out, and gunning fuckers down with his work tool. After the hearts of people stopped beating and the bodies were pallid without gore, he carried the carcasses upstairs, loading the corpses into his helicopter, and flying away toward his house of transgression. His kitchen was ornamented in a French manner with skulls, and the soffit was adorned with the leftovers of bones.

He went to sleep after drinking a strong liquor, when suddenly death started talking to the lunatic, saying, "I want to see more pain, grief, and sorrow on planet earth." It spoke into the ear of the man with a low volume frequency. "I want you to make my maker happy and smiling up in hell. Rape those pretty angels so I can watch and obtain gratification when you violently abuse, kill, and eat the holy children of God and the devil. And if you will do my request, we both will be promoted up in hell into a higher position of so-called eternal damnation. For your creator knows about the spiritual hell and heaven. Kill everyone on Earth, if you can."

"Yes," Lucifer said. "The kitchen, cemetery, morgue and crematorium are my favorite places for this pastime as I don't know them and I don't know if they are kids of the devil or God. I will kill them all. I kill Holy God and I kill the devil because I was programmed to kill. I don't know what is holy and what is evil, so I kill for fun."

Holy said, "I collect human souls by sending them up to heaven or up to hell for further education, and your soul will be taken up to scorching cold because you are the devil and the souls of those whom you have killed will be taken up to the paradise of Elysium, heaven. Concepts of good killers and evil killers. Zero money intended to be death. As you can see, there are guns on sale together with human meat. Only I have the power to forgive good killers." Holy one said. "I disagreed with holy zero myself, the word 'faith' and sinners on earth. People refused to use condoms and were condemned; as a result you can see they started a war, and I had no choice but to become a gatekeeper by separating good from evil and collecting human souls, redirecting them into an appropriate place after death. That is why my name is holy." The holy one spoke from the universe that she created by saying, "i wrote commandment number one, which stands for thou shall not kill, or murder, but the devil killed me; that is why I created the star gate and heaven for good souls up in outer space, and I created the cosmic gate and hell for evil souls. There is a microcosm and macrocosm; according to my commandment, I will separate good killers from evil killers. The souls of good killers will be forgiven and accepted into the lower regions of heaven. The souls of evil killers will be taken into hell fire forever, and the souls of people who killed zero people will be taken up to heaven forever. I made different levels of nirvana up and down in paradise to educate the enlightened souls of good people."

The insane guy woke up trying to recreate and remember his dream, but he was not able to; he forgot everything. His hands were bloody, so he washed them before calling another prostitute.

After one hour of sucking on him, she said, "I want a hundred bucks."

The discourteous man said, "I will give you twenty dollars for sucking, my friend; you can take it, or you can leave."

The young slut fought with the guy; he became angry and said, "I will give you one last chance," but she didn't take the money. So he got his long blade and sliced her pretty face and mouth with it. "What a stupid bitch," the teaser said. "I can't believe she didn't take the option when I was offering it to her; now I have to clean my brand-new wooden floor from her nasty bloody shit and make it look nice again."

After a couple of hours, he called ten more girls to do a suctorial competition to see which had the best mouth and who had sucking skills. Ten hours later he picked two of them, offering them a bounty by giving each of them two hours of uninterrupted cunnilingus. After a while he told everyone to walk downstairs into the cellar to finish the devilish fucking contest by fingering each other. Yes, ten hot out-of-their-mind models said, "We want you to show us what a real heavy fuck is all about." He took an arbalest with arrows and struck them with it, then he grabbed a doubled-bladed Indian halide knife and started cutting them like they were soft animals from a zoo. The spirit of a sadistic sicko incarnated into him, advising him which way was more professional to dismember sinew on to a clean cut, with no veins or vessels.

The soul of the Holy God came down from universe, saying, "I am sending my angels down to Earth to clean Gaia from the evil children of the devil by annihilating and destroying the weapons of humans." She said to her supernatural beings, "Fly down on sinful Earth and offer humans a choice to confess, or be destroyed as at the end of time and life, I will collect human souls by teleporting them up to heaven and hell."

"Fine," the man said, "I will never repent of my sins in front of her heavenly puppets." By taking another evil tool from his collection, he continued to assassinate the holy fuckers of hell; he kidnapped more people. An angel found him while he was eating his sacrifice and started talking to him, trying to convince Al Qatil in reverse action to turn away from his sinful actions by preaching the Holy Bible to him and explaining the word "sin." The messenger of God flew around him trying to deaden the evil man, but for some reason she could not. Every time she flew near him, her wings burned from his fire. She tried to use her magic sword to break the protective blazing sphere around him, but she didn't have the power to destroy the orbicular flaming ball. The devil man captured the angel with his hands and cut her wings off with his sharp razor, cooking the heavenly beings the same night and selling their supernatural bodies to hungry followers of Buddha. A Chinese kitchen was very busy making profitable transactions.

Five more angels of death flew toward the location of the murder, trying to put him to death, but they could not do it; Al Qatil was too powerful; he took a fishing net and captured angels of heaven in to his evil cages, which he had gathered during his lunch break. While eating their beautiful wings, he took them out of the cage one by one and roasted the faithful cherubs inside the furnace. Holy God looked down from heavenly dimension number five on the evil man, unable to believe the outcome. The question was spoken into existence: "How is it possible that a man is stronger and has more power than angels?"

An answer came from the dimension number six: "I gave my evil son power over angels by allowing him to do anything he wants on Earth."

"Okay," the holy spirit of God said, "in that case, I will come down to Earth personally, and I will kill your evil son." So that was that. The meat grinder started working, making crushing sounds; Chort walked into his kitchen to adjust and fix the detrimental mechanism.

One week later minotaur man decided to do a mass massacre of people on a football field as he had tired of meat butchering. He found a nice semiautomatic rifle. He bought one thousand bullets of ammunition, ten explosive timed grenades, fourteen small bombs, and drove toward a football stadium. He put a mask on and used an employee entrance to get inside, carrying the rifle and grenades under his coat. He installed explosives under the seats of people and took the detonator with him. When the stadium was filled with fans and the game had started, he pressed the button and a stadium fired up as if with New Year's fireworks. When the crowd started to panic, he pulled out his gun and began shooting everyone, trying to kill as many people as possible. After five minutes of shooting, he escaped using an exit he had prepared for himself two days earlier. Taking the mask and gloves off, he threw them into the garbage, jumped into his car, and drove toward the bar to see more news of the local city. After a few shots of vodka with cranberry juice, he asked the bartender, "Can you turn on the TV so I can watch the news channel?" Every channel was talking about an accident that had just happened; everyone was talking about an evil act that happened that morning in the small city. Lucifer sat and enjoyed watching his evil activity. "Less people is better," he said with a loud voice to a bartender. "Right?"

"I am not sure about your philosophy," the girl replied.

The Satan man asked the girl, "What are you doing tonight after work?"

The girl answered, "I don't have any plans yet."

The man asked her, "Would you like to go in to the cinema with me tonight?"

She said, "I already have a boyfriend."

The killer said, "You are very beautiful, and I would like to give you a present," and he gave her a golden necklace with a diamond.

The girl accepted the gift and said, "Okay, tomorrow I will be available for a supper with you." The next day he picked his girlfriend up from the bar and took her to a local restaurant. She ordered a bloody beefsteak, and he ordered a drink saying, "I am not hungry." After a while the cannibal man asked the girl, "Would you like to come in to my house tonight and have sex with me?"

The girl said, "Okay, let's go." When they arrived at his house, they fucked; the girl heard something from the basement, like somebody crying and calling for help. She asked the devil man, "What is that I hear? Is it the voice of somebody in your basement?"

The evil man said, "I don't know what it is; let's go and see together."

When the girl walked into the room of death, she realized what was going on. She found a maidservant on the floor, naked and pleading to be saved. He told her, "Now you know my hidden evil secret, and I will not kill you if you will agree on my terms and conditions; you do have options. What is your choice?"

She cried and said, "Okay, okay, just don't kill me. I will do anything you want." So he fucked her without a condom and ejaculated inside of her six times; after that he locked her next to a metal bed. Taking the second dame, he separated her body with a mechanical separator into little cubes of meat, removing her wrist; he was cooking it on a stove and giving it for food to both of them.

The devil man said, "Now you have become like me, knowing good and evil. I will not kill you, but you will be helping me in the kitchen and basement with the kidnapping and murder of people and preparation of food."

The girl looked at Lucifer man, and a tear fell from her eye.

He also said, "We are going to a police station, and you will shoot six cops to prove to me your worthiness."

The devil gave her a gun, and they drove up next to a law enforcement station; they walked inside, and the angel began shooting everyone inside of the building.

Lucifer said, "Now that you have proved to me you are capable of cold-blooded murder, I will reward you" and they drove to a hotel room and fucked there all night.

Crazy Chort bought parts of a sniper rifle from an internet website and assembled it, putting it into a sport bag; he drove into a big crowded city to practice and gain quality experience using living targets. It was Sunday, and he climbed the staircase of a tall business building all the way to the top for the clear view, good lookout observation, and shooting. Setting down a rifle on the cement, he screwed a massive suppressor on it and began his training exercises. Looking through a scope, he aimed at one of the pretty blondes who were crossing the pedestrian crosswalk. He pressed a trigger, and the large caliber bullet made a ten-inch hole in her beautiful head.

His next target was a fat banker; he took aim, saying, "It will be a pleasure to send this one into another dimension." The bullet exited the back side of the guy's brain, making no sound and leaving a pink mess on the pavement. His third choice was a group of workers who were standing in front of an antique building and talking about their life problems and family issues. The evil shooter said to himself, "I am so glad I will release those men from the sufferings of life. By taking their lives from them, I will make a big present to everyone as the souls of the men I am about to take will rest in peace forever; also I will add them to my collection of good memories." He took them out one by one, until five dead fuckers were lying on the ground bleeding similar to a fucking cunt. Burgundy streams of blood were flowing down the street sewer. *Very well*, the exterminator thought to himself, *now there are seven beings less on Earth, and I have a big list to complete in the future.* After the testing of the new weapon was over, he returned in to his house to rest as the next day he would continue to clean large towns from the invasion of the human species.

The wicked man opened a school for people, a place where he taught virgin souls how to kill other folks. He was offering training to newcomers, to those who had never killed before; he taught them techniques by offering lessons. He named his class "execution of the innocent lamb." Believe it or not, one hundred people came to his class for education, and the lesson was murder for the first time.

The evil man said, "I will train you, and I will give you skills and knowledge, so after you graduate from my school, you will become professional assassins. And today will be your first lesson." Giving each person a weapon of choice, he gave them a brief explanation on human anatomy. When he finished, he said, "Now you know the weak spots of a human body, and it will be easy for you to terminate your opposer by cutting theirs veins and main arteries."

He separated the one hundred people into groups of two and said, "I will lock each pair in the room, leaving them there until one is dead, so your goal is to survive by killing your opponent. You will have a choice to kill or to be killed. If you are scared to kill and have changed your mind, I want to know right now. Think about it, and tell me your decision, and if you are afraid, I will send you home. You don't have to continue your schooling."

Seventy adults stepped out of the line, saying, "We do not agree with your rules and teachings: we didn't sign up to die."

"Fine," Lucifer said, "you don't have to do it and stay here any longer." He showed them the exit and walked with them outside, executing them in front of a basketball court by shooting them down with a Mini Gatling. Subsequently, he returned to the classroom and continued the lesson by locking the first pair into a translucent glass room; the rest of the apprentices could watch the tournament and learn from the mistakes of a loser. The first combat was between two young guys. One had a black belt in karate and kickboxing; the second was a three-hundred-pound bodybuilder. After ten minutes of bloody sparring, the boxer guy had brain failure and heart damage. The big muscle guy was beaten and stabbed sixteen times in the gut, neck, back, iliac artery, and inferior vena cava.

His body wallowed on the carpet, calling for medical help. The survivor took a silver sword and ended the life of the defeated man.

The next violent confrontation was between a capoeira dance martial art girl and a shaolin kung fu monk. They were invited into a red room; after a handshake and agreement to continue the death fight, the weapon was handed to a fighters, and they immediately attacked each other.

The capoeira girl jammed the neck of the monk between her legs, pushing hard into his carotid artery, putting him to sleep in ten seconds. The evil teacher said to the girl, "I want you to finish him," so she took a war hammer and smashed it into the head of a shaolin master, leaving a bloody, colorful, slippery surface on the floor. The doors opened, and the attractive dancer was awarded a degree. The next two people were crazy soldiers who had returned from Syria and Iraq; one was Caucasian, and the other was Arab. Both were mentally ill and had paranoia. The instructor opened glass doors and welcomed the veterans by saying, "It is an honor to meet legends in my school, particularly first timers." They walked inside and started punching each other with their elbows, knees, and legs. Both knew different mix fighting styles, such as boxing, jiujitsu, and tae kwon do; also, each had a militant knife. The guy who served in hot spots of Syria said to the Iraqi dude, "I will eat your tongue after I cut it out." He used a bone break style by clinching the arms of his opponent and breaking his wrists, radius ulna bones, elbow joints, and the middle connection of his shoulder and arm. The white guy was lying on his back, cursing the Arab fighter by saying, "Your nation stinks, just like your little shit country." The huge Muslim took concertina wire out of his pocket, wrapping it around the neck of the vanquished European guy and tightened it, using all his power and strength, until the eyes of his rival came out of his eye sockets. The door was unlocked; freedom and a trophy were given to the winner.

The archangel decided to buy parts of a nuclear warhead from the black market of European countries, so he flew to Europe and arranged a meeting with a gun dealer saying, "I brought cash, and I would like to buy parts of a bomb, together with plutonium and uranium."

"No problem," the gun seller said, "you got it, but first I would like to see my money."

The killer opened a suitcase full of one-hundred-dollar bills and said, "Now that you have seen your money, I would like to see the parts of my nuclear bomb."

The dealer brought the parts of a nuclear weapon to him, together with the enriched plutonium and uranium. They shook hands, and the deal was over.

Later Lucifer assembled the nuclear armament by putting parts and components together, using paper instructions. Then he put it inside of a van and drove into the downtown of a major city.

There he reprogrammed it with a cell phone signal as a detonator. When he had finished, he flew back to the United States, making a videotape of himself warning the European Union and NATO of nuclear explosions in major European cities of Eurasia.

He said, "And if you think I am bluffing, I will detonate one of my blasting devices." He said, "I want six billion dollars transferred to my bank account by tomorrow" and gave them his bank account number. Then he said, "You have twenty-four hours to transfer my money, and if you don't comply with my terms and conditions, I will blow up the second bomb." He sent ten copies of the recordings to a different locations, including the White House, the United Nations, the Chinese government, and so on. The next morning he received a phone call from a Pentagon military general.

The voice said, "First, prove to us you are serious and real about threat, and second, you must—"

Lucifer interrupted the general and said, "Turn on the TV, and switch to the news TV channel" as he pressed the button of a detonator at the same time. "Now you know I am serious, and you have twenty hours to transfer the money. End of conversation."

He woke up the next morning and checked his bank account. Six billion dollars had been deposited into his bank account. "Well," he said, "now we are in business."

He asked his girlfriend, "Where would you like to go on vacation?"

She said, "I would like to fly to Dubai in the United Arab Emirates."

"No problem," he said, "I will have a private jet waiting for you." The next morning he asked her, "What else would you like to do?"

She said, "I would like to kill and eat people."

The djinn said, "Your wish is my command. Done." Three beautiful guys were invited into a room with an evil girl inside of it.

Lucifer offered her a choice of weapons, including a knife, ax, machete, and a sword. She picked up knife, and her hands shook as she thought about killing those people, as she had done it only once before. The guys pleaded with her not to hurt them, but she said, "Sorry, dears, but I already ate from the tree of good and evil." She slit open the innocent men with a sharp knife, then she cut the heart out of a guy and ate it. Then she killed the rest of men by slicing their necks and chests with an ax. She said to her boyfriend the devil, "I would like to fuck you right here, lying on the bodies of these dead people." Two hours later the girl said, "I had a very deep orgasm when I was killing those men and you were fucking me deep."

"Cool," Lucifer said and left.

When he returned to the hotel room seven hours later, food was on the table and supper was ready. "Good job, honey," he said. "I like the way you take care of me."

Both sat in the kitchen and began eating the meat of the men she had murdered eight hours ago. He asked her, "How did you cook the meat? Are you willing to give me the recipe?" Then he asked her, "What are you thinking about, my angel?"

She said, "I was thinking about having sex with five young males and females; also my desire and night imagination is to kill them in our room after sex. Will you arrange it and make my dream come true, darling?"

"No problem," he said, and one hour later, five guys and girls were fucking the angel in every hole she had. After four hours of sex, the evil man offered her a huge variety of torture tools and options; she began bisecting the group, inflicting severe pain on all five of them. She was brutally punishing them using a scalpel, then she took an electric device and began sending two thousand volts through the body of a guy who had no feet and wrists. It was her method of maltreatment. The evil man set up a video camera in the middle of the room and began recording.

Then the devil said to her, "I want you to cut the head of a big muscular guy off." She did what he asked; she forced another guy to eat the leg and drink the blood of the man. He ate, then she took scissors and cut his penis off, killing the last guy and a girl using a machete.

She said, "Okay, now I am satisfied watching their pain and suffering. I am tired of bloody games; let's pack the bodies into the garbage bags and throw them into the dumpster. Will you help me?"

"Of course I will help you, my angel," the devil said, and they packed meat and bones into the trash bags.

They found a homeless man and paid him fifty dollars to dump the bags. The bum took the bags filled with human corpses to the dumpster.

The next morning they flew into Miami, Florida, to continue their bloody hobbies.

Angel said, "i want an Uzi, and I also want two teens boy, and a girl; let's kidnap them from a school.

"Awesome," Lucifer replied, "I see no problem doing it." They drove a rental car near the college and sat there, awaiting for postgraduates to come out from the building. The bell rang at 2:00 p.m., and the learners finished their lessons and began exiting the school.

The evil couple stepped out of the car; Angel said, "I can't believe we will rape those beautiful bunnies together in our new evil house."

"Yes," the devil man said, "and we are going brutally chop their legs and hands off, making them experience severe physical pain and unbearable suffering."

Angel started talking with two eighteen- and nineteen-year-old handsome teens, introducing herself as a teacher of the English language. She said, "Your parents paid for extra time, so take a seat please" and opened the doors of her car.

Both the boy and girl didn't mind and sat in the back seat of the car as they drove toward the house. When they arrived, the teenagers asked angel, "Where are we?"

She said, "We are in the private house, and we will learn new English words here."

The guy was so excited as studying new words was his favorite activity.

The girl said, "I like to read too."

Lucifer said, "Excellent, I think we have everything we need."

One hour later all four arrived at the house, and the killers pretended to be very smart teachers as they walked inside. The cannibal closed the door behind the teens, telling Angel, "The students are in your possession now; you can do whatever you want with them." The evil woman was filed with temptation and mandative to one single thought about cutting them slowly with a meat grinder and burning them with fire. They sat on a couch and began talking.

She asked the grown adults to introduce themselves and then asked the guy, "Have you ever thought about kissing your friend?"

The guy said, "I don't think this is a part of the lesson."

Angel said, "Yes, of course it is not a part of the lesson, but would you like to see your friend naked? Be honest with me right now."

The guy replied, "To be honest, yes, I would like to see her naked, and I would like to fuck her as well, but she does not know about it."

Angel took his nineteen-year-old cock and began sucking; he ejaculated in her mouth. Then she talked the girl into having sex with her and her friend. The angel had sex with them for three hours. They were fucking and kissing each other; devil man walked in, bringing a meat grinder and the collection of a meat cutting tools with him.

He said to Angel, "Watch how a professional does his job." He took a large cleaver and began waving it in front of the guy's face, making him feel fear and horror. Later on he used pliers and a little hammer to take the teeth of the boy out. The boy was screaming and crying. Then the evil man removed his penis and testicles, telling the guy to swallow his own genitals.

He did as he was told because he had no choice. The killer had big, sharp scissors for metal cutting. He began fucking the girl, and after he finished, he forced her to eat her friend. Angel was reading a book to the girl, teaching her the etiquette of dining and washing shitholes while she ate the internal organs of her friend.

She told her, "You have a very beautiful body, and it turns me on a lot when I see you naked." Then she stuck two fingers into her young vagina, saying to the girl, "Do you understand what just happened?"

The girl was crying and yelling, "Stop, please stop. You are hurting me; don't hurt me."

But the evil desire of Angel was growing in an arithmetic progression; she had three orgasms while she was harming the young couple. She grabbed her soft hair with her left hand and a sharp knife with the right hand, separating the head of the teen girl from her shoulders as she looked directly into her eyes. She licked her lips, then she lubricated her own vagina with blood and began masturbating. They cooked the bodies of the teens with fire, baking them and drinking their blood, listening to classical music, and talking about life and death.

Angel said, "The meat was very delicious."

"I am glad you find this amusing," the devil man said. One week later Lucifer said, "Do you have any plans or ideas? What are we going to do next?"

Angel said, "We must blow up the holy temples of Jesus Christ and temples of God during a service. Whenever it's full of people. Thus we can prove our worthiness to our father, the devil, who is in hell."

This idea blew up in the minds of killers fast; he loved his girlfriend's clever thinking. So they bought a lot of TNT and dynamite. Satan called his friend that dealt with guns and asked for timing bombs and explosives. One day later the goodies arrived, and they left the house, mining three churches, two Buddhist temples, one Hindu temple, and one mosque with the heavy explosives. They blew up the places when people were inside for a service, praying.

The devil asked Angel, "What is the meaning of life?"

She said, "Life is the opposite of death; life has no meaning; it is the biological desire of the human species."

The tyrant said, "Yes, that's the correct answer; life is a steak."

She said, "I know how we can kill the children of God."

"Yes, yes," the cannibal man said, "that is exactly what we are going to do."

Angel said, "I love you, shaitan."

The despot said, "Thanks. I like you a lot too, angel." The next morning they flew to Hong Kong and brought an offering to their father, the devil. This time they hired four men and paid them ten thousand dollars each to kidnap people. They went to the beach to pick up ten good-looking souls for an altar of immolation. The bodyguards caught the men and women and threw them into the bus to transport them on to a remote location for murder. It was an open field in the forest with many tools and much equipment for cutting and removing the organs of people.

They waited until the Sun went down so they could praise the maker of hell by sacrificing innocent people to him. When the sky became dark, they used a dagger to slice the spines and throats of the praying people. Blood was sprinkling like a fountain of wealth. They drained the blood of five people into the buckets and tubes and were swimming in the blood of those people they had just killed.

The evil man took his sword and showed the edge of it to those that were still alive, saying, "Death is near, and all of you will die tonight. How would you like me to kill you, fast or slow?"

All five were scared and feared for their lives. They supplicated to their dominator, asking for mercy, but he didn't want to cease his joyfulness, so he beheaded the first of them with a fast move of his hand. Picking up the bleeding head of the guy, he showed it to the rest of people, making them feel shock and fear of death.

He drank the man's blood and continued beheading them one by one, praising the almighty devil in the night sky. After he collected bodies and heads of the dead people, he stacked them into the bus for transportation.

They drove to a house to grind up the bodies and to donate meat to a local churches and nonprofit organizations; this way poor and homeless bums will be able to eat and be happy.

The next morning they flew to Sydney, Australia, and sat thinking about their next bloody game to entertain themselves. They visited an arts and craft store to buy tools for wood- and metal-cutting. The idea was is to make chairs, kitchenware, and various forms of art made of human skeletons and bones. The repressive man said, "I will decorate my house inside with furniture that will be made of human skulls and bones."

Angel said, "I will help you, honey, to make your dream come true."

After that they fucked for three hours nonstop. As the stars shone late in the evening, the evil couple went out to hunt for their new victims.

They found three people near a concert hall for opera and instrumental music. The evil girl said to them, "Excuse me, my boyfriend and I are looking for three people for a short project to do ministry tasks. We pay five thousand dollars to each person for two days of work; would you be interested in participating?"

The two girls and one guy looked at each other, and said, "Yes, of course, for five thousand, we don't mind helping you."

"Great," she said, "let's meet at this address on Monday so I can give you assignments." She gave them a business card.

The next morning the doorbell rang, and the new furniture walked into the house. It was hilarious for angel and the evil man because the innocents didn't know they would be murdered that night for their bones to make a throne for an angel to sit and dine on. They seated the guests in the main room on a couch, offering them a meal. All three said, "No thanks, I am not hungry."

One girl asked if she and her friends could see the honorarium first. "Sure," the evil couple replied, "the money is not a problem, but first let us have some sexual perversion with you."

After those words the three friends became nervous saying, "We don't understand what are you talking about."

"Well," Lucifer said, "perhaps I can explain it to you better," and he showed them the iron meat cutter. Angel took her clothes off, saying to her boyfriend, "Let me have voyeurism before you kill them."

"Sure," the devil replied, "you can do whatever you want with them." Then Angel fucked the guy and commanded the girls to lick her vagina. The fully developed characters didn't want to do what she was telling them to do, but they had to obey; otherwise the devil man would slice them like a butcher slices meat at the grocery store.

After two hours of sex with Angel, the devil man gave her a handsaw and a butterfly knife, telling her while laughing loudly, "Now I want you to cut them."

"No, stop, don't do it," the girls and the guy supplicated, but the evil woman didn't have any spark of good in her. She began cutting the girls with a saw, removing their thighbones and shinbones. Then she took her knife and began opening the chest of a guy and a girl, cutting their still alive bodies, and educating herself on the human anatomy.

"Good job," the devil man said. "I am proud of you; you are a good student. Now I want you to separate their flesh from the bones and make sure the bones are clean of meat. The skeletons shall shine before I craft them with my tools," and he drafted a drawing on a piece of paper. It was a picture of a chair he was planning to construct, and he made a design of it.

Angel packed the body parts, stacking them into the boxes filled with ice.

"Would you please give me a glass of blood?" the devil asked his girlfriend.

"Yes, of course my love," she said, and brought him a big glass of still-warm blood with ice, saying, "I hope you will thirst no more, dear."

The evil couple was walking not far from the city of Brazil and talking about God's commandment "Thou shall not kill, or murder."

Lucifer told his girlfriend, "I never understood life and almighty God, but I understand death very well. Look at me, I have killed so many people, and no one stopped me from murdering life; so my point is, there is no God because I killed Holy God, and no one cares about people."

Angel said, "I agree with you, my love, there is no God on Earth." Stars sent a bright light down to Earth so intense it blinded Angel's eyes for a second. She said, "I have a plan; let's buy a restaurant and serve human meat in it to other people. Then we will see how they eat the flesh of their fellow humans."

"Yes," the devil man replied, "it is a wonderful idea; that is why I like you so much, my wise girl, because you always give me good advice."

"I will euthanize people, and I will help you to cook them, honey," she said.

"Very well. I am happy I finally found a helper for myself," the devil man replied.

They bought a building with a big kitchen in it and hung a sign on the door: "Open to the public." Then they abducted fifteen people from the neighborhood and brought them into the kitchen. They printed out a paper menu with a choice of the meals made out of human flesh and wrote "human meat" under the pictures of the food. In four hours the doorbell rang, and five hungry customers walked into the restaurant. The evil companions gave them a menu and waited for an order. To the big surprise of the demons, the people weren't scared of the menu; in fact they ordered food worth two hundred dollars.

"Okay," Angel and the evil spirit said, "your dinner will be ready in twenty minutes."

The psychopath said to his girlfriend, "Make sure they are not using mobile phones, and if you see anyone using a telephone, let me know and I will take care of them; I can't allow them to call the police on us."

"Sure," Angel said. "If I see them using cell phones, I will help you to kill them."

"Yes, very well," the man said. "Dinner is ready." And five meals on the big plates were served to their customers.

The first meal was human bones and ribs with tendered flesh on it, slowly baked on fire. The second plate had human heads on it that were cooked with corn, green peppers, and lemons, and the third plate had human organs on it like the liver, heart, kidneys, lungs, male and female genitals. It was steamed and smoked in the oven and served with garlic, onion, mashed potato, apples, and grapefruit. Dish number four included human hips, legs, and calves together with the arms and shoulders decorated with rosemary, green onion, tomatoes, beets, and carrot. Angel brought the food and set it on the table right in front of the guys and the girls.

They were scared when they saw the human flesh served right in front of them and said, "We thought it was a joke when we were reading the menu."

"Oh no, it is not a joke," the evil couple replied. "First, we want you to eat and finish your meal, and if you cooperate and eat, you will be set free. If you refuse to do what we are telling you, you will die here tonight and become a meal for somebody else, so eat it now."

The visitors ate the human meat, crying.

After dinner was over, Angel said, "Okay, now you are free to go. Go now, and don't tell anyone what happened." They opened the door, and five lucky and mentally ill people ran outside to save their lives. The evil girl and the king of hell were walking on a beach in India near a beautiful Hindu temple. The man told his girlfriend, "We can do everything we want on Earth; what would you like to do?"

The girl said, "Let's buy thirty acres of land and build a graveyard on it. We will abduct fifty people and make an evil game; we will force them to kill and bury each other. We will give them a lot of weapons, and then we will tell them only ten people who survive will walk away alive from the cemetery." So that was that; they caught fifty people from an ashram: twenty-five females and twenty-five males. Then they brought them onto a battlefield with a tall concrete fence around it, closing the big gate behind them. When all fifty players were inside the yard, the devil man explained to them the rules of the game, telling them the reason why they were brought there, and unloaded a trailer full of weapons. It had battle axes, halberds, maces, swords, flails, spears, crossbows, sickles, and tomahawks. The game host had a Kalashnikov rifle in his hands. He said, "I will stand near the gate and control the playground, so it's now time to kill each other; only ten of you will walk away alive, and your time is ticking." He shot one guy in the head to prove his word and the seriousness of the situation to the rest of a crowd.

No one could believe in the reality of life and death, but this was real. One girl grabbed a sword and killed a guy standing next to her, then the rest of the crowd ran toward the weapon pile. Five minutes later all forty-eight people had knives and axes in their hands. They fought each other, trying to kill to survive. Blood and dead bodies were everywhere.

The man with a gun counted the number of dead people on the ground. After about thirty minutes of brutal massacre and slaughter, forty dead people lay on the ground with no sign of life in them. "Well done." The spirit of the devil spoke. "Now I want you to bury your friends in the graves, and then you are free to go home."

After the bodies of the people were underground, the man opened the gate, and ten morally crazy Hindus walked outside, escaping the hell they had just been through.

"How did you like being the eyewitness to the death-match, my angel?" the devil man asked his girlfriend.

She answered, "I was so excited and hot during the entertainment; I enjoyed watching them dying a lot."

The evil freak said, "I want to fuck you right now and give you my thanks for everything you did for me, my love."

And they fucked on the burial ground.

Two weeks later the fallen angel man said to his girl, "I have an idea about what we will do today. We will build a temple to my father, the devil. We will murder and execute people inside a crematorium using a wide variety of killing techniques."

Lucifer invested one million dollars into a project of construction to build a house of worship. One week later the shrine was ready and open to the public. Believers walked in and out of the cathedral until one hundred people were praying inside the sanctum.

The devil man and his bitch locked the doors of the house, the so-called holy place, capturing naive people inside of it. Lucifer gave his girlfriend a sharp two-edged sword and said, "There are one hundred people inside of the trap we made, and I want to see you killing fifty of them using the sword I gave you."

He had a loaded gun and controlled the crowd from attacking his woman. Angel began cutting people's heads off with the shining blade. The crowd panicked, so the devil man shot twenty of them right away, discharging ten magazines of fifty-caliber bullets.

When the flock of sheep was quiet, Lucifer spoke. He had prepared a speech four days earlier, writing it on a piece of paper. He said, "Today, all of you will die a painful and horrible death. Do you have any questions before my girlfriend and I begin extermination and mass execution?" he asked the crowd.

People cried and pleaded for mercy. "Please don't kill us. Please stop; don't hurt us," but the Satan man took a large ax and a guy, laying his head on a block and chopping it off. People watched with wide-open eyes of disbelief. Then the man took ten more girls and guys and lined them up in front of a guillotine, explaining the procedure of how they would be lynched on the table of death. He told every one of his victims, "I want you to fuck each other, so I can watch and receive rejoicing and happiness."

Twenty out-of-their-mind guys and girls undressed in front of him and began sexual intercourse, fucking each other everywhere.

"Enough," the man said. "It is time to die; bring your sinful assholes to the altar," he commanded. Angel began the process of beheading as they grieved and pleaded for pardoning inside the house of pain and death.

After the slaughter was over, the evil girl told her boyfriend, "It is over, and there is no one left alive here; we killed all of them."

"Yes," Lucifer said, "you are correct; everyone is dead. Now I want you to help me with the dead bodies." They piled up the bodies in the center of the temple.

After one hundred dead cadavers were placed in one spot, the man said, "I want you to spray gasoline everywhere inside of the building and bring eight barrels of petrol." Firing up a cigarette, he threw it on a pile of the people he had just killed.

The building fired up like a Lewes bonfire. The evil couple left, watching the temple becoming flaming wooden coal.

"What do you want to do next?" The man asked his female partner.

She said, "I am starving, and I would like to eat."

"No problem," the demon replied, and a twenty-year-old guy was invited into the room of Angel. The evil woman played with her toy, whom she had bought for one night from an escort agency. She took a blade and stuck it into his gut, opening it up and taking his intestines out. The guy watched her and his own intestines, unable to understand his own death and asking her, "Why?" His body was still alive, but technically speaking he was dead. She ate his body without cooking it in front of him, telling him not to cry and giving him hope by saying, "Relax, everything will be okay; you will die soon." After this she extracted his liver and heart. She sang him a song, and his eyes closed from pain and shock, and he died. Angel had a very delicious dinner, breakfast, and lunch. The next morning the enraged man told his girlfriend about a new idea that had birthed in his mind when he was sleeping. He said, "I will invite twenty beautiful and sinless souls, and I will torment them for you, so you can educate yourself watching me putting them to death slowly. I will buy a new video camera so you can make a recording of me causing them excruciating pain."

"Yes, my love, no problem," she said to her boyfriend. "I hope you will enjoy the process of torture and sadism." The devil made ten thousand invitation flyers to a porn party at his house, printing them out and giving them away to people everywhere. He prepared rooms for the bloody horror and cannibal orgy.

When twenty people came into his house the next evening for a porn film shoot, he invited everyone to walk inside and take a look around the house. It was decorated as a playboy mansion and there were pictures of naked people on the walls and ceiling. Erotic toys were everywhere.

"Outstanding," the girlfriend of the evil man said, "we have enough people. Now we can start recording the movie." Lucifer locked the doors of the house, turned his video camera on, and started making a film. The first part was about sucking dicks, licking vaginas, fucking and masturbating like crazy with each other. The dark angel asked her beloved for permission to join an orgy for a couple of hours. He said, "Okay, you can join the sex party, but don't forget about the final, brutal end."

"Of course I remember," she said.

Everybody undressed and began lovemaking for four hours, licking assholes, fucking and engaging in hardcore gay and lesbian pornography.

Satan took up a saber and gave a stiletto to his girlfriend, asking the movie actors, "Did you like playing with each other?"

Everyone said, "Yes, we enjoyed the sex."

"Good job," he said. "Now it is time for a reward. I will pay you back."

He cut one guy from the top to a bottom with a sharp saber. Half of the body fell to the right, and the second half fell to the left. Blood sprinkled on the faces of the nearby people. The viewers were paralyzed from watching the live murder of the guy they had just been fucking. Then the killer took a katana Japanese sword and started beheading nine people without mercy. He saved ten people for his girl to play with; the evil girl nailed five to a wooden wall. This way she had better access to their internal body organs. She opened their chests and abdomens, took out their organs, and watched them crying and moaning in pain.

She told the remaining group to "fuck the dead bodies of the people I have just killed." While they were fucking the dead corpses, angel masturbated as she watched them. "Well done," Lucifer said. "I'm proud of you, my angel, and now I want you to tell me the names of every organ you extracted and ate. This way I know you are a clever student and have done your homework. And don't forget, you have five more people to kill."

"Thank you very much," she replied. "I do the best I can to make you and myself happy." Angel took a hatchet and scythe, telling her prey, "I want you to bow down in front of me." They did as she asked. With a wide swing, she decapitated them, and their heads dropped on the floor. She wiped the blood from her scythe and continued the process of cutting. The young adults were begging not to be killed, but Angel was like a wild beast from the jungle. She bit the throat of a girl, ripping off pieces of meat out and chewing them, using the hatchet at the same time; it was a bloody nightmare.

The warlord told his girlfriend, "I will show you the true nature of humankind."

"Yes, please show me," Angel said. They walked into an armory shop, purchasing five hundred pistols, one hundred automatic rifles, thirty sniper rifles, and one thousand boxes of ammunition. The devil man hired thirty soldiers, paying them $100,000 each for completion of the project. The assignment was to kill rich politicians and judges at a summit in Moscow. The thirty special-force fighters were born and raised to kill; they were given training to remove the heads of the government permanently. The devil gave his girlfriend a video camera for recording the executions. A blacklist of people who were presidents and prime ministers and would be given the death penalty. When a vice president was giving a speech about the world economic crisis, snipers sat one mile away from the building, controlling the conference. When the dome of the cathedral was full of congress people and judges, the devil gave the command to kill, and the soldiers shot everyone inside the building. "What a brilliant picture," Satan said. "Look at them; no more fat pigs in the chairs of the world governments."

"Yes," the girlfriend of a devil man said. "It is sick as fuck, and I had an orgasm watching them die."

The evil man said to his girlfriend, "You will have a lot of food after my guys finish the assassinations."

They took the bodies of the dead people, undressed them, and sold them to an African American restaurants for twenty thousand dollars.

The next morning the destroyer decided to rob the Bureau of Engraving and Printing. He bought a bazooka, fifty antitank grenades, a heavy machine gun, and two Gunto military swords for himself and his girlfriend from a World War II gun dealer. They drove to a building where billions of dollars was printed every day and waited for the workers to load an armored truck with $50 million. When it left the thug and his girlfriend followed it in their van. They drove for fifty miles, and when the bulletproof truck was near a county road without witnesses, they blew up the truck using a bazooka and grenades. After the truck flipped, they stepped out of the van and fired at everyone until the last security guard was dead. They opened the truck and loaded bags with cash into their van, driving away into a forest.

Angel said, "We must find a place where we can check the money bags and securely arrange them in our basement."

When they drove to a house, the bad man said, "We have a lot of money, so what would you like to do next?"

Angel said, "Let's build a war machine so people will destroy themselves faster, because it is too much work for us."

"What a wonderful suggestion," the bandit said. "I like your proposition and your superintelligent mind." They hired ten technicians, ten physicists, five architects, five engineers, and ten constructors to create a space mirror that would orbit the Earth, generating concentrated solar power into a laser beam, capable of destroying entire cities within a couple of hours. The weapon was ready one year after the beginning of a project. When it was ready, they launched a rocket up into a space together with the satellite and the weapon affixed to it. The devil gave Angel a key to a remote control, saying, "Now you have the power to destroy the entire human race; all you have to do is to press a button on that electronic device and choose which city you would like to explode. It's as simple as that," and they laughed.

The house was empty as the fiend and his girlfriend were traveling around the world, entertaining themselves by making bloody horror in every town they went to. This time the man took a crossbow with arrows, an assassin saber, and steel strangulation wire to choke his prey. Hunting and killing for food was his most liked activity. He stepped out of his helicopter, carrying the weapons behind his back. He went to a crowd of people and started an archery tournament, shooting eleven people with sharp arrows, beheading five of them with the Chinese saber, and strangling two females using wire in front of everyone. People ran away in fear of the hunter. After the main part of the bloody performance was over, the devil man commanded his bodyguard to collect and load the bodies into the helicopter for further kitchen work. The human meat was ground and sold to a church owner who was a priest. The priest gave them $25,000 for eighteen dead bodies and made a supper for his church members.

The evildoer was hungry and thirsty for young blood and souls, so he decided to capture twenty teenagers from their houses. He developed a plan for the kidnapping by knocking on the door of a house and asking if they had a room for rent. Every time someone opened the door to him, he shocked them with a taser gun and prepared them right there inside of their own houses by taking their skin off and enjoying their groans and pleas to stop the horror and malicious actions. Lucifer laughed loudly, understanding the power he had over his victims. His body shook as he watched the bleeding pieces of meat die right in front of him. He said, "I have power over you; I can take away your life from you, if I want to." He cut them slowly, watching their reaction, as he stared directly into their pupils at the moment of death, saying, "I want to see the light of your soul, and I also want to see your soul leaving your body as I take your life from you with my dagger." He inserted the sharp dirk into the throat of a beautiful girl, licking her blood and observing the moment of death in her eyes, but he saw neither her soul nor spirit, only one hundred pounds of meat on the floor with no sign of life in it. "Well," he said, "I guess there is no soul." He picked her body up from the floor and began the standard procedure of butchering and cooking.

The meat pies were ready in sixty minutes from the time of heating on the stove. The meat eater was happy eating his own work of art. Lucifer sat and thought about the taste of the girl he had killed one and a half hour ago. The evil man took his favorite weapon, a small hatchet and a rope, and went out to a crowded place to catch his new prey. He walked into a concert hall to hear performance of classical music. While sitting and listening to Vivaldi, he was choosing his targets for a future fleshy and bloody pastime with his new toys. A young couple sat near him, so he started talking to them and introducing himself as a movie producer.

He asked them, "Are you lesbians?"

They said, "Yes, we are lesbians."

"What a surprise," he said. "I record sexy videos on tape, and I would like to invite you in to my house for a session. I pay five thousand dollars for a video recording. Would you like to accept my offer?"

"Wow, that's a lot of money," the two friends remarked.

Lucifer exclaimed, "If you're keen, my car is waiting outside; in this envelope is your upfront payment for your time and cooperation" and he gave them $2,500 as a trust agreement.

The girls accepted the offer, laughing at their good fortune. Fifteen minutes later the two adults and the cannibal drove toward the house of their demise.

The nice-looking man, who was a very handsome devil, told his goddesses of love, "You can do anything you want in my house; just make sure you prepare yourself for a porn shoot."

The girls played erotic games in his house, taking each other's clothes off and licking their clitorises and labia as the guy held the video camera making a film, fantasizing at the same time about cutting them with a razor blade in front of a mirror. After around fifty minutes of dildo fucking and licking, the evil guy joined them for another hour, binding them up with a rope around their legs and hands. The happy females did not realize their lives would end tonight in this house.

They were smiling and playing games, thinking it was all part of a movie plan. Finally, when his dream came true, and the blade was in his hand, he cut the faces of the pretty women with it. Pleading voices filled the house of the devil, asking for mercy. He took a sharp surgery tool that he had stolen from the hospital and opened the flesh by cutting their arms and legs, watching and observing the last seconds of life in their bodies. While one of them was still alive, he undressed her body and fucked the almost-dead girl. Her breasts and nipples were bleeding, and her liver was removed. She died crying with bloody tears. The second girl he cooked inside the fireplace using a blowtorch, skewers, and a smoker. He put the smoked meat into storage and saved it there for future hungry days.

And then Holy God came out of a star gate down to Earth in its own spirit, which was irradiated with supreme astronomical content and unlimited knowledge about the geosphere and Van Allen radiation belt. The animated perispirit was working outside of the space and time continuum and being timeless, making corrections and fixing the disorder of chaos into which solid ground was so deeply submerged over millions of years. It could see, hear, and read without the human body. First, the spirit of Holy God killed the maker of hell and the devil. Second, hell was conquered and a voice proclaimed, "Now I control entry and portals and stand in power of heaven, and hell, so the spirit of every human who died on Earth will go to an appropriate place after death, according to their deeds on earth."

The meat factory was functioning at its normal pace, and the doorway into paradise and Abaddon was opening and closing every five to six seconds. The human soul and spirit collector was tuned like a musical, melodious instrument according to zeros and ones. Then Holy God created a time machine on Earth in case something went wrong and evil people took advantage of good people and sinners killed good people. The matrix would be rewritten back in time, and the murdered victims of an evil crimes would be brought back in to life after their death into an undefined moment of time, giving good people a second chance in life as it was not their fault or decision to die. It was given to them as a gift from the holy one; resurrected people would have no memories of their death.

A Christian guy was living near the evil man's house. He was out taking his usual evening walk before dinnertime. As he was running, he suddenly saw a light inside of a nearby house and a shadow with a knife behind the curtain. Pausing, he checked it out and walked nearer the window, trying not to make a noise. He looked into a small gap between the wall and the frame and witnessed the horror inside. The man inside was making clothes out of a young female he had recently stabbed to death; her body was moving on the floor toward an open door. The bad man was using a bone knife to extract her ribcage, and through it, into the back of the girl, a bone knife pierced the spine. He took it out and stuck it back in repeatedly, until her body did not move at all. He sat on the chair next to her and began removing and taking her skin off to make a winter coat. The Christian guy stood outside watching, unable to believe the happening was real. He ran toward his house to get his gun, rushing to come back and shoot the devil man. He broke the window with a stone and jumped inside the house, where Lucifer stood before him, chewing the still-beating heart of the girl. The good guy pointed the gun at him and said, "Why are you doing this? What made you commit such an evil act? Answer me!"

The cannibal said, "I am the devil, and I have killed more people than you can imagine, and I ate them also. I can give you anything you desire: money, success, women. What would you like? You can kill me right now, or you can let me live, and I will make any of your wishes come true."

The Christian guy hesitated for a second and said, "I will give you some time, but before I shoot and kill you, I want an explanation about why you became a devil man."

The cannibal said to him, "You know, human flesh is so tasty. You definitely should try it, and by the way, I have a meal in my refrigerator right now. Would you like to eat it?"

"No," the good guy said. "It is wrong to eat people, and it is wrong to kill them."

"Why is it wrong?" the devil asked. "These people are going to die anyway, so why not kill them and eat them?"

The good guy answered, "It is morally wrong and immoral."

"It is not immoral to me," the devil said. "Also, I have a collection of movies in my living room. Would you like to walk there with me? I will show you and explain more."

"Yes, please, show it to me," the guy said, having strong faith in God he would not be harmed. They walked together into his main room, sat on a sofa, and began watching the films. The cannibal turned on the video player and showed him the recordings; the guy sat crying, telling the devil man, "I can't believe it is real."

"Yes, it is real," Lucifer answered with an electronic voice from hell, "and I am the real devil from hell. I kill humans because I hate Holy God and I hate people. In fact, I know there is no God on Earth and there never was. Look, there are so many people on Earth, and they multiply every day like fucking rabbits. They pray to the creator of Earth every day, the so-called almighty God, but the maker of sky and Earth does not help humans and does not answer their prayers; somebody has to do the damned work. Do you agree with me? I kill human beings, and I eat sin, which is human flesh, so I eat sinners. If you kill me, you will become the devil also, and you will join me in hell because Holy God said, 'You shall not murder or kill.' So the choice is yours. Kill me, and you will join me in hell, or you let me live my life, and I will make you God himself on Earth."

The Christian guy paused for a second and then said, "I will not go to hell after I kill you as you are the devil and it is okay to eliminate your kind from the surface of Earth." The spirit of Holy God embodied the flesh of the Christian dude pointing the barrel of a gun at the evil man as he pressed the trigger. Lucifer fell on the floor laughing and died.

The good guy started exploring the murderer's house. Walking into the bedroom, he discovered a young lady lying on a bed and sleeping.

Awakening her, he asked, "Are you okay, and what is your name?"

She said, "My name is Angel; can you save me?" The guy took her hand and they ran outside together, leaving the house of terror. The evil girl didn't tell the guy she was the girlfriend of the devil himself; instead she introduced herself as a hostage and victim. After four weeks of friendship with the nice, good guy, during which they fucked every night, Angel said, "I am so glad you saved me; I thought he would kill me, but you broke into the house and saved me. You're my hero."

"It is not a big deal," the guy replied, talking to the girl. The furious woman sat thinking about lunch. She was so used to eating human flesh, and her new boyfriend was vegetarian, so she decided to kill and eat him at night during sex with a metal stick that she sharpened with a sharpening stone. While he was lying down on the bed and she was on top of him, jumping up and down on his dick, he ejaculated inside of her, and she struck the guy with the stick, making puncture wounds in his body. After her lover was dead, she removed his head and began masturbating using his head as dildo, and eating his penis, which she had amputated. The ghost of her dead boyfriend Lucifer came out from hell and said, "I am so proud of you, my angel, and pleased you are doing my work, as I didn't have enough time to finish."

"Yes," she said to the spirit of the devil, "I will continue to do your work on Earth to make you happy in hell." Angel lived in the house of the guy she had just killed for another two months before she moved on to another house as she was homeless. She also had no money as Lucifer did not leave her any cash. So she walked into her dressing room and opened her wardrobe full of fancy clothes.

She put them on in front of a looking glass and did her makeup, making herself look sexy to cast a spell on any future boyfriend. Two hours later she walked into a fancy hotel to get to know a group of guys who were having a gay party on the first floor. The evil woman sat next to them ordering drinks from the barman. The guys spoke to her; each had a strong erection as they thought about sex.

She said to herself, "Well, I guess five dicks is even better than one" aloud; she asked, "Would you like to fuck me?"

The guy said, "My friends and I have a condominium not far from here, and we would like to invite you in to our place."

Her expectation was fulfilled, and all five guys ejaculated into her mouth. In about an hour, she opened her purse and took out a little pistol with a suppressor. She walked toward the hungry guys, who were begging her for more sex, and shot all of them one by one, leaving one guy for herself to satisfy her own sexual desire.

She enjoyed her new house and a meal. She fucked the guy in the morning, afternoon, and evening until his dick could not stay rigid. In two weeks she fucked him all the way to death. As the years went by, the evil woman, Angel, killed one hundred guys in the same way, traveling around the world, visiting new places and exploring new houses. She met new guys in every city she flew to; as a result every meeting had the same brutal end in the kitchen with her cooking a cannibalistic dinner, but every day she thought about the experiences with her first boyfriend five years ago, the devil man who forced her pure, sinless, virgin soul to become that of an evil, dark angel. It was too late to repent since her satanic cult had gone too far, and she knew God would never forgive her for the evil actions she had done and the murders she had committed. She didn't believe in God and did not care about spirituality. She knew Holy God was dead as she had killed him personally many times. Angel purchased an airplane ticket to Rome, Italy, asking heaven, "What is love?" But the spirit was silent, and no one answered her question. "Okay," she said, "there is no love without money, and certainly zero money is death." She walked into a gun store and ordered a nice forty-five caliber pistol with a stainless steel light suppressor from a catalog for five hundred euros. The arms dealer gave Angel the gun and said, "This is an excellent choice, and here are the free accessories that come with your new purchase; if you take good care of it, it will last you forever."

She took the weapon and walked outside with it, driving onto the main highway and mixing herself with the crowd of cars on the road. Driving near a sanctuary with a cross, she parked near the building and walked inside of a temple, starting a conversation with monks who were working inside. She said, "I need spiritual and physical help. Would you be so kind as to offer me your assistance and aid?" The monks looked at angel's naked legs, and the wild animal instincts made them sexually aroused. The holy monks could not resist sin and temptation.

They started talking to her about her life problems.

The evil woman said, "I rent a room not far from here, and my sister is lying in the bed there; she needs exorcism of the demons inside her as she does not have a boyfriend and is very lonely. I will pay you four hundred euros if you agree to come with me and get to know my younger sister intimately by showing her what a real man is all about and eject the evil spirit out of her." The monks looked at each other, and the almighty dollar started singing them a song. The woman and two young priests drove to her house and went inside. They asked her, "Where is your sister?"

Angel said, "I lied to you to lure you into my house because my eros and passion is too strong, and I want you to show me what real love is." She said, "Get down on your knees, and lick my clitoris now, and if you will not facilitate, I will shoot you right here, right now. You have only one option, and the only choice you have today is to eat my vaginal orifice's lips until I am pleased, happy, and satisfied."

The two brothers undressed in front of her and began a long two-hour lick. After five orgasms and expulsion of fluids, she proclaimed, "I am satisfied, but I still don't know what love is." Then she shot them, cooked, and ate them the same night. She ate love, and it was very delicious.

Reading the Bible, she was trying to find answers and spiritual peace before killing herself. She went to a deserted place to see stars up in the night sky; she sat and was thinking about hell and heaven, observing and watching stars. Grabbing a loaded gun, she committed suicide.

God continued to destroy the weapons of humans by demolishing them and eliminating everything, starting with nuclear weapons and finishing with guns. When Earth was cleaned of its armament of military equipment, international peace was formed as a result. Ten thousand more angels were sent down to Earth to break down and obliterate prisons of evil buildings, eradicating mortal, evil people from the land and their immoral wicked homes. Holy God took on the appearance of a jinn to mix with the world, acting as male and female human to understand sinners, good and evil people, feeding them with animals, as the maker of heaven knew the past, present, and future fate of planet earth. Jinn sat inside of her virtual library reading and downloading five thousand languages from her house up in the galaxy down on Earth. The being was educating people to see who deserved to go to a higher level of paradise and who should stay on Earth or go to hell. A new human was born and died every hour on Earth, and their soul continued to learn in heaven by reading the matrix, pages of a virtual reality book. The leftovers of quantum computers created galactic net and an electro-photonic web for teachings. The physical realm was building by itself; reality was working the way it was supposed to, keeping people wondering if there was a heaven and hell after death. The molecular and atomic levels were functioning within their normal parameters, supporting and sustaining human bodies, observing spirituality, and awaiting the internet-souls of its children on a terrestrial sphere. Everything was downloaded into a matrix in different varieties and forms to make people happy and smile. The digital makers of money came into sight from dimension number four, making calculations using its computerized calculator and speaking into the 3D realm of humans. "I made a plurality of mathematical trigonometry on Earth to make people happy, but as a result, the rich people stole from the poor people and the poor people killed the rich, and the wealthy killed the destitute for money, selling the flesh of their fellow brothers and sisters because of extreme poverty and hunger. Time ticked into the future, and more people became victims of moolah; the poor died, and the rich were blissful. Then we decided to make weapons and give it to people for self-defense. But they started wars, killing each other for no reason. Our dimension of time was exposed, and people found the entrance into our world by traveling into the past and back into the future, predicting the stock market. That is why we were condemned to hell from the beginning of creation." The holy jinn was writing his books, reading decimals at the same time. Aljana and Aljahim were his favorite places of attendance. The soul of the almighty walked on the surface of a planet, collecting the phantoms of dead bodies and scanning them to see if they had a deadly sin on them.

Death spoke from hell, talking to people and persuading them to become disbelievers, turn away from their faith, rejecting Holy God as the maker of earth, paradise, and Hades by making themselves irreligious atheists. The spirit of the devil was saying repeatedly, "Kill, kill," and the holy spirit of God said repetitively, "Don't kill."

The holy one wrote a law, in accordance with which the souls of good killers would be forgiven and accepted into the lower areas of heaven for further education. The souls of evil killers would never be forgiven and would be taken into an imaginary nightmare of hell forever. The souls of those who killed zero would enter paradise after death, and the souls of the good ones who were murdered or killed would enter the utopia of Elysium forever. The souls of evil ones who were murdered or killed would go into the freezer of nightmare forever. The souls of good people who committed suicide would go up to heaven forever, and the souls of evil people who committed suicide would stay in Hades forever. The same laws applied to jinn, angels, or any other beings on Earth or up in the multiverse.

She said, "I don't care what you eat, or whom you eat, but the only thing I care about is your soul and body, and that is why I wrote this decree."

Entrance into spiritual heaven was programmed by the vibration of a voice. The wave of the true Holy God had a special intonation. "Please don't kill."

Recognition was initiated at approximately the speed of sound, or faster. Hell and heaven, zero and one—that is how it was, and that is how it always would be, holy zero killed zero, and holy one is the commandment "Thou shall not kill." Or good killer and evil killer. The souls of holy zeros who killed zero or were murdered by good or evil killers would be taken to paradise. If good killers killed humans—those with the title of holy zero on them—the soul of the killer would stay in hell forever. If good killers killed evil killers, the souls of good killers would be in heaven. If evil killers killed good killers, or a holy one, the soul of the evil killer would stay in hell forever. If a good killer killed another good killer, the souls of both would go to heaven. If an evil killer killed another evil killer, the souls of both evil killers would go to hell of never-ending combat. Consequently, a binary language was made together with the digital world of a computerized matrix grid, where each letter represented as a certain amount of numbers, zeros, and ones: 01.

The number zero is 00110000, and the number one is 00110001.

A 01000001 a 01100001 B 01000010 b 01100010 C 01000011 c 01100011 d 01000100 d 01100100 E 01000101 e 01100101 F 01000110 f 01100110 G 01000111 g 01100111 H 01001000 h 01101000 I 01001001 I 01101001 J 01001010 j 01101010 K 01001011 k 01101011 l 01001100 l 01101100 M 01001101 m 01101101 N 01001110 n 01101110 o 01001111 o 01101111 P 01010000 p 01110000 Q 01010001 q 01110001 r 01010010 r 01110010 s 01010011 s 01110011 T 01010100 t 01110100 U 01010101 u 01110101 V 01010110 v 01110110 W 01010111 w 01110111 X 01011000 x 01111000 y 01011001 y 01111001 Z 01011010 z 01111010

Five billion people were working for the devil, and five billion were working for a righteous God. Both had an army of fighters; they fought for money and justice to prove to themselves the existence of heaven and hell after death.

The soldiery was well trained and prepared to erase their enemy from the face of an orb; a weapon of nonhuman origin was designed and manufactured for military forces and their troops. They attacked the holy people of Holy God first, so the saints didn't have many options but to protect themselves by fighting back. Four billion people were erased, killed on the combat zone of war; heaven was crowning good killers, and their souls were promoted to an angelic levels of paradise serving divine powers. The souls of evil assassins were taken into the dimension number six and were locked there for eternity. The souls of innocent, hallow, just men were killed during war action and taken to the utopia of paradise forever. Half of the terrestrial orb belonged to the devil, and the other half was owned by God.

The devil knew he and his evil children would never leave hell because of the unforgiveable sins they had committed while being on Earth as humans, so they rebelled against the holy people and holy spirits of God by confusing, misleading, and giving them the wrong information about truth and reality, spirituality, and existence after and before the death of the physical body.

Satan spoke from his secret place on Earth to people and said, "Look at yourself and your holy maker; you are nothing but flesh and bones. No one can help you, and nobody cares about your pain and suffering, so why do you pray to your omnipotent God, who claimed to have made heaven and earth? With all God's unlimited, preeminent power, he could not save them from death and stop me from killing two billion people since the birth of Christ. Where was the maker of your planet when death destroyed half of the population by sending fire, tornadoes, earthquakes, floodwaters, indigence, illness, and disease that walked among you and took your lives from you for no reason? Bow down to me and pray to me; glorify my house, my name, and my angels of death, and I will accept you into my kingdom of diablo." The voice of the devil spoke into the subconscious of all humans. "If you have not killed anyone, I want you to kill at least one human, and then I will accept you into my house forever; after you kill, you will be my child. I, the true and only God, in the little sphere of your so-called home. You will see a galaxy full of stars with your own eyes like no one else among your own kind, for my house stretches up into the sky, and I open hidden gates of the cosmos only to the chosen ones."

One billion people joined Lucifer in the lower regions of the underworld as the temptation of the promised never-ending life after death and rich lifestyle were too attractive to turn down. The kids of the devil accepted the offer and killed, creating a ritual and secret society by meeting each other in private places and offering confused souls a pistol, asking them to kill and join the devil's organization for unlimited wealth and money. Every day the ground swallowed the new sacrifices.

Dead flesh, graveyards, and crematoria worked twenty-four hours a day nonstop, as sorrow and bloody-red colored clouds gathered up in the noosphere. Nature itself was crying by sending rain. Thousands of dead bodies were burned every day. The anger of Holy God was great. Thunder and lightning electrified the air and destroyed estates, as the holy one became a killer, and no one cared if he or she was good or bad. The military factory never slept. War was declared. People were possessed with an evil virus, and everyone tried to assassinate weak people. Hospitals saved their soldiers who fought in the war. The planet became a living hell for kids, leaving no variants to survive. They prayed to an open sky, but instead of hope and salvation, another bomb was exploded. Holy zeros who killed zero walked and thought about whether to kill or not to kill. One hundred million people committed suicide as they could not resist such a flattering offer to fly to heaven before their biological clock ended. Every time they bought guns, five out of ten bastards shot themselves in a temple to see what would happen after death, releasing themselves from the pain of the earthly world and sinful body. Humanity's diseased population grew every day, as evil workers and followers of the devil made plans of destruction. Holy zeros were losing their holiness by shooting people at night, converting themselves from zero into one. They did it, calling themselves gods of the earth and sky. The killers were above the holy law, and due to a lack of knowledge, they played gods, traveling to foreign countries, decreasing the number of people on the globe by slaughtering other men, and increasing the amount of those whom they did not like.

They collected numbers and memories for their judgment day after death, if there was to be one.

The artificial devil made a special bank account for the killers. For every man or woman they slayed, one hundred ounces of golden coins were deposited into the account of the killers as a reward for their brave actions, for pressing a trigger without fear. The word "faith" became something distant from reality, as people did not believe and did not want to know the meaning of it. Meat was cooking, and no one knew what they should believe in as pain was just as real as death. Holy God and its angels did not give up on the unbelievers; they flew everywhere faster than the speed of light, creating invisible tunnels up to interstellar space, helping humans with faerie magic hidden from human eyesight. Believers talked to those who had no faith, explaining fallen angels and who Holy God was. Those whose eyes were opened to the painful truth showed faithful Christians and religious societies the truth about life and death by taking a knife and saying, "If a holy, almighty, powerful God exists, then we want to see how she will stop us from spilling innocent blood," but no one stopped them from sin, and nobody said a single word to them. Silence was above and below them, and there was no one out there to save the lives that were taken so easily.

Beings from far distant constellations arrived and visited Earth to see for themselves if it was true; they could not believe that a highly advanced civilization was destroying themselves with atomic weapons. An interplanetary summit was arranged to save life. Superadvanced technology was brought to Earth to solve the problems of global suffering. A statement was made that if the maker of Earth did not care about life and death, then we would intervene and offer our support to those who asked for it. One billion humans were evacuated from Earth to neighboring planets to save the species from self-destruction. They were sent through the vertical and horizontal teleporter rings, which were constructed above and under certain places on Earth.

Intergalactic eyes observed humans in the day and nighttime; holy zero was the leader of spirituality in paradise and the enormity of hell. Whenever people were awake, they lived normal lives, having no memory of the world of dreams and the places they traveled during the night.

Whenever they slept and awakened, they did not bother themselves much with the question of what slumber or dormancy were. But the world of dreams was much more real than the world of the flesh in which they lived after awakening. A lot of people could not wake up in the morning, and their self-consciousness searched for an exit as they became lost inside their own reverie, lucid dreaming, coma, or whatever it was called in our world. Confused by reality and a sleep paralysis, they could not come back into the 3D realm and open their eyes. This deep state of mind was a spiritual death. It happened when the devil took the soul of watchmen from them, or when the observer had no control over his or her own destiny inside of a dream. Whenever a good or an evil person was dying or was killed watching his or her dream-fantasia, they were awakened into another lucid dream at the same time without knowing the truth or being able to distinguish reality from the dreamy fantasy. At that moment they felt as if they had died for real or had been killed, but in the present life, or illusory mental imagery, they were fully alive.

The holy ten and Christ controlled the entrance and portals from the world of visionary dreamers into our world of humans. The moment of transfer from and to was like a puzzle made of little pieces that assembled and disassembled the image of this world. The devil lived inside of a day or night together with Holy God. To understand good there had to be comprehension of the opposite as evil. A good God was prevailing over the evil forces of nightmares, controlling the actions of cartoons, or in some cases films, which people were watching at night and day every time their subliminal mind was disconnected from the 3D realm and taken into a fantasy of holy jinn. Both worlds were intertwined to keep one lonely from humans and no human wraiths out there as the number was infinite. Whenever good or evil humans were killing other good or evil human beings, intelligent or unintelligent, guilty or not guilty, the cosmic gate and the star gate descended onto the foundation from the upper heavens, taking the souls and bodies of those dead or alive women or men up to a palace of divinity, or the atrocity of hell, which was like a prison without walls, for judgment day.

The holy one, together with Christ, judged the good and evil killers, up in the megacosm, which was made of light. Choice was always given to them, but many of them made the wrong decisions in life.

Holy God protected the holy zeros from the evil forces of evil ones. And when good people became victims of evil people, the earth shook from a quake, lightning, and thunder. The power of the devil grew, and jokes about killers were funny. The hydrosphere was laughing, sending rain down on the ground and making the rest of the biological organisms smile.

Those who understood the immoral deity of darkness cried as well. Good killers or good ones were matted as they killed guiltlessly by a miscarriage, and it made them doubt themselves, whether they were good or evil. Evil killers or evil ones were confused as well as they thought they were good killers, but surely they were bad. An all-seeing quanta reflector was looking inside of pupils, recreating the actuality in which they were living by projecting starlight down on them. One universe, and that is why we are made of zeros and ones, sounds, letters, words, meanings, etcetera.

Molecules, DNA, and nucleic acid double helixes were designed and seeded in as many places of our galaxy as possible by an alien race before the Sun and the Earth were placed in orbit. Just like waves on the beaches of the coastline, everything was vibrating. Knowledge about self and the world around it is what makes atoms so strong.

Sound dominated over silence, and silence was absorbing the sound. Thus it was made neutral. Nuclear transmutation as a result of atomic transmogrification from a subatomic level into molecular complicated structures. The great lie was everywhere, keeping people without knowledge about who they really were by nature of their existence. When truth was revealed to those individuals who had conversance, the world of vibrations and celestial organisms arose from an unending oblivion of the rectangular matrices' array. Hypnosis was used to mesmerize incoherent animals, or so-called people. Supernal creatures were teaching foolish humanoids from upper heaven the meaning of words. The holy law was hidden from people to perplex them about the afterlife. The solar system was traveling around the Milky Way, and the globe was orbiting around its own axis and the Sun. Stars rose and disappeared from the horizon. Five millennia hereinafter, the world reached its highest peak of an ascension from the wavering point of view; but null and one always was a mystery to everyone. Evil dimension six was sealed with its superstrong invisible walls and the gates of hell until the present day.

We were working underground in our laboratory, having no clue what we were about to expose to this world. When we launched our atom smasher, powering it up with four hundred terra volts for another experiment, to open a window into the future, instead of an electron beam, we were exposed to some sort of dark matter energy, which flew out of a time tunnel, speaking some foreign language we had never heard of before. That substance killed half of our team instantly within a second of inhaling it. The rest of the crew, who were behind thick, strong, translucent alloy glass were watching, and their hair became white in five minutes from the horror they witnessed. A laser projection of theirs storing memories was replayed to us on a large, color light projector screen. The being was conscious; it flew out of the time tunnel through an airduct and up into the atmosphere, and beyond. Our artificial satellites made a video recording of it; after everything was calm and an unknown invasion was over, we called it the evil ghost from the future. If only we knew what we had done. But we didn't know; later on we figured it out, but it was too late as it had already happened. We had cracked the entrance of a dimension number six by an accident, trying to walk into a far future. So after recalculating the parameters of the final destination, the point of arrival was moved one second back from six to five.

When teleportation was successful and our bodies were gathered back together, none of us recognized each other as our physical bodies were no longer made of flesh and bones. We had mutated into cartoon sort of characters, and the physical laws of nature didn't bother us any longer. We could see, hear, feel, and move objects with our minds. We became immortals by overcoming death, and the whole world around us was like an animated fairy tale. It was Earth, but a different type of it. The ground was stiff; also it could become soft, if we desired so. We flew and walked using the power of our minds and imagination. Everything listened to us with every thought we had and every word we spoke; matter adapted to our will. We became one with everything, fusing together complicated structures of matter and turning our fantasies into reality.

A chemical substance rebuilt itself from our input and the thoughts reflected from our intellect into the mirror of the mind. After being in that world for an unknown period of time, we could not distinguish reality from a dreamy fantasy. We decided it was heaven itself; half of our team stayed there forever, and nine of us returned to a 3D realm to finish what we had started by exploring the world behind the gate of hell.

We realized there were two types of time machines: One was made by nature or God. It resembled a mechanism with Earth inside the apparatus; it was recording history every fifteen minutes and saving it onto a global hard drive. The second was designed by us people, so after the decision was made to open hell's doors again, we prepared ourselves to see the worst. A group stepped inside, and our bodies reappeared on the other side. There was a fiery heat and freezing cold; screenshots of animals and people before and after death were everywhere. They were recorded nonstop in every corner of a flat geometrical world that was always changing its form and shape, showing us more and more of the devil. First it was a cube, then it became a hypercube, and so on. Every time there were more rooms and labyrinths; it was endless. A giant digital spider appeared from behind, capturing us. It was scanning the database of our stored memories into its storage processor unit through our eye lenses and brains. I assume it was an arachnoid judge that found nothing interesting to attract its attention.

Seven of my teammates were given freedom; one friend and I were pulled into a world of wide webs. I don't know how long I was there, but after witnessing nightmares and experiencing bodily pain sensations, the system spewed me out of its mainframe. I still had my dialing device on me to call home; I pushed the button and signaled to my people, and my body was sucked into a wormhole that took me straight back into the lab. I returned from hell, or whatever it was called. After the exploration was over, we counted our losses and plusses. A lot of men were missing from our mission, so we recruited and hired more people for these dangerous trips. Every time we opened a hole in space and time, giving it new coordinates, the network was rebuilding by itself, showing us what to expect from the new worlds in the past and future. AI helped us travel to mysterious places of our galaxy.

The year 2020: from the birth of Christ to the present day. Aurora, in the city of Chicago, Illinois. They built Fermi Laboratories or Time Core in the future, underground city that is hidden from human eyes, covered up to confuse people from the truth, making it look like it is a department of energy. They built underground tunnel five hundred miles long where they performed time travel experiments with extraterrestrial civilizations, which flew to earthly orbit in the year 1400. They discovered time was relevant and alternate realities existed by opening windows in time and space into the past and future. In this way they uncovered the so-called God particle. Immortality is what people had always searched for.

A lifetime was not enough to create a quality soul inside a human body, so we traveled back in time to extend the lifetime of our bodies using a particle collider. The one in the present met the one in the past, and if the one who came from the future into the past met himself or herself back in time, and, if the one who came from the future into the past died, the second one, or the one who was in the past would still keep on living. Practical immortality through futuristic technology's so-called atom smasher. Cheating death, or tricking it, was a goal of our lifetimes. As we move from the present into the future, the present becomes the past, and the future becomes the present. He traveled back in time and into the future to extend his lifetime up to one thousand years, to create a superpowerful and superintelligent soul inside of him by means of reading realistic or virtual web archives. Endless bookshelves inside of a computer mind calling itself God, or one year. The one who speaks, reads, and understands all languages of Earth and beyond our terrestrial sphere. Decoding symbols of the other planets, consciousness was learning to connect itself with the supreme intellect of the galaxy maker.

Entrance into CERN was not given to everyone. The retina of an eye was scanned by a nanothin magnifying glass, zooming in and out to the back side of a brain's pineal gland with an ultraviolet scanner and capturing reflections before giving inside access to the makers and users of it. His name was sound. He survived on Earth by revealing secrets to the rest of the people who had no clue about what was going on in reality and what was reality. They hired him as an electromechanical technician to work on a large hadron collider in Geneva, Switzerland. He assembled parts, drew diagrams, calibrated experimental and support equipment, performed a radioactive alignment of electron beams, and stabilized hardware. They were adjusting the core of the largest particle accelerator.

After about six months of daily labor helping his coworkers, he was accidently exposed to an experiment. When they launched it for another test, a portal opened, and people from the very far future stepped inside into our time line, giving us an electromagnetic portable time travel device. They told us they retrieved it from hell itself by copying it and reconstructing it into a quantum device. The gadget was made of futuristic parts and powered itself from a dark matter energy source, which also was very small and convenient to carry. The dark matter energy source fed itself from a godly power, or the so-called crucifixion of Christ. Reality suddenly changed in front of him, and at that moment they explained how artificial intelligence was not able to process the first commandment. It crushed, they gave him a tour of a virtual reality of our planet and the recorded history of it starting with the year 01. Whereas they were able to go back in time as far as five billion years, one hundred billion people who lived on Earth died, but memory is still stored in the global software. He was given the offer to become a time traveler by going back and forward on a registry recording, or life, fixing life-threatening situations by saving lives and establishing justice. First, they tested him by giving him a choice to kill himself or to shoot his friend. He aimed at his temporal bone, triggering the last bullet in the chamber. He died, and that is how he found out he was immortal. Money was not a problem as he played winning lotto numbers every week, which he brought with him from the future. In present days we play in coordinates at the Grand Canyon, not far from Las Vegas.

Winning lottery numbers—New York lotto results archive from year 1978:

Saturday 30th December 1974: 28 29 30 32 38 23
Saturday 23rd December 1978: 7 9 11 18 34 38 1
Saturday 16th December 1978: 1 11 15 16 17 37 39
Saturday 9th December 19782: 14 20 27 29 34 40
Saturday 2nd December 1978: 1 5 8 15 28 38 26
Saturday 25th November 1978: 8 13 28 29 37 38 5
Saturday 18th November 1978: 2 4 6 22 29 37 30
Saturday 29th December 1979: 3 4 5 6 13 25 33
Saturday 22nd December 1979: 3 7 8 18 25 35 33
Saturday 15th December 1979: 2 9 11 15 30 32 18
Saturday 8th December 1979: 12 13 21 22 25 34 8
Saturday 1st December 1979: 1 14 19 25 27 28 38

Saturday 24th November 1979: 10 11 22 24 28 38 2
Saturday 17th November 1979: 4 10 11 31 32 36 28
Saturday 10th November 1979: 2 20 24 33 37 38 6
Saturday 3rd November 1979: 1 4 22 25 33 39 11
Saturday 27th October 1979: 8 19 24 27 37 38 40
Saturday 20th October 1979: 6 14 19 20 23 34 1
Saturday 13th October 1979: 3 7 22 24 26 33 2
Saturday 6th October 1979: 12 13 14 17 21 33 3
Saturday 29th September 1979: 8 17 22 30 32 35 20
Saturday 22nd September 1979: 3 10 21 26 34 40 25
Saturday 15th September 1979: 4 5 8 17 22 23 33
Saturday 8th September 1979: 6 8 17 29 30 39 31
Saturday 25th august 1979: 2 10 14 16 28 35 6
Saturday 18th august 1979: 8 14 18 21 36 39 9
Saturday 11th august 1979: 3 4 14 32 34 39 21
Monday 6th august 1979: 7 17 22 23 32 35 2
Sunday 29th July 1979: 17 20 21 23 30 31 4
Saturday 21st July 1979: 2 10 15 22 39 40 29
Saturday 14th July 1979: 1 5 18 26 36 38 2
Saturday 7th July 1979: 3 5 10 17 21 23 14
Saturday 30th June 1979: 7 20 23 27 36 40 19
Saturday 23rd June 1979: 1 2 4 7 9 15 24
Saturday 16th June 1979: 3 22 25 26 27 35 20
Saturday 9th June 1979: 1 12 17 19 27 35 28
Saturday 2nd June 1979: 2 13 20 22 25 35 37
Saturday 26th May 1979: 4 11 21 22 24 31 15
Saturday 19th May 1979: 6 9 10 13 18 20 39
Saturday 12th May 1979: 19 27 28 29 33 36 11
Saturday 5th May 1979: 7 9 12 19 26 40 30
Saturday 28th April 1979: 8 11 12 17 21 39 22
Saturday 21st April 1979: 14 25 26 31 33 37 19
Saturday 14th April 1979: 2 8 10 18 21 28 36
Saturday 7th April 1979: 1 5 8 13 25 33 20
Saturday 31st March 1979: 12 16 20 25 37 39 34

Saturday 24th March 1979: 4 6 10 26 32 35 34
Saturday 17th March 1979: 1 13 16 25 29 38 26
Saturday 10th March 1979: 5 7 12 16 19 29 13
Saturday 3rd March 1979: 1 11 23 24 28 40 16
Saturday 24th February 1979: 3 5 17 22 26 40 14
Saturday 17th February 1979: 18 19 27 28 34 35 11
Saturday 10th February 1979: 1 20 21 23 25 26 5
Saturday 3rd February 1979:11 21 27 30 32 36 13
Saturday 27th January 1979: 2 13 21 30 32 35 18
Saturday 20th January 1979: 1 8 12 14 34 38 16
Saturday 13th January 1979: 4 8 14 32 35 37 20
Saturday 6th January 1979: 8 13 19 22 24 36 16
Saturday 27th December 1980: 12 17 21 29 30 40 1
Saturday 20th December 1980: 1 21 22 31 34 38 36
Saturday 13th December 1980: 8 11 32 34 35 36 18
Saturday 27th December 1980: 12 17 21 29 30 40 1
Saturday 20th December 1980: 1 21 22 31 34 38 36
Saturday 13th December 1980: 8 11 32 34 35 36 18
Saturday 6th December 1980: 12 31 32 34 35 38 33
Saturday 29th November 1980: 5 8 18 20 21 38 7
Saturday 22nd November 1980: 1 10 13 32 33 37 40
Saturday 15th November 1980: 10 18 22 29 32 37 2
Saturday 8th November 1980: 5 7 8 16 28 36 15
Saturday 1st November 1980: 8 9 25 37 38 40 26
Saturday 25th October 1980: 3 11 16 23 38 40 1
Saturday 18th October 1980: 5 8 9 17 31 40 36
Saturday 11th October 1980: 5 20 22 29 31 40 23
Saturday 4th October 1980: 5 7 12 15 20 27 35
Saturday 27th September 1980: 6 10 32 33 34 40 31
Saturday 20th September 1980: 1 10 12 15 28 39 25
Saturday 13th September 1980: 12 19 23 28 32 38 7
Saturday 6th September 1980: 7 13 16 19 25 38 12
Saturday 30th August 1980: 3 5 28 33 36 37 22
Saturday 23rd August 1980: 1 11 14 30 32 40 23

Saturday 16ᵗʰ August 1980: 6 10 13 16 18 38 9
Saturday 9ᵗʰ August 1980: 3 7 15 23 37 38 25
Saturday 2ⁿᵈ August 1980: 2 16 20 32 33 39 34
Saturday 26ᵗʰ July 1980: 9 13 15 21 23 26 25
Saturday 19ᵗʰ July 1980: 5 18 25 29 30 38 26
Saturday 12ᵗʰ July 1980: 6 9 10 17 18 35 33
Saturday 5ᵗʰ July 1980: 9 15 31 33 38 39 4
Saturday 28ᵗʰ June 1980: 11 22 25 32 33 40 26
Saturday 21ˢᵗ June 1980: 13 17 32 36 37 39 19
Saturday 14ᵗʰ June 1980: 9 15 18 21 28 39 8
Saturday 7ᵗʰ June 1980: 7 19 23 27 30 34 38
Saturday 31ˢᵗ May 1980: 10 16 31 32 38 39 29
Saturday 24ᵗʰ May 1980: 7 11 23 24 25 26 31
Saturday 17ᵗʰ May 1980: 5 9 19 31 32 38 3
Saturday 10ᵗʰ May 1980: 2 5 15 30 33 36 9
Saturday 3ʳᵈ May 1980: 7 9 15 19 20 29 17
Saturday 26ᵗʰ April 1980: 1 4 21 27 38 39 14
Saturday 19ᵗʰ April 1980: 2 17 28 30 37 40 22
Saturday 12ᵗʰ April 1980: 3 9 15 16 22 31 8
Saturday 5ᵗʰ April 1980: 8 12 17 19 20 36 13
Saturday 29ᵗʰ March 1980: 10 22 23 31 32 33 25
Saturday 22ⁿᵈ March 1980: 2 3 13 34 35 38 24
Saturday 15ᵗʰ March 1980: 1 18 26 33 36 37 19
Saturday 8ᵗʰ March 1980: 7 11 15 23 27 31 28
Saturday 1ˢᵗ March 1980: 6 12 14 17 24 28 7
Saturday 23ʳᵈ February 1980: 3 9 19 20 28 34 26
Saturday 16ᵗʰ February 1980: 11 12 14 20 22 34 38
Saturday 9ᵗʰ February 1980: 2 11 12 14 15 23 18
Saturday 2ⁿᵈ February 1980: 7 8 20 23 26 36 6
Saturday 26ᵗʰ January 1980: 9 12 13 14 16 20 36
Saturday 19ᵗʰ January 1980: 21 24 30 31 38 39 1
Saturday 12ᵗʰ January 1980: 4 10 11 13 24 31 28
Saturday 5ᵗʰ January 1980: 9 10 14 24 34 37 38
Saturday 26ᵗʰ December 1981: 4 17 18 26 37 40 27

Saturday 19th December 1981: 5 7 9 26 35 37 25
Saturday 12th December 1981: 2 9 12 16 18 25 17
Saturday 5th December 1981: 10 18 24 26 29 33 39
Saturday 28th November 1981: 12 15 18 28 30 32 31
Saturday 21st November 1981: 1 2 8 10 28 34 33
Saturday 14th November 1981: 3 14 22 24 25 29 27
Saturday 7th November 1981: 2 22 29 32 34
Saturday 31st October 1981: 13 14 21 24 33 34 7
Saturday 24th October 1981: 7 10 17 19 34 40 33
Saturday 17th October 1981: 3 6 17 19 22 25 14
Saturday 10th October 1981: 3 14 19 34 38 40 12
Saturday 3rd October 1981: 6 8 21 22 29 39 35
Saturday 26th September 1981: 3 17 19 25 28 40
Saturday 19th September 1981: 1 6 16 17 19 27
Saturday 12th September 1981: 3 18 20 23 33 34
Saturday 5th September 1981: 2 11 16 18 29 39 14
Saturday 29th August 1981: 9 14 16 22 35 40 27
Saturday 22nd August 1981: 2 3 9 34 36 40 13
Saturday 15th August 1981: 3 7 9 25 27 39 26
Saturday 8th August 1981: 1 20 28 29 35 40 31
Saturday 1st August 1981: 12 14 16 25 34 39 38
Saturday 25th July 1981: 2 9 10 15 19 36 3
Saturday 18th July 19816 7 8 11 32 35 15
Saturday 11th July 1981: 7 10 15 24 30 34 21
Saturday 4th July 1981: 6 11 20 29 31 34 1
Saturday 27th June 198117 22 23 26 31 37 4
Saturday 20th June 1981: 4 5 12 30 36 38 40
Saturday 13th June 1981: 2 10 12 15 25 37 34
Saturday 6th June 1981: 10 12 28 32 36 38 2
Saturday 30th May 1981: 1 2 3 7 32 35 21
Saturday 23rd May 1981: 7 8 20 27 28 35 10
Saturday 16th May 1981: 10 17 18 22 30 40 13
Saturday 9th May 1981: 3 5 10 28 33 35 4
Saturday 2nd May 1981: 4 8 18 19 26 27 20

Saturday 25th April 1981: 4 24 27 29 31 36 22
Saturday 18th April 1981: 10 12 22 23 25 31 36
Saturday 11th April 1981: 10 13 14 20 31 32 24
Saturday 4th April 1981: 2 6 17 18 32 36 23
Saturday 28th March 1981: 4 10 15 26 28 29 12
Saturday 21st March 1981: 13 14 26 31 34 36 32
Saturday 14th March 1981: 12 14 20 23 25 29 22
Saturday 7th March 1981: 2 6 9 20 27 31 5
Saturday 28th February 1981: 4 9 10 18 20 22 24
Saturday 21st February 1981: 3 10 15 20 25 27 18
Saturday 14th February 1981: 1 20 26 34 38 40 19
Saturday 7th February 1981: 8 20 26 28 32 37 31
Saturday 31st January 1981: 21 29 34 35 36 40 26
Saturday 24th January 1981: 5 6 11 17 21 28 8
Saturday 17th January 1981: 3 24 26 32 35 40 12
Saturday 10th January 1981: 1 4 11 18 19 30 26
Saturday 3rd January 1981: 22 23 27 28 36 39 38
Saturday 18th December 1982: 6 7 8 19 33 40 36
Saturday 11th December 1982: 4 6 14 21 26 31 5
Saturday 4th December 1982: 1 4 23 27 34 36 24
Saturday 27th November 1982: 1 2 9 16 34 40 15
Saturday 20th November 19823 8 9 16 39 40 18
Saturday 13th November 1982: 2 5 16 30 32 37 38
Saturday 6th November 1982: 9 15 16 24 26 27 28
Saturday 30th October 1982: 6 15 23 27 32 38 19
Saturday 23rd October 1982: 9 20 21 33 35 39 3
Saturday 16th October 19821 23 29 30 32 35 18
Saturday 9th October 1982: 2 14 30 34 37 40 33
Saturday 2nd October 1982: 7 12 15 24 28 32 27
Saturday 25th September 1982: 3 16 19 20 33 34 24
Saturday 18th September 1982: 5 12 15 17 20 29 33
Saturday 11th September 1982: 6 19 20 23 24 27 8
Saturday 4th September 1982: 3 4 9 10 15 36 33
Saturday 28th August 1982: 1 4 9 25 33 40 22

Saturday 21st August 1982: 4 16 19 20 21 27 37
Saturday 14th August 1982: 4 8 13 28 34 36 27
Saturday 7th August 19827 12 15 18 34 39 17
Saturday 31st July 1982: 6 13 17 23 30 38 5
Saturday 24th July 1982: 8 13 14 29 32 38 21
Saturday 17th July 1982: 12 15 23 29 32 39 4
Saturday 10th July 1982: 5 7 9 10 19 37 27
Saturday 3rd July 1982: 2 3 8 19 24 39 10
Saturday 26th June 1982: 7 9 19 25 26 28 37
Saturday 19th June 1982: 1 11 14 27 37 39 16
Saturday 12th June 1982: 3 5 12 15 29 39 1
Saturday 5th June 1982: 10 14 18 22 26 36 3
Saturday 29th May 19826 18 24 28 29 39 5
Saturday 22nd May 1982: 3 23 24 29 35 38 2
Saturday 15th May 1982: 9 12 17 22 25 31 5
Saturday 8th May 1982: 4 8 15 20 35 37 1
Saturday 1st May 1982: 9 13 18 23 34 40 21
Saturday 24th April 198212 16 18 26 36 37 15
Saturday 17th April 1982: 5 14 17 23 24 36 34
Saturday 10th April 1982: 6 23 28 29 38 39 24
Saturday 3rd April 1982: 2 17 20 23 28 37 31
Saturday 27th March 1982: 3 4 6 21 23 31 25
Saturday 20th March 1982: 4 8 14 15 29 35 36
Saturday 13th March 1982: 3 4 9 13 31 34 22
Saturday 6th March 1982: 2 7 9 16 23 27 38
Saturday 27th February 1982: 11 15 19 20 29 34 23
Saturday 20th February 1982: 9 12 16 26 35 39 11
Saturday 13th February 1982: 4 6 14 27 29 34 28
Saturday 6th February 1982: 1 2 12 18 24 35 7
Saturday 30th January 1982: 3 13 17 19 35 38 21
Saturday 23rd January 1982: 2 3 5 15 22 33 28
Saturday 16th January 1982: 3 10 14 17 24 40 39
Saturday 9th January 1982: 3 9 13 23 29 33 36
Saturday 2nd January 1982: 2 23 26 33 38 40 14

Saturday 31ˢᵗ December 1983: 12 18 22 24 29 36 7
Wednesday 28ᵗʰ December 1983: 1 7 8 28 31 39 11
Saturday 24ᵗʰ December 19831 5 19 28 38 39 37
Wednesday 21ˢᵗ December 1983: 9 18 24 40 42 44 5
Saturday 17ᵗʰ December 1983: 3 12 15 17 38 43 40
Wednesday 14ᵗʰ December 1983: 5 6 14 16 30 33 29
Saturday 10ᵗʰ December 1983: 3 4 11 23 24 35 14
Wednesday 7ᵗʰ December 1983: 16 17 18 32 38 44 39
Saturday 3ʳᵈ December 1983: 10 11 13 25 27 40 23
Wednesday 30ᵗʰ November 1983: 4 13 19 24 32 38 21
Saturday 26ᵗʰ November 1983: 6 13 17 22 32 42 4
Wednesday 23ʳᵈ November 1983: 7 17 20 24 28 42 37
Saturday 19ᵗʰ November 1983: 6 14 19 28 32 41 17
Wednesday 16ᵗʰ November 1983: 3 18 27 30 35 40 23
Saturday 12ᵗʰ November 1983: 7 11 22 34 36 41 28
Wednesday 9ᵗʰ November 1983: 3 10 19 34 36 38 15
Saturday 5ᵗʰ November 1983: 10 22 31 37 39 40 29
Wednesday 2ⁿᵈ November 1983: 2 10 18 21 25 34 39
Saturday 29ᵗʰ October 1983: 3 15 22 26 40 42 8
Saturday 22ⁿᵈ October 1983: 7 20 21 26 27 36 28
Saturday 15ᵗʰ October 1983: 9 13 16 22 33 34 14
Saturday 8ᵗʰ October 1983: 5 10 11 18 35 39 14
Saturday 1ˢᵗ October 19835 6 12 16 36 40 10
Saturday 24ᵗʰ September 19832 6 15 20 26 30 17
Saturday 17ᵗʰ September 1983: 7 21 24 31 32 33 40
Saturday 10ᵗʰ September 1983: 4 5 10 19 24 29 20
Saturday 3ʳᵈ September 1983: 10 11 15 17 27 29 22
Saturday 27ᵗʰ August 1983: 4 13 15 19 23 34 27
Saturday 20ᵗʰ August 1983: 8 10 15 34 36 40 7
Saturday 13ᵗʰ August 1983: 7 13 18 20 22 33 4
Saturday 6ᵗʰ August 1983: 7 14 15 21 30 36 16
Saturday 30ᵗʰ July 1983: 9 15 18 25 27 28 38
Saturday 23ʳᵈ July 1983: 3 9 20 21 28 31 37
Saturday 16ᵗʰ July 1983: 2 7 16 17 36 37 20

Saturday 9th July 1983: 3 7 8 14 31 35 11
Saturday 2nd July 1983: 7 27 29 32 35 40 2
Saturday 25th June 1983: 9 15 26 36 39 40 21
Saturday 18th June 1983: 10 16 27 33 37 40 9
Saturday 11th June 1983: 2 21 22 31 36 40 7
Saturday 4th June 1983: 6 13 20 21 28 30 38
Saturday 28th May 19831 6 8 14 23 35 11
Saturday 21st May 1983: 2 4 5 16 21 22 7
Saturday 14th May 1983: 2 5 12 14 30 38 9
Saturday 7th May 1983: 3 6 22 25 30 38 36
Saturday 30th April 1983: 1 7 16 29 34 37 17
Saturday 23rd April 19833 4 5 16 20 23 31
Saturday 16th April 1983: 3 5 14 17 24 27 23
Saturday 9th April 1983: 8 23 29 30 32 38 18
Saturday 2nd April 1983: 6 11 15 20 22 37 36
Saturday 26th March 1983: 18 23 26 30 34 38 3
Saturday 19th March 1983: 10 21 23 28 32 37 2
Saturday 12th March 1983: 1 10 12 17 22 40 25
Saturday 5th March 1983: 12 15 24 30 34 40 17
Saturday 26th February 1983: 1 6 7 16 27 30 2
Saturday 19th February 1983: 4 19 23 28 35 40 27
Saturday 12th February 1983: 2 13 18 24 34 40 21
Saturday 5th February 1983: 4 7 13 18 26 30 34
Saturday 29th January 1983: 22 26 27 33 36 38 3
Saturday 22nd January 1983: 8 14 30 32 36 38 4
Saturday 15th January 1983: 10 12 17 26 29 31 15
Saturday 8th January 1983: 14 16 18 27 32 36 12
Saturday 1st January 1983: 12 14 22 25 27 28 9
Saturday 29th December 1984: 14 17 24 33 34 39 44
Wednesday 26th December 1984: 3 19 23 31 42 44 20
Saturday 22nd December 1984: 2 15 23 35 38 39 13
Wednesday 19th December 19847 22 24 32 34 42 16
Saturday 15th December 1984: 2 5 9 18 25 44 6
Wednesday 12th December 1984: 13 20 32 33 36 39 26

Saturday 8th December 1984: 1 15 21 24 35 38 30
Wednesday 5th December 1984: 2 10 19 27 34 37 41
Saturday 1st December 1984: 2 6 33 40 41 44 7
Wednesday 28th November 1984: 2 12 14 29 30 33 24
Saturday 24th November 1984: 32 34 35 36 40 43 19
Wednesday 21st November 1984: 1 14 20 26 34 41 12
Saturday 17th November 1984: 15 23 39 40 41 44 28
Wednesday 14th November 1984: 3 15 17 27 30 31 36
Wednesday 7th November 1984: 10 23 25 32 39 40 24
Saturday 3rd November 1984: 3 12 15 28 38 40 11
Wednesday 31st October 1984: 1 9 13 33 38 43 20
Saturday 27th October 1984: 1 6 8 17 39 42 5
Wednesday 24th October 1984: 4 7 9 17 19 44 30
Saturday 20th October 1984: 6 25 26 30 34 44 13
Wednesday 17th October 1984: 1 10 22 26 36 38 20
Saturday 13th October 1984: 5 10 24 29 30 41 38
Wednesday 10th October 1984: 2 9 12 17 25 40 23
Saturday 6th October 198417 18 34 35 36 39 42
Wednesday 3rd October 1984: 1 9 14 20 25 42 18
Saturday 29th September 1984: 2 10 15 30 39 44 6
Wednesday 26th September 1984: 6 12 13 36 40 41 24
Saturday 22nd September 1984: 6 14 27 28 38 40 17
Wednesday 19th September 1984: 5 12 26 27 31 42 1
Saturday 15th September 1984: 10 15 16 30 33 38 6
Wednesday 12th September 1984: 4 16 17 33 40 42 10
Saturday 8th September 1984: 1 15 17 26 30 43 8
Wednesday 5th September 1984: 9 16 28 29 35 44 20
Saturday 1st September 1984: 14 18 24 25 27 32 7
Wednesday 29th August 1984: 1 6 24 29 37 44 42
Saturday 25th August 1984: 5 10 12 29 31 39 18
Wednesday 22nd August 1984: 3 27 35 42 43 44 21
Saturday 18th August 1984: 2 3 8 12 17 34 24
Wednesday 15th August 1984: 16 31 32 38 42 44 37
Saturday 11th August 19847 8 14 21 22 24 34

Wednesday 8th August 1984: 5 17 22 23 28 38 10
Saturday 4th August 1984: 5 6 14 21 24 39 15
Wednesday 1st August 1984: 1 15 20 28 32 40 9
Saturday 28th July 1984: 9 10 27 30 32 42 39
Wednesday 25th July 1984: 1 5 17 18 38 42 44
Saturday 21st July 1984: 5 11 14 15 40 42 31
Wednesday 18th July 1984: 10 19 30 31 43 44 40
Saturday 14th July 1984: 11 14 25 32 34 43 23
Wednesday 11th July 1984: 5 16 20 24 33 40 18
Saturday 7th July 1984: 3 6 14 26 31 33 28
Wednesday 4th July 1984: 18 25 30 37 39 44 4
Saturday 30th June 19846 8 21 24 27 41 7
Wednesday 27th June 1984: 3 14 22 27 36 42 37
Saturday 23rd June 1984: 7 8 11 26 30 35 42
Wednesday 20th June 1984: 6 7 26 31 33 38 2
Saturday 16th June 1984: 5 20 22 23 30 39 21
Wednesday 13th June 1984: 6 18 19 25 29 39 12
Saturday 9th June 1984: 1 13 15 30 33 36 19
Wednesday 6th June 1984: 11 20 27 35 41 42 28
Saturday 2nd June 1984: 4 8 17 21 23 38 40
Wednesday 30th May 1984: 3 5 10 18 20 26 43
Saturday 26th May 1984: 6 19 21 29 31 40 36
Wednesday 23rd May 1984: 5 7 11 14 16 37 8
Saturday 19th May 1984: 9 13 17 23 31 33 14
Wednesday 16th May 1984: 15 25 26 30 35 43 29
Saturday 12th May 1984: 3 9 22 31 36 38 11
Wednesday 9th May 1984: 6 22 24 35 41 42 5
Saturday 5th May 1984: 5 17 23 29 31 36 11
Wednesday 2nd May 1984: 12 14 23 25 33 37 41
Saturday 28th April 1984: 8 18 23 24 40 43 22
Wednesday 25th April 1984: 2 22 28 34 37 39 14
Saturday 21st April 1984: 17 28 29 32 41 42 38
Wednesday 18th April 1984: 13 17 29 37 39 43 31
Saturday 14th April 1984: 5 16 19 24 32 35 12

Wednesday 11th April 1984: 18 19 20 33 34 43 16
Saturday 7th April 1984: 3 4 14 16 42 43 25
Wednesday 4th April 1984: 10 11 13 19 25 41 42
Saturday 31st March 1984: 7 9 21 28 29 43 35
Wednesday 28th March 1984: 13 14 17 21 31 33 11
Saturday 24th March 1984: 9 10 17 20 23 31 2
Wednesday 21st March 1984: 8 18 23 30 34 39 17
Saturday 17th March 1984: 2 3 5 33 39 42 19
Wednesday 14th March 1984: 12 18 29 33 37 43 39
Saturday 10th March 1984: 4 16 17 25 32 37 24
Wednesday 7th March 1984: 2 14 23 26 41 44 17
Saturday 3rd March 1984: 2 26 36 40 41 44 33
Wednesday 29th February 1984: 12 15 27 30 32 40 38
Saturday 25th February 1984: 9 15 19 26 37 38 30
Wednesday 22nd February 1984: 6 19 21 29 30 36 10
Saturday 18th February 1984: 7 11 15 29 35 37 23
Wednesday 15th February 1984: 1 8 10 18 27 35 15
Saturday 11th February 1984: 10 19 24 29 36 42 1
Wednesday 8th February 198410 16 19 20 30 37 18
Saturday 4th February 1984: 7 8 26 28 34 37 17
Wednesday 1st February 1984: 3 5 15 17 19 27 34
Saturday 28th January 1984: 17 26 31 32 35 40 4
Wednesday 25th January 1984: 2 6 29 34 38 43 8
Saturday 21st January 1984: 4 12 14 15 20 35 17
Wednesday 18th January 1984: 5 10 11 14 18 43 17
Saturday 14th January 1984: 1 8 10 19 27 35 38
Wednesday 11th January 1984: 3 24 32 36 38 42 29
Saturday 7th January 1984: 7 11 12 28 41 43 19
Wednesday 4th January 1984: 1 6 16 18 34 44 38
Monday 30th December 1985: 11 14 17 22 28 38
Saturday 28th December 1985: 20 25 28 38 46 48 44
Wednesday 25th December 1985: 2 13 19 32 39 46 18
Monday 23rd December 1985: 5 7 28 34 35 36
Saturday 21st December 1985: 2 13 18 22 27 34 48

Wednesday 18th December 1985: 2 21 22 24 44 47 10
Monday 16th December 1985: 1 15 16 20 33 38
Saturday 14th December 1985: 6 8 11 20 21 46 14
Wednesday 11th December 1985: 4 5 13 17 22 30 40
Monday 9th December 1985: 4 7 11 18 34 38
Saturday 7th December 1985: 6 14 17 20 32 44 42
Wednesday 4th December 1985: 9 12 15 19 25 30 28
Monday 2nd December 1985: 5 11 17 18 33 37
Saturday 30th November 1985: 4 6 32 34 38 41 16
Wednesday 27th November 1985: 11 21 25 27 33 39 3
Monday 25th November 1985: 1 6 21 26 27 40
Saturday 23rd November 1985: 2 21 25 27 34 36 33
Wednesday 20th November 1985: 3 7 8 17 26 45 32
Monday 18th November 1985: 8 10 14 15 36 40
Saturday 16th November 1985: 10 23 29 30 31 45 5
Wednesday 13th November 1985: 4 5 9 12 20 37 41
Monday 11th November 1985: 17 18 24 35 36 40
Saturday 9th November 1985: 22 37 39 40 41 42 26
Wednesday 6th November 1985: 13 18 20 26 32 46 19
Monday 4th November 1985: 1 11 13 18 33 35
Saturday 2nd November 1985: 1 5 7 14 23 36 22
Wednesday 30th October 1985: 11 20 28 31 33 41 25
Monday 28th October 1985: 3 9 23 31 34 36
Saturday 26th October 1985: 7 15 30 35 47 34 2
Wednesday 23rd October 1985: 2 25 29 36 47 48 34
Monday 21st October 1985: 1 4 21 27 29 33
Saturday 19th October 1985: 6 13 24 41 42 45 38
Wednesday 16th October 1985: 3 9 15 21 39 46 38
Monday 14th October 1985: 4 7 18 23 34 38
Saturday 12th October 1985: 1 4 6 7 12 48 39
Wednesday 9th October 1985: 13 22 24 33 34 37 14
Monday 7th October 1985: 1 10 13 27 34 37
Saturday 5th October 1985: 5 21 24 33 38 41 8
Wednesday 2nd October 1985: 4 8 15 19 22 26 17

Monday 30th September 1985: 13 14 16 25 26 28
Saturday 28th September 1985: 4 8 13 33 38 42 29
Wednesday 25th September 1985: 9 21 23 27 30 36 26
Monday 23rd September 1985: 6 18 22 26 32 39
Saturday 21st September 1985: 6 19 33 34 41 42 38
Wednesday 18th September 1985: 17 20 25 29 36 43 21
Monday 16th September 1985: 5 10 18 22 24 40
Saturday 14th September 1985 10 14 17 25 35 42 27
Wednesday 11th September 1985: 1 5 7 26 31 37 32
Monday 9th September 1985: 2 13 18 24 30 39
Saturday 7th September 1985: 5 19 21 29 34 38 46
Wednesday 4th September 1985: 3 8 16 24 41 46 32
Monday 2nd September 1985: 2 4 15 19 26 35
Saturday 31st August 1985: 2 6 17 20 28 46 15
Wednesday 28th August 1985: 11 13 15 19 40 45 34
Monday 26th August 1985: 1 2 3 8 27 34
Saturday 24th August 1985: 10 12 36 38 41 45 5
Wednesday 21st August 1985: 14 17 22 23 30 47 33
Monday 19th August 1985: 10 12 17 18 36 37
Saturday 17th August 1985: 7 14 26 40 45 46 48
Wednesday 14th August 1985: 1 4 12 23 42 46 29
Monday 12th August 1985: 6 8 24 33 35 40
Saturday 10th August 1985: 12 24 32 34 38 47 40
Wednesday 7th August 1985: 7 13 23 24 28 39 38
Monday 5th August 1985: 3 13 18 20 29 38
Saturday 3rd August 1985: 10 14 18 20 22 43 13
Wednesday 31st July 1985: 4 8 10 16 22 45 36
Monday 29th July 1985: 1 4 17 24 29 30
Saturday 27th July 1985: 10 24 25 26 36 39
Wednesday 24th July 1985: 1 3 16 28 42 47
Monday 22nd July 1985: 16 19 22 33 34 39
Saturday 20th July 1985: 7 14 27 42 44 46
Wednesday 17th July 1985: 9 12 20 23 37 47
Monday 15th July 1985: 14 22 24 28 36 38

Saturday 13th July 1985: 5 7 25 33 34 37
Wednesday 10th July 1985: 1 14 24 26 28 37
Monday 8th July 1985: 1 18 24 29 32 36
Saturday 6th July 1985: 6 8 22 24 25 37
Wednesday 3rd July 1985: 6 17 25 26 35 43
Monday 1st July 1985: 1 2 13 19 28 30
Saturday 29th June 1985: 7 18 21 25 40 46
Wednesday 26th June 1985: 1 2 4 6 24 39
Monday 24th June 1985: 1 3 11 32 34 35
Saturday 22nd June 1985: 32 33 34 38 39 47
Wednesday 19th June 1985: 2 7 11 24 41 44
Monday 17th June 19853 11 14 24 27 32
Saturday 15th June 198521 23 28 33 38 46
Wednesday 12th June 1985: 2 3 13 30 34 41 31
Monday 10th June 1985: 2 9 15 20 30 33
Saturday 8th June 1985: 11 27 32 39 44 48
Wednesday 5th June 1985: 3 12 14 19 27 28 33
Monday 3rd June 19851 2 3 31 38 40
Saturday 1st June 1985: 10 15 19 22 35 39
Wednesday 29th May 1985: 7 11 24 29 31 42 16
Monday 27th May 1985: 13 18 26 28 32 35
Saturday 25th May 1985: 17 18 33 34 47 48
Wednesday 22nd May 1985: 11 13 14 18 24 33 19
Monday 20th May 1985: 14 23 26 34 39 40
Saturday 18th May 1985: 7 13 26 38 43 45
Wednesday 15th May 1985: 14 23 24 32 41 42 27
Monday 13th May 1985: 9 19 20 26 28 32
Saturday 11th May 1985: 2 16 17 29 33 44
Wednesday 8th May 1985: 14 20 22 29 33 41 21
Monday 6th May 1985: 16 20 22 23 32 36
Saturday 4th May 1985: 11 15 23 28 36 39 3
Wednesday 1st May 1985: 4 10 18 22 36 38 19
Saturday 27th April 1985: 1 14 25 28 39 40 35
Wednesday 24th April 1985: 3 9 18 20 26 43 10

Saturday 20th April 1985: 9 15 27 37 39 44 29

Wednesday 17th April 1985: 9 24 25 28 39 41 37

Saturday 13th April 1985: 5 7 10 28 30 42 24

Wednesday 10th April 1985: 7 10 17 18 29 34 27

Saturday 6th April 1985: 16 18 19 21 25 36

Wednesday 3rd April 1985: 13 15 23 28 29 31 4

Saturday 30th March 1985: 1 2 3 23 33 43 37

Wednesday 27th March 198514 15 17 28 29 38 4

Saturday 23rd March 1985: 3 4 21 33 34 44 38

Wednesday 20th March 1985: 3 6 12 20 26 32 22

Saturday 16th March 1985: 1 8 12 21 43 44 25

Wednesday 13th March 1985: 6 7 9 22 33 43 3

Saturday 9th March 1985: 6 15 28 35 36 41 9

Wednesday 6th March 1985: 11 18 24 31 33 34 9

Saturday 2nd March 1985: 1 17 21 25 32 35 28

Wednesday 27th February 1985: 10 20 22 23 25 39 17

Saturday 23rd February 1985: 3 4 9 32 33 36 21

Wednesday 20th February 1985: 1 11 19 22 25 26 35

Saturday 16th February 1985: 4 15 19 23 25 42 14

Wednesday 13th February 1985: 7 15 17 28 29 36 44

Saturday 9th February 1985: 3 8 15 20 26 40 21

Wednesday 6th February 1985: 6 8 16 21 26 34 44

Saturday 2nd February 1985: 3 5 8 14 20 32 33

Wednesday 30th January 1985: 3 9 20 25 31 39 11

Saturday 26th January 1985: 4 6 13 16 18 27 28

Wednesday 23rd January 1985: 16 29 30 31 43 44 19

Saturday 19th January 1985: 15 28 29 33 36 39 13

Wednesday 16th January 1985: 3 7 15 16 26 35 2

Saturday 12th January 1985: 16 22 24 25 36 42 28

Wednesday 9th January 1985: 1 2 16 17 18 25 31

Saturday 5th January 1985: 5 9 24 25 35 36 11

Wednesday 2nd January 1985: 4 7 8 14 31 42 3

Wednesday 31st December 1986: 1 3 18 21 25 41 46

Monday 29th December 1986: 3 4 20 24 29 37

Saturday 27ᵗʰ December 19862 6 27 39 45 47 32
Wednesday 24ᵗʰ December 1986: 5 9 12 19 27 43 32
Monday 22ⁿᵈ December 1986: 5 15 18 28 29 33
Saturday 20ᵗʰ December 1986: 23 25 30 38 43 44 3
Wednesday 17ᵗʰ December 1986: 1 2 14 26 32 48 20
Monday 15ᵗʰ December 1986: 15 19 24 30 36 38
Saturday 13ᵗʰ December 1986: 7 12 15 21 24 33 17
Monday 8ᵗʰ December 1986: 5 9 11 12 21 25
Saturday 6ᵗʰ December 1986: 9 16 24 27 40 43 2
Wednesday 3ʳᵈ December 1986: 19 23 26 27 37 44 42
Monday 1ˢᵗ December 1986: 2 5 16 24 33 39
Saturday 29ᵗʰ November 1986: 11 13 24 29 34 43 6
Wednesday 26ᵗʰ November 1986: 12 15 16 27 45 46 44
Monday 24ᵗʰ November 1986: 8 10 11 18 29 40
Saturday 22ⁿᵈ November 1986: 4 8 17 25 31 34 36
Wednesday 19ᵗʰ November 1986: 4 9 25 28 32 39 8
Monday 17ᵗʰ November 1986: 9 21 25 30 37 39
Saturday 15ᵗʰ November 1986: 6 8 22 33 37 45 42
Wednesday 12ᵗʰ November 1986: 4 13 16 18 28 40 36
Monday 10ᵗʰ November 1986: 4 8 11 15 16 18
Saturday 8ᵗʰ November 1986: 18 21 24 36 45 47 20
Wednesday 5ᵗʰ November 1986: 9 10 14 26 32 33 15
Monday 3ʳᵈ November 1986: 1 11 19 20 29 33
Saturday 1ˢᵗ November 1986: 1 14 20 21 39 45 6
Wednesday 29ᵗʰ October 1986: 7 32 34 38 44 47 3
Monday 27ᵗʰ October 1986: 2 4 7 11 24 33
Saturday 25ᵗʰ October 1986: 2 3 4 27 35 42 12
Wednesday 22ⁿᵈ October 1986: 5 9 25 27 33 39 31
Monday 20ᵗʰ October 1986: 6 11 15 20 23 33
Saturday 18ᵗʰ October 1986: 1 7 22 28 38 42 48
Wednesday 15ᵗʰ October 1986: 10 11 18 22 40 45 6
Monday 13ᵗʰ October 1986: 6 13 23 32 36 40
Saturday 11ᵗʰ October 1986: 19 21 23 28 30 37 48
Wednesday 8ᵗʰ October 1986: 14 15 35 38 41 47 21

Monday 6th October 198612 17 20 25 31 37
Saturday 4th October 1986: 2 3 11 35 44 46 32
Wednesday 1st October 1986: 6 16 18 34 35 46 26
Monday 29th September 1986: 2 3 13 21 31 40
Saturday 27th September 1986: 3 9 16 35 37 45 33
Wednesday 24th September 1986: 2 9 15 23 31 32 33
Monday 22nd September 1986: 1 9 20 27 38 40
Saturday 20th September 198614 18 26 33 40 45 34
Wednesday 17th September 1986: 2 6 17 18 26 46 4
Monday 15th September 1986: 4 6 9 16 19 36
Saturday 13th September 1986: 11 21 23 41 43 47 29
Wednesday 10th September 1986: 7 16 25 26 37 39 8
Monday 8th September 1986: 2 13 16 18 19 29
Saturday 6th September 1986: 2 17 27 42 43 44 34
Wednesday 3rd September 1986: 3 9 11 21 34 47 45
Monday 1st September 1986: 6 9 13 14 21 30
Saturday 30th August 1986: 13 14 19 20 23 45 42
Wednesday 27th August 1986: 9 17 19 21 30 44 47
Monday 25th August 1986: 6 13 17 22 28 38
Saturday 23rd August 1986: 18 19 33 36 39 41 48
Wednesday 20th August 1986: 4 6 21 25 34 38 41
Monday 18th August 1986: 7 12 14 25 34 36
Saturday 16th August 1986: 17 21 22 24 31 47 30
Wednesday 13th August 1986: 13 16 26 30 41 44 29
Monday 11th August 1986: 8 10 11 15 26 39
Saturday 9th August 1986: 3 16 32 34 38 42 21
Wednesday 6th August 1986: 1 2 4 6 21 25 30
Monday 4th August 1986: 15 23 28 34 35 39
Saturday 2nd August 1986: 6 13 26 28 32 34 4
Wednesday 30th July 1986: 13 14 33 34 39 48 1
Monday 28th July 1986: 8 18 19 22 29 38
Saturday 26th July 1986: 11 15 17 25 37 48 43
Wednesday 23rd July 1986: 4 9 28 30 40 44 2
Monday 21st July 1986: 1 4 5 10 20 33

Saturday 19th July 1986: 4 15 25 29 33 48 22
Wednesday 16th July 1986: 9 14 15 19 20 28 34
Monday 14th July 1986: 2 9 18 33 35 38
Saturday 12th July 1986: 13 17 20 35 41 48 22
Wednesday 9th July 1986: 2 13 25 33 43 48 21
Monday 7th July 1986: 6 8 15 16 21 32
Saturday 5th July 1986: 1 6 9 14 35 48 39
Wednesday 2nd July 1986: 17 21 29 37 41 46 48
Monday 30th June 1986: 3 24 29 33 34 36
Saturday 28th June 1986: 3 18 31 36 39 47 19
Wednesday 25th June 1986: 3 9 33 34 42 43 27
Monday 23rd June 1986: 17 23 26 27 34 35
Saturday 21st June 1986: 7 8 16 17 23 34 21
Wednesday 18th June 1986: 1 4 16 23 34 36 14
Monday 16th June 1986: 1 12 16 25 36 38
Saturday 14th June 1986: 1 22 23 28 39 40 29
Wednesday 11th June 1986: 2 4 24 31 42 46 6
Monday 9th June 1986: 5 18 23 27 33 38
Saturday 7th June 1986: 15 19 22 26 28 41 31
Wednesday 4th June 1986: 9 12 17 20 22 37 44
Monday 2nd June 1986: 6 10 19 25 26 39
Saturday 31st May 1986: 8 10 20 41 42 48 3
Wednesday 28th May 1986: 4 7 12 18 25 46 37
Monday 26th May 1986: 6 20 21 25 32 39
Saturday 24th May 1986: 9 21 29 36 46 48 44
Wednesday 21st May 1986: 3 8 22 27 32 42 38
Monday 19th May 1986: 1 9 12 21 33 38
Saturday 17th May 1986: 10 11 25 43 44 48 34
Saturday 17th May 1986: 10 11 25 43 44 48 34
Wednesday 14th May 1986: 1 8 20 25 29 34 21
Monday 12th May 1986: 10 13 20 22 29 31
Saturday 10th May 1986: 16 17 20 31 36 48 33
Wednesday 7th May 1986: 7 8 15 20 22 41 42
Monday 5th May 1986: 6 16 18 27 28 36

Saturday 3rd May 1986: 7 8 14 30 43 46 21
Wednesday 30th April 1986: 10 13 21 22 28 31 3
Monday 28th April 1986: 1 5 8 19 26 40
Saturday 26th April 1986: 7 8 18 37 47 48 34
Wednesday 30th December 1987: 6 21 24 29 31 36 37
Monday 28th December 1987: 4 10 17 22 24 39
Saturday 26th December 1987: 18 24 28 35 41 46 47
Wednesday 23rd December 1987: 3 8 20 26 34 46 29
Monday 21st December 1987: 4 14 27 28 36 39
Saturday 19th December 1987: 19 23 27 33 35 43 29
Wednesday 16th December 1987: 7 15 19 21 25 44 36
Monday 14th December 1987: 4 7 9 20 26 30
Saturday 12th December 1987: 15 19 25 29 33 41 18
Wednesday 9th December 1987: 9 10 12 15 25 31 23
Monday 7th December 1987: 6 15 17 25 29 30
Saturday 5th December 1987: 9 13 17 22 23 28 48
Wednesday 2nd December 1987: 1 18 19 29 31 33 13
Monday 30th November 1987: 7 11 21 25 27 39
Saturday 28th November 1987: 9 20 31 38 39 44 23
Wednesday 25th November 1987: 2 6 12 22 24 28 13
Monday 23rd November 1987: 3 5 8 9 25 39
Saturday 21st November 1987: 1 6 17 37 41 44 4
Wednesday 18th November 1987: 8 14 29 38 45 46 42
Monday 16th November 1987: 9 16 21 23 28 32
Saturday 14th November 1987: 6 7 14 16 18 24 33
Wednesday 11th November 1987: 12 14 18 31 32 36 28
Monday 9th November 1987: 2 10 15 18 25 26
Saturday 7th November 1987: 19 24 34 35 40 47 43
Wednesday 4th November 1987: 3 16 17 21 24 34 23
Monday 2nd November 1987: 1 10 28 29 30 32
Saturday 31st October 1987: 2 18 25 33 36 39 41
Wednesday 28th October 1987: 2 11 12 23 24 40 44
Monday 26th October 1987: 1 2 10 22 24 30
Saturday 24th October 1987: 28 29 31 38 44 48 4

Wednesday 21ˢᵗ October 1987: 12 16 27 36 45 48 19
Monday 19ᵗʰ October 1987: 1 14 23 25 32 35
Saturday 17ᵗʰ October 1987: 8 9 37 41 42 43 39
Wednesday 14ᵗʰ October 1987: 4 13 20 22 36 46 37
Monday 12ᵗʰ October 1987: 3 14 21 22 27 28
Saturday 10ᵗʰ October 1987: 3 6 21 33 36 37 38
Wednesday 7ᵗʰ October 1987: 5 20 22 31 32 35 40
Monday 5ᵗʰ October 1987: 7 22 26 28 33 34
Saturday 3ʳᵈ October 1987: 3 20 34 35 37 46 4
Wednesday 30ᵗʰ September 1987: 2 18 28 30 46 48 41
Monday 28ᵗʰ September 1987: 1 2 3 6 29 36
Saturday 26ᵗʰ September 1987: 1 15 17 28 34 41 26
Wednesday 23ʳᵈ September 1987: 2 23 24 34 42 47 39
Monday 21ˢᵗ September 1987: 1 5 15 24 39 40
Saturday 19ᵗʰ September 1987: 18 19 23 34 41 45 39
Wednesday 16ᵗʰ September 1987: 4 12 19 24 45 46 2
Monday 14ᵗʰ September 1987: 3 5 12 26 27 38
Saturday 12ᵗʰ September 1987: 10 11 14 16 46 47 7
Wednesday 9ᵗʰ September 1987: 1 2 19 42 43 44 15
Monday 7ᵗʰ September 1987: 7 9 13 19 23 28
Saturday 5ᵗʰ September 1987: 4 9 14 25 28 33 32
Wednesday 2ⁿᵈ September 1987: 6 13 30 32 42 44 11
Monday 31ˢᵗ August 1987: 9 14 16 21 31 34
Saturday 29ᵗʰ August 1987: 20 24 27 36 37 48 7
Wednesday 26ᵗʰ August 1987: 18 22 29 35 37 38 26
Monday 24ᵗʰ August 1987: 7 8 11 19 20 22
Saturday 22ⁿᵈ August 1987: 5 8 15 28 35 45 29
Wednesday 19ᵗʰ August 1987: 9 11 12 17 22 40 32
Monday 17ᵗʰ August 1987: 11 20 21 30 39 40
Saturday 15ᵗʰ August 1987: 2 6 20 27 42 45 39
Wednesday 12ᵗʰ August 1987: 14 22 24 27 29 32 12
Monday 10ᵗʰ August 1987: 9 10 26 27 36 37
Saturday 8ᵗʰ August 1987: 4 10 13 44 45 46 40
Wednesday 5ᵗʰ August 1987: 6 21 30 33 44 48 15

Monday 3rd August 1987: 2 10 15 17 34 39
Saturday 1st August 1987: 9 11 12 25 35 37 45
Wednesday 29th July 1987: 5 15 24 29 33 47 43
Monday 27th July 1987: 11 16 20 28 29 33
Saturday 25th July 1987: 2 22 24 25 26 39 29
Wednesday 22nd July 1987: 8 19 21 41 46 48 2
Monday 20th July 1987: 12 20 35 37 38 39
Saturday 18th July 1987: 2 3 24 29 33 45 39
Wednesday 15th July 1987: 2 22 33 37 39 42 48
Monday 13th July 1987: 7 11 12 15 27 40
Saturday 11th July 1987: 22 24 25 26 32 35 27
Wednesday 8th July 1987: 17 30 33 34 36 45 1
Monday 6th July 1987: 5 16 26 27 32 37
Saturday 4th July 1987: 6 13 26 29 36 46 2
Wednesday 1st July 1987: 7 12 26 28 34 48 16
Monday 29th June 1987: 3 4 5 10 13 30
Saturday 27th June 1987: 5 16 18 19 22 34 36
Wednesday 24th June 1987: 19 26 29 34 39 48 23
Monday 22nd June 1987: 7 21 25 29 32 34
Saturday 20th June 1987: 8 12 20 24 43 46 23
Wednesday 17th June 1987: 2 10 11 15 32 47 35
Monday 15th June 1987: 4 6 7 12 25 36
Saturday 13th June 1987: 6 15 17 21 43 47 11
Wednesday 10th June 1987: 2 17 32 41 46 47 35
Monday 8th June 1987: 16 18 20 21 23 40
Saturday 6th June 1987: 12 16 20 26 36 43 5
Wednesday 3rd June 1987: 7 23 24 27 28 30 46
Monday 1st June 1987: 9 13 18 19 26 28
Saturday 30th May 1987: 27 28 32 34 40 42 41
Wednesday 27th May 1987: 8 13 14 17 21 43 29
Monday 25th May 1987: 2 4 6 18 34 37
Saturday 23rd May 1987: 3 15 18 20 30 38 27
Wednesday 20th May 1987: 15 21 23 27 29 47 35
Monday 18th May 1987: 3 11 12 20 22 24

Saturday 16th May 1987: 7 12 24 37 42 45 39
Wednesday 13th May 1987: 2 10 14 29 40 42 24
Monday 11th May 1987: 3 7 20 30 38 39
Saturday 9th May 1987: 8 10 15 21 23 29 11
Wednesday 6th May 1987: 12 16 22 27 38 47 28
Monday 4th May 1987: 4 8 11 19 28 32
Saturday 2nd May 1987: 11 17 24 31 32 40 4
Wednesday 29th April 1987: 3 5 11 18 19 25 23
Monday 27th April 1987: 4 10 15 16 21 32
Saturday 25th April 1987: 17 28 30 34 42 48 4
Wednesday 22nd April 1987: 3 6 11 19 29 43 8
Monday 20th April 1987: 3 9 13 21 22 24
Saturday 18th April 1987: 6 15 23 27 35 40 32
Wednesday 15th April 1987: 6 18 21 26 45 47 22
Monday 13th April 1987: 2 9 10 17 22 34
Saturday 11th April 1987: 9 11 21 29 43 44 24
Wednesday 8th April 1987: 5 7 12 13 23 27 35
Monday 6th April 1987: 3 9 20 21 31 37
Saturday 4th April 1987: 4 12 14 17 18 27 20
Wednesday 1st April 1987: 3 18 26 36 46 48 20
Monday 30th March 1987: 19 23 24 26 29 38
Saturday 28th March 1987: 3 12 25 37 46 47 8
Wednesday 25th March 1987: 7 22 34 40 43 47 35
Monday 23rd March 1987: 7 9 11 14 19 21
Saturday 21st March 1987: 6 9 11 15 38 46 2
Wednesday 18th March 1987: 1 11 14 19 25 29 16
Monday 16th March 1987: 4 5 15 23 25 39
Saturday 14th March 1987: 1 5 20 24 34 42 26
Wednesday 11th March 1987: 24 32 35 40 44 48 27
Monday 9th March 1987: 2 6 12 20 24 26
Saturday 7th March 1987: 3 19 22 26 40 47 20
Wednesday 4th March 1987: 6 22 24 27 35 45 31
Monday 2nd March 1987: 2 11 12 13 28 33
Saturday 28th February 1987: 7 10 13 25 34 41 26

Wednesday 25th February 1987: 16 19 29 35 37 38 41

Monday 23rd February 1987: 5 12 25 27 30 32

Saturday 21st February 1987: 4 6 24 39 44 45 13

Wednesday 18th February 1987: 10 19 22 29 34 48 2

Monday 16th February 1987: 2 10 11 16 20 22

Saturday 14th February 1987: 5 18 37 40 41 44 13

Wednesday 11th February 1987: 23 25 33 34 36 37 15

Monday 9th February 1987: 4 12 20 26 27 39

Saturday 7th February 1987: 17 27 30 42 44 45 20

Wednesday 4th February 1987: 5 16 24 27 37 44 17

Monday 2nd February 1987: 10 14 25 28 33 34

Saturday 31st January 1987: 9 11 19 21 42 47 15

Wednesday 28th January 1987: 4 11 15 19 22 31 33

Monday 26th January 1987: 8 12 20 22 26 29

Saturday 24th January 1987: 12 15 18 31 44 45 1

Wednesday 21st January 1987: 1 11 12 26 31 45 17

Monday 19th January 1987: 2 7 9 16 21 25

Saturday 17th January 1987: 6 7 28 36 41 43 9

Wednesday 14th January 1987: 2 3 4 25 27 47 10

Monday 12th January 1987: 2 7 18 27 33 34

Saturday 10th January 1987: 4 9 15 21 29 30 27

Wednesday 7th January 1987: 2 12 18 24 45 46 19

Monday 5th January 1987: 7 23 31 34 36 40

Saturday 3rd January 1987: 3 9 14 22 27 48 5

Saturday 31st December 1988: 2 13 20 24 46 49 14

Wednesday 28th December 1988: 13 38 39 46 47 48 4

Monday 26th December 1988: 9 10 13 19 26 38

Saturday 24th December 1988: 28 30 36 44 51 53 49

Wednesday 21st December 1988: 1 9 23 26 33 42 39

Monday 19th December 1988: 3 20 26 30 31 32

Saturday 17th December 1988: 4 9 21 24 27 50 34

Wednesday 14th December 1988: 2 6 11 13 33 37 43

Monday 12th December 1988: 4 8 11 13 18 22

Saturday 10th December 1988: 17 22 24 25 32 36 27

Wednesday 7th December 1988: 1 6 9 20 22 32 8
Monday 5th December 1988: 2 7 10 13 33 39
Saturday 3rd December 1988: 1 8 13 18 28 48 19
Wednesday 30th November 1988: 3 5 18 37 40 48 42
Monday 28th November 1988: 3 12 15 24 25 28
Saturday 26th November 1988: 4 7 42 46 47 52 45
Wednesday 23rd November 1988: 3 19 28 40 48 54 11
Monday 21st November 1988: 6 11 14 19 33 40
Saturday 19th November 1988: 20 21 22 27 46 48 11
Wednesday 16th November 1988: 9 23 33 49 51 54 32
Monday 14th November 1988: 2 6 10 30 33 36
Saturday 12th November 1988: 3 4 8 35 47 48 33
Wednesday 9th November 1988: 6 18 32 36 39 49 50
Monday 7th November 1988: 13 23 26 29 31 37
Saturday 5th November 1988: 9 13 25 30 43 47 20
Wednesday 2nd November 1988: 12 28 35 42 44 51 14
Monday 31st October 1988: 2 10 11 25 32 34
Saturday 29th October 1988: 5 8 15 27 29 31 14
Wednesday 26th October 1988: 1 8 14 15 51 52 11
Monday 24th October 1988: 1 7 27 30 33 39
Saturday 22nd October 1988: 7 9 13 21 34 43 47
Wednesday 19th October 1988: 17 24 30 36 37 42 18
Monday 17th October 1988: 4 5 16 18 39 40
Saturday 15th October 1988: 3 5 18 23 41 47 1
Wednesday 12th October 1988: 13 23 26 38 42 46 22
Monday 10th October 1988: 1 4 15 27 31 32
Saturday 8th October 1988: 4 8 19 21 22 44 12
Wednesday 5th October 1988: 1 11 14 22 51 52 2
Monday 3rd October 1988: 12 15 17 21 27 36
Saturday 1st October 1988: 3 4 5 10 53 54 49
Wednesday 28th September 1988: 1 21 25 30 45 48 4
Monday 26th September 1988: 15 16 18 23 33 37
Saturday 24th September 1988: 20 27 30 31 42 53 48
Wednesday 21st September 1988: 7 21 26 37 43 50 31

Monday 19th September 1988: 4 15 24 25 26 28
Saturday 17th September 1988: 6 16 29 30 32 40 44
Wednesday 14th September 1988: 9 22 24 32 37 49 31
Monday 12th September 1988: 2 13 15 28 37 40
Saturday 10th September 1988: 3 12 13 16 24 27 4
Wednesday 7th September 1988: 4 10 16 21 23 40 26
Monday 5th September 1988: 2 3 4 5 24 39
Saturday 3rd September 1988: 11 18 22 25 44 48 7
Wednesday 31st August 1988: 5 8 29 37 41 47 14
Monday 29th August 1988: 7 11 15 31 35 36
Saturday 27th August 1988: 3 29 41 44 49 51 6
Wednesday 24th August 1988: 4 12 23 37 50 53 18
Monday 22nd August 1988: 13 16 17 33 34 39
Saturday 20th August 1988: 3 17 24 29 31 38 26
Wednesday 17th August 1988: 12 17 20 31 32 49 2
Monday 15th August 1988: 11 14 21 25 33 36
Saturday 13th August 1988: 3 6 15 17 26 29 46
Wednesday 10th August 1988: 7 21 26 35 40 52 14
Monday 8th August 1988: 5 11 22 28 29 40
Saturday 6th August 1988: 8 26 27 31 50 52 11
Wednesday 3rd August 1988: 17 24 25 26 27 34 46
Monday 1st August 1988: 4 14 15 18 36 40
Saturday 30th July 1988: 4 10 12 20 38 48 36
Wednesday 27th July 1988: 1 12 15 26 30 39 46
Monday 25th July 1988: 6 8 27 30 33 40
Saturday 23rd July 1988: 7 12 24 40 53 54 16
Wednesday 20th July 1988: 5 7 14 27 31 51 11
Monday 18th July 1988: 1 8 15 26 30 37
Saturday 16th July 1988: 5 16 21 31 33 35 25
Wednesday 13th July 1988: 1 4 21 31 36 38 19
Monday 11th July 1988: 10 12 14 18 35 39
Saturday 9th July 1988: 2 5 15 19 25 35 10
Wednesday 6th July 1988: 6 11 17 19 24 48 25
Monday 4th July 1988: 2 12 20 22 35 37

Saturday 2nd July 1988: 7 20 29 45 47 49 22
Wednesday 29th June 1988: 13 27 31 32 37 53 20
Monday 27th June 1988: 5 11 14 26 28 31
Saturday 25th June 1988: 2 17 22 25 29 45 43
Wednesday 22nd June 1988: 6 23 26 34 43 44 5
Monday 20th June 1988: 12 17 19 24 32 33
Saturday 18th June 1988: 7 21 29 38 40 48 12
Wednesday 15th June 1988: 11 31 32 33 35 44 49
Monday 13th June 1988: 4 7 9 12 13
Saturday 11th June 1988: 1 3 12 26 49 54 17
Wednesday 8th June 1988: 2 8 20 24 30 43 54
Monday 6th June 1988: 7 15 24 35 36 38
Saturday 4th June 1988: 20 24 30 33 39 45 17
Wednesday 1st June 1988: 7 11 25 26 39 47 22
Monday 30th May 1988: 6 14 19 21 25 27
Saturday 28th May 1988: 14 35 39 45 48 49 47
Wednesday 25th May 1988: 1 8 11 31 32 33 25
Monday 23rd May 1988: 2 4 8 22 26 32
Saturday 21st May 1988: 6 14 18 25 31 33 27
Wednesday 18th May 1988: 3 8 21 40 41 48 54
Monday 16th May 1988: 1 3 7 12 19 27
Saturday 14th May 1988: 7 10 20 22 26 46 29
Wednesday 11th May 1988: 1 8 12 13 23 28 52
Monday 9th May 1988: 9 15 18 24 29 39
Saturday 7th May 1988: 5 16 18 31 37 54 34
Wednesday 4th May 1988: 2 15 16 18 41 49 30
Monday 2nd May 1988: 3 6 7 31 32 34
Saturday 30th April 1988: 15 19 21 25 30 38 24
Wednesday 27th April 1988: 8 9 11 45 48 51 28
Monday 25th April 1988: 2 13 18 28 33 40
Saturday 23rd April 1988: 2 3 4 11 13 41 43
Wednesday 20th April 1988: 12 27 42 43 44 46 48
Monday 18th April 1988: 13 15 30 35 37 38
Saturday 16th April 1988: 12 13 22 40 43 46 29

Wednesday 13th April 1988: 4 12 27 36 45 46 21

Monday 11th April 1988: 1 16 26 31 37 38

Saturday 9th April 1988: 17 21 28 35 39 40 23

Wednesday 6th April 1988: 17 24 27 31 39 43 47

Monday 4th April 1988: 12 15 20 21 33 34

Saturday 2nd April 1988: 4 15 16 18 22 33 34

Wednesday 30th March 1988: 4 8 18 33 38 45 41

Monday 28th March 1988: 7 8 17 21 28 32

Saturday 26th March 1988: 5 12 20 28 39 46 15

Wednesday 23rd March 1988: 16 21 23 33 44 46 9

Monday 21st March 1988: 4 13 14 24 34 39

Saturday 19th March 1988: 3 5 14 20 25 48 8

Wednesday 16th March 1988: 13 18 28 35 42 44 5

Monday 14th March 1988: 3 20 25 26 35 37

Saturday 12th March 1988: 5 9 17 22 30 32 47

Wednesday 9th March 1988: 9 19 21 22 31 41 34

Monday 7th March 1988: 11 16 17 24 34 39

Saturday 5th March 1988: 2 5 11 31 38 40 36

Wednesday 2nd March 1988: 3 7 28 33 45 46 25

Monday 29th February 1988: 1 6 23 24 27 34

Saturday 27th February 1988: 5 13 14 24 32 37 45

Wednesday 24th February 1988: 1 19 27 34 39 43 23

Monday 22nd February 1988: 10 14 15 20 31 39

Saturday 20th February 1988: 2 7 28 31 39 43 30

Wednesday 17th February 1988: 16 22 27 40 42 45 36

Monday 15th February 1988: 1 5 6 7 21 31

Saturday 13th February 1988: 7 15 22 23 36 40 31

Wednesday 10th February 1988: 1 4 6 8 22 33 17

Monday 8th February 1988: 4 5 6 9 15 23

Saturday 6th February 1988: 3 7 18 28 34 46 10

Wednesday 3rd February 1988: 9 18 23 36 40 42 10

Monday 1st February 1988: 4 7 11 13 18 27

Saturday 30th January 1988: 16 27 28 32 37 43 26

Wednesday 27th January 1988: 9 16 18 33 43 47 30

Monday 25th January 1988: 7 12 20 21 26 35
Saturday 23rd January 1988: 2 6 27 36 37 41 23
Wednesday 20th January 1988: 11 14 22 30 44 48 36
Monday 18th January 1988: 6 9 15 26 38 39
Saturday 16th January 1988: 4 20 23 31 35 37 46
Wednesday 13th January 1988: 8 20 24 28 30 43 15
Monday 11th January 1988: 4 6 9 10 25 30
Saturday 9th January 1988: 15 18 25 30 41 46 43
Wednesday 6th January 1988: 24 29 32 34 44 45 16
Monday 4th January 1988: 1 7 10 17 19 40
Saturday 2nd January 1988: 3 4 7 23 38 45 14
Saturday 30th December 1989: 9 13 21 38 46 47 27
Wednesday 27th December 1989: 8 22 30 40 49 54 31
Tuesday 26th December 1989: 7 17 25 35 36 40
Saturday 23rd December 1989: 20 22 28 29 37 44 30
Wednesday 20th December 1989: 2 3 7 14 35 49 39
Monday 18th December 1989: 5 17 23 27 29 36
Saturday 16th December 1989: 12 16 39 41 44 47 52
Wednesday 13th December 1989: 8 10 13 23 41 44 47
Monday 11th December 1989: 9 15 19 26 28 32
Saturday 9th December 1989: 4 6 19 28 30 51 2
Wednesday 6th December 1989: 7 21 24 36 41 48 25
Monday 4th December 1989: 10 14 16 28 34 38
Saturday 2nd December 1989: 11 14 28 31 35 38 42
Wednesday 29th November 1989: 2 3 31 32 35 46 23
Monday 27th November 1989: 7 22 23 30 33 38
Saturday 25th November 1989: 9 20 41 48 50 54 23
Wednesday 22nd November 1989: 1 8 23 39 4448 34
Monday 20th November 1989: 3 7 10 12 17 39
Saturday 18th November 1989: 1 5 11 30 31 53 52
Wednesday 15th November 1989: 9 18 23 26 33 43 36
Monday 13th November 1989: 19 20 29 30 33 40
Saturday 11th November 1989: 1 8 29 32 43 44 41
Wednesday 8th November 1989: 3 9 32 36 38 42 11

Monday 6th November 1989: 2 11 13 15 17 37
Saturday 4th November 1989: 20 29 42 46 50 52 8
Wednesday 1st November 1989: 2 5 11 31 52 53 48
Monday 30th October 1989: 12 15 25 32 37 39
Saturday 28th October 1989: 6 23 30 38 48 51 5
Wednesday 25th October 1989: 6 10 17 39 46 49 24
Monday 23rd October 1989: 8 19 20 23 30 39
Saturday 21st October 1989: 2 18 25 32 34 40 3
Wednesday 18th October 1989: 1 4 11 12 48 50 29
Monday 16th October 1989: 10 14 20 22 25 39
Saturday 14th October 1989: 3 12 31 43 46 52 24
Wednesday 11th October 1989: 14 24 36 37 47 49 7
Monday 9th October 1989: 5 17 21 27 28 37
Saturday 7th October 1989: 7 8 26 29 32 51 44
Wednesday 4th October 1989: 4 7 17 32 49 53 28
Monday 2nd October 1989: 2 5 7 22 32 37
Saturday 30th September 1989: 7 12 16 28 50 51 42
Wednesday 27th September 1989: 4 20 23 31 40 54 16
Monday 25th September 1989: 6 13 15 16 33 34
Saturday 23rd September 1989: 9 13 15 31 48 54 29
Wednesday 20th September 1989: 2 3 22 33 40 50 20
Monday 18th September 1989: 5 9 11 14 20 35
Saturday 16th September 1989: 6 21 33 35 36 46 20
Wednesday 13th September 1989: 5 17 34 37 48 53 4
Monday 11th September 1989: 8 14 23 29 32 40
Saturday 9th September 1989: 7 15 19 22 33 53 52
Wednesday 6th September 1989: 20 25 28 29 35 42 22
Monday 4th September 1989: 2 9 12 15 25 29
Saturday 2nd September 1989: 3 4 9 13 26 50 27
Wednesday 30th August 1989: 3 11 20 36 40 47 46
Monday 28th August 1989: 14 18 31 35 36 37
Saturday 26th August 1989: 8 16 20 32 40 51 21
Wednesday 23rd August 1989: 2 14 18 20 39 46 16
Monday 21st August 1989: 4 11 14 29 31 39

Saturday 19th August 1989: 2 22 30 39 44 46 13
Wednesday 16th August 1989: 1 2 11 21 40 49 19
Monday 14th August 1989: 8 11 12 22 35 38
Saturday 12th August 1989: 4 6 13 16 24 49 10
Wednesday 9th August 1989: 21 24 29 42 43 44 41
Monday 7th August 1989: 4 9 14 21 23 38
Saturday 5th August 1989: 4 6 14 29 51 54 5
Wednesday 2nd August 1989: 4 21 22 37 40 41 5
Monday 31st July 1989: 5 8 17 22 29 34
Saturday 29th July 1989: 18 29 31 36 42 44 13
Wednesday 26th July 1989: 32 35 40 44 52 53 27
Monday 24th July 1989: 1 10 11 13 27 38
Saturday 22nd July 1989: 6 22 25 29 39 54 30
Wednesday 19th July 1989: 20 22 32 34 39 54 41
Monday 17th July 1989: 5 8 20 21 26 35
Saturday 15th July 1989: 2 3 15 19 32 33 48
Wednesday 12th July 1989: 1 4 9 16 24 32 26
Monday 10th July 1989: 5 8 13 26 33 36
Saturday 8th July 1989: 1 17 32 33 37 39 6
Wednesday 5th July 1989: 20 21 23 28 32 54 14
Monday 3rd July 1989: 1 3 4 11 14 31
Saturday 1st July 1989: 6 9 17 29 42 50 12
Wednesday 28th June 1989: 4 5 20 31 39 40 10
Monday 26th June 1989: 2 4 6 7 13 36
Saturday 24th June 1989: 4 10 31 33 40 42 21
Wednesday 21st June 1989: 16 26 28 30 43 54 49
Monday 19th June 1989: 2 6 18 21 24 34
Saturday 17th June 1989: 9 18 27 39 40 48 10
Wednesday 14th June 1989: 4 5 14 26 46 54 42
Monday 12th June 1989: 13 16 22 35 36 38
Saturday 10th June 1989: 20 33 44 45 48 54 21
Wednesday 7th June 1989: 24 26 38 39 41 54 2
Monday 5th June 1989: 2 6 14 17 28 31
Saturday 3rd June 1989: 4 7 11 32 34 43 10

Wednesday 31st May 1989: 6 7 12 41 45 54 43
Monday 29th May 1989: 9 23 33 35 36 39
Saturday 27th May 1989: 4 8 19 30 46 54 36
Wednesday 24th May 1989: 3 15 24 27 28 47 23
Monday 22nd May 1989: 1 17 18 22 32 39
Saturday 20th May 1989: 4 34 36 39 46 54 9
Wednesday 17th May 1989: 7 9 10 15 17 33 47
Monday 15th May 1989: 1 15 25 29 33 38
Saturday 13th May 1989: 4 8 12 13 47 49 37
Wednesday 10th May 1989: 3 7 10 12 16 19 31
Monday 8th May 1989: 8 12 21 28 33 38
Saturday 6th May 1989: 2 30 43 46 48 53 12
Wednesday 3rd May 1989: 18 21 35 36 45 52 46
Monday 1st May 1989: 4 17 20 21 28 34
Saturday 29th April 1989: 15 21 29 34 38 42 10
Wednesday 26th April 1989: 2 14 28 34 48 50 22
Monday 24th April 1989: 12 14 18 21 30 32
Saturday 22nd April 1989: 9 11 15 25 37 52 17
Wednesday 19th April 1989: 3 12 26 29 44 49 35
Monday 17th April 1989: 7 11 17 26 31 39
Saturday 15th April 1989: 6 19 31 37 38 41 42
Wednesday 12th April 1989: 5 38 41 44 47 48 29
Monday 10th April 1989: 2 6 9 11 14 34
Saturday 8th April 1989: 11 23 29 32 35 48 37
Wednesday 5th April 1989: 13 26 30 31 43 44 34
Monday 3rd April 1989: 6 7 16 18 24 27
Saturday 1st April 1989: 2 14 18 19 43 46 40
Wednesday 29th March 1989: 1 8 18 27 46 49 20
Monday 27th March 1989: 4 6 8 17 23 35
Saturday 25th March 1989: 6 21 39 41 48 53 31
Wednesday 22nd March 1989: 5 28 35 38 48 54 7
Monday 20th March 1989: 4 12 20 23 33 34
Saturday 18th March 1989: 7 30 40 45 50 52 36
Wednesday 15th March 1989: 5 13 27 32 41 52 37

Monday 13th March 1989: 9 16 18 19 22 26
Saturday 11th March 1989: 1 24 25 31 35 47 51
Wednesday 8th March 1989: 12 13 15 25 52 53 20
Monday 6th March 1989: 3 5 7 19 22 34
Saturday 4th March 1989: 2 8 28 34 38 44 9
Wednesday 1st March 1989: 17 21 22 33 42 52 13
Monday 27th February 1989: 5 12 16 17 21 24
Saturday 25th February 1989: 3 16 23 34 37 53 41
Wednesday 22nd February 1989: 1 5 12 19 44 50 32
Monday 20th February 1989: 1 6 7 24 33 38
Saturday 18th February 1989: 11 13 14 30 50 54 29
Wednesday 15th February 1989: 12 14 20 26 28 49 36
Monday 13th February 1989: 8 12 14 27 37 40
Saturday 11th February 1989: 3 5 12 14 45 46 26
Wednesday 8th February 1989: 13 28 29 37 39 50 9
Monday 6th February 1989: 1 17 19 20 29 37
Saturday 4th February 1989: 7 20 21 24 39 51 27
Wednesday 1st February 1989: 3 9 19 40 42 54 52
Monday 30th January 1989: 5 7 12 26 34 40
Saturday 28th January 1989: 27 33 34 35 42 49 15
Wednesday 25th January 1989: 1 13 18 33 41 46 12
Monday 23rd January 1989: 6 10 14 15 25 39
Saturday 21st January 1989: 5 8 12 21 22 40 42
Wednesday 18th January 1989: 2 6 21 22 30 48 52
Monday 16th January 1989: 5 6 23 34 38 40
Saturday 14th January 1989: 18 20 33 34 40 51 46
Wednesday 11th January 1989: 13 16 30 40 44 48 14
Monday 9th January 1989: 7 10 23 28 32 34
Saturday 7th January 1989: 2 3 5 8 10 35 50
Wednesday 4th January 1989: 6 14 15 41 45 51 2
Monday 2nd January 1989: 1 2 10 17 39 40
Monday 31st December 1990: 2 3 7 11 26 39
Saturday 29th December 1990: 7 13 18 37 46 47 52
Wednesday 26th December 1990: 14 20 30 35 38 48 8

Monday 24th December 1990: 4 11 20 36 37 39

Saturday 22nd December 1990: 10 12 14 19 21 54 37

Wednesday 19th December 1990: 21 23 28 39 53 54 9

Monday 17th December 1990: 1 8 20 31 35 38

Saturday 15th December 1990: 18 19 36 48 49 53 2

Wednesday 12th December 1990: 10 14 17 41 50 54 5

Monday 10th December 1990: 5 9 10 22 27 34

Saturday 8th December 1990: 3 15 21 27 40 53 46

Wednesday 5th December 1990: 1 8 10 14 16 35 7

Monday 3rd December 1990: 2 7 10 19 23 27

Saturday 1st December 1990: 16 17 24 46 49 51 41

Wednesday 28th November 1990: 11 19 22 42 50 54 17

Monday 26th November 1990: 1 14 16 23 24 32

Saturday 24th November 1990: 18 19 22 36 37 52 5

Wednesday 21st November 1990: 3 12 15 17 42 45 43

Monday 19th November 1990: 14 19 23 29 34 40

Saturday 17th November 1990: 3 11 24 34 39 47 40

Wednesday 14th November 1990: 7 12 16 39 42 50 54

Monday 12th November 1990: 1 13 20 30 38 39

Saturday 10th November 1990: 1 7 34 40 42 48 19

Wednesday 7th November 1990: 3 8 13 24 25 44 41

Monday 5th November 1990: 6 7 22 23 25 27

Saturday 3rd November 1990: 8 19 35 37 43 53 50

Wednesday 31st October 1990: 8 13 18 19 44 47 36

Monday 29th October 1990: 2 5 7 15 17 38

Saturday 27th October 1990: 7 13 15 21 33 35 44

Wednesday 24th October 1990: 2 21 27 32 37 54 46

Monday 22nd October 1990: 14 21 22 27 28 34

Saturday 20th October 1990: 16 20 21 33 37 52 25

Wednesday 17th October 1990: 2 11 26 36 38 39 48

Monday 15th October 1990: 1 4 19 26 31 32

Saturday 13th October 1990: 3 10 12 17 43 49 47

Wednesday 10th October 1990: 4 11 26 29 42 45 9

Monday 8th October 1990: 10 13 15 21 28 32

Saturday 6th October 1990: 9 23 32 37 43 45 30
Wednesday 3rd October 1990: 4 7 18 38 46 50 30
Monday 1st October 1990: 5 11 13 14 16 39
Saturday 29th September 1990: 2 10 11 18 26 35 27
Wednesday 26th September 1990: 5 23 39 43 44 48 47
Monday 24th September 1990: 1 3 8 23 25 28
Saturday 22nd September 1990: 1 3 6 16 43 54 15
Wednesday 19th September 1990: 8 9 10 11 27 45 35
Monday 17th September 1990: 5 21 25 34 39 40
Saturday 15th September 1990: 2 29 34 41 42 49
Wednesday 12th September 1990: 1 16 24 39 43 45 27
Monday 10th September 1990: 3 8 14 30 31 34
Saturday 8th September 1990: 21 23 34 38 46 47 40
Wednesday 5th September 1990: 2 4 11 20 24 32 22
Monday 3rd September 1990: 5 21 24 28 31 38
Saturday 1st September 1990: 8 15 26 29 32 38 37
Wednesday 29th August 1990: 10 14 18 40 49 52 44
Monday 27th August 1990: 14 20 21 32 35 38
Saturday 25th August 1990: 19 32 35 39 45 47 33
Wednesday 22nd August 1990: 8 14 15 21 27 42 7
Monday 20th August 1990: 1 20 26 33 37 39
Saturday 18th August 1990: 8 15 16 32 40 44 5
Wednesday 15th August 1990: 3 12 22 29 34 39 38
Monday 13th August 1990: 8 20 21 27 33 34
Saturday 11th August 1990: 4 7 19 32 35 54 5
Wednesday 8th August 1990: 16 20 31 42 50 53 15
Monday 6th August 1990: 13 15 18 26 31 40
Saturday 4th August 1990: 4 12 21 30 35 44 41
Wednesday 1st August 1990: 8 18 22 31 39 41 11
Monday 30th July 1990: 11 12 15 23 25 37
Saturday 28th July 1990: 6 10 11 19 21 53 49
Wednesday 25th July 1990: 2 18 25 44 49 53 22
Monday 23rd July 1990: 3 9 13 16 19 31
Saturday 21st July 1990: 3 5 6 26 31 39 13

Wednesday 18th July 1990: 5 8 15 18 22 48 35
Monday 16th July 1990: 4 6 23 24 27 29
Saturday 14th July 1990: 1 8 14 41 50 52 49
Wednesday 11th July 1990: 6 9 16 29 52 2
Monday 9th July 1990: 5 18 19 20 21 34
Saturday 7th July 1990: 4 9 17 24 25 43 53
Wednesday 4th July 1990: 3 10 19 24 28 44 23
Monday 2nd July 1990: 5 8 14 19 26 33
Saturday 30th June 1990: 3 8 36 37 45 50 21
Wednesday 27th June 1990: 3 18 28 33 37 51 14
Monday 25th June 1990: 1 10 19 24 27 39
Saturday 23rd June 1990: 7 13 25 34 40 53 41
Wednesday 20th June 1990: 12 21 27 34 44 51 19
Monday 18th June 1990: 1 11 12 24 25 37
Saturday 16th June 1990: 8 15 18 35 38 40 39
Wednesday 13th June 1990: 2 12 14 23 27 42 11
Monday 11th June 1990: 2 18 21 31 32 33
Saturday 9th June 1990: 11 18 31 32 33 52 46
Wednesday 6th June 1990: 3 15 29 33 37 46 49
Monday 4th June 1990: 1 2 4 17 31 36
Saturday 2nd June 1990: 6 16 20 31 44 47 2
Wednesday 30th May 1990: 7 17 43 45 46 47 53
Monday 28th May 1990: 2 6 12 15 17 36
Saturday 26th May 1990: 3 8 13 31 32 51 54
Wednesday 23rd May 1990: 5 11 13 18 35 48 21
Monday 21st May 1990: 5 17 21 23 29 40
Saturday 19th May 1990: 13 15 19 29 48 53 10
Wednesday 16th May 1990: 3 8 20 23 25 32 48
Monday 14th May 1990: 5 8 19 24 33 38
Saturday 12th May 1990: 15 16 23 41 43 52 42
Wednesday 9th May 1990: 3 25 28 35 44 50 20
Monday 7th May 1990: 8 12 17 22 25 28
Saturday 5th May 1990: 11 13 21 26 27 29 49
Wednesday 2nd May 1990: 1 16 24 31 42 43 51

Monday 30th April 1990: 3 6 12 24 35 37
Saturday 28th April 1990: 3 14 16 20 41 53 28
Wednesday 25th April 1990: 1 11 24 25 26 33 31
Monday 23rd April 1990: 5 8 9 21 25 34
Saturday 21st April 1990: 12 13 15 19 29 51 41
Wednesday 18th April 1990: 33 34 40 43 47 54 30
Monday 16th April 1990: 8 14 23 28 29 36
Saturday 14th April 1990: 1 17 22 30 32 38 35
Wednesday 11th April 1990: 6 14 24 32 34 51 48
Monday 9th April 1990: 1 18 22 26 32 40
Saturday 7th April 1990: 14 18 26 44 47 53 46
Wednesday 4th April 1990: 8 16 26 43 47 53 42
Monday 2nd April 1990: 7 8 14 24 25 27
Saturday 31st March 1990: 1 16 18 19 26 36 6
Wednesday 28th March 1990: 26 30 37 40 46 53 17
Monday 26th March 1990: 6 7 25 30 31 36
Saturday 24th March 1990: 13 15 19 20 36 53 41
Wednesday 21st March 1990: 11 13 15 18 35 46 30
Monday 19th March 1990: 1 5 12 20 27 33
Saturday 17th March 1990: 1 20 39 40 41 42 7
Wednesday 14th March 1990: 26 32 43 47 51 52 24
Monday 12th March 1990: 1 5 19 22 26 38
Saturday 10th March 1990: 8 14 28 36 40 47 5
Wednesday 7th March 1990: 3 9 18 41 43 46 13
Monday 5th March 1990: 7 19 24 25 26 31
Saturday 3rd March 1990: 11 16 31 35 40 49 30
Wednesday 28th February 1990: 17 28 30 33 47 52 27
Monday 26th February 1990: 13 21 25 26 32 33
Saturday 24th February 1990: 5 15 31 33 38 54 16
Wednesday 21st February 1990: 3 7 22 25 39 49 34
Monday 19th February 1990: 22 23 27 28 34 38
Saturday 17th February 1990: 14 23 25 30 36 47 37
Wednesday 14th February 1990: 13 21 23 26 31 50 14
Monday 12th February 1990: 6 7 8 9 13 38

Saturday 10th February 1990: 8 18 37 38 39 42 20
Wednesday 7th February 1990: 3 12 21 22 27 33 50
Monday 5th February 1990: 2 9 23 30 32 40
Saturday 3rd February 1990: 1 5 7 18 22 25 40
Wednesday 31st January 1990: 3 6 15 40 43 51 41
Monday 29th January 1990: 16 20 35 36 37 40
Saturday 27th January 1990: 9 40 42 47 52 53 3
Wednesday 24th January 1990: 3 10 34 47 48 49 43
Monday 22nd January 1990: 4 32 34 35 37 39
Saturday 20th January 1990: 5 6 8 19 31 32 17
Wednesday 17th January 1990: 13 21 27 30 35 48 47
Monday 15th January 1990: 5 6 20 21 28 31
Saturday 13th January 1990: 6 13 14 24 34 54 49
Wednesday 10th January 1990: 4 21 32 33 48 53 39
Monday 8th January 1990: 17 21 22 33 34 38
Saturday 6th January 1990: 18 25 26 32 42 44 11
Wednesday 3rd January 1990: 11 12 16 28 38 46 29
Monday 1st January 1990: 14 15 21 29 36 39
Monday 30th December 1991: 6 8 9 13 19 27
Saturday 28th December 1991: 7 22 31 43 48 54 11
Thursday 26th December 1991: 1 7 16 43 51 54 50
Monday 23rd December 1991: 6 8 10 12 17 18
Saturday 21st December 1991: 4 5 9 19 50 52 17
Wednesday 18th December 1991: 8 11 14 18 41 50 36
Monday 16th December 1991: 1 2 5 18 26 29
Saturday 14th December 1991: 12 15 18 29 42 47 37
Wednesday 11th December 1991: 4 10 16 40 48 50 29
Monday 9th December 1991: 3 10 24 28 33 35
Saturday 7th December 1991: 4 25 26 34 42 47 50
Wednesday 4th December 1991: 4 6 22 23 29 50 33
Monday 2nd December 1991: 11 22 24 27 30 31
Saturday 30th November 1991: 14 31 33 49 50 54 27
Wednesday 27th November 1991: 19 24 25 32 34 54 8
Monday 25th November 1991: 4 5 14 16 32 33

Saturday 23rd November 1991: 4 10 27 29 35 50 13
Wednesday 20th November 1991: 13 16 17 20 45 46 1
Monday 18th November 1991: 1 14 15 19 27 40
Saturday 16th November 1991: 8 18 28 29 34 36 35
Wednesday 13th November 1991: 3 29 32 36 44 49 41
Monday 11th November 1991: 5 18 20 28 35 36
Saturday 9th November 1991: 13 26 27 38 44 45 2
Wednesday 6th November 1991: 1 7 10 31 46 53 33
Monday 4th November 1991: 2 8 9 14 30 36
Saturday 2nd November 1991: 1 6 7 22 39 44 52
Wednesday 30th October 1991: 11 14 28 38 44 54 34
Monday 28th October 1991: 7 10 14 26 28 38
Saturday 26th October 1991: 19 20 37 42 44 54 21
Wednesday 23rd October 1991: 23 27 28 31 37 44 17
Monday 21st October 1991: 1 7 9 27 28 32
Saturday 19th October 1991: 3 13 18 47 48 49 54
Wednesday 16th October 1991: 7 22 33 44 45 49 15
Monday 14th October 1991: 1 7 16 31 32 40
Saturday 12th October 1991: 5 17 34 38 47 53 11
Wednesday 9th October 1991: 7 9 17 31 41 43 4
Monday 7th October 1991: 14 15 17 23 24 32
Saturday 5th October 1991: 10 20 24 29 52 54 49
Wednesday 2nd October 1991: 23 31 34 45 49 50 17
Monday 30th September 1991: 2 22 26 32 34 39
Saturday 28th September 1991: 2 4 6 9 17 21 52
Wednesday 25th September 1991: 3 17 35 41 47 54 43
Monday 23rd September 1991: 13 15 23 26 30 32
Saturday 21st September 1991: 6 8 27 33 45 54 20
Wednesday 18th September 1991: 8 9 22 26 34 38 47
Monday 16th September 1991: 4 6 13 21 30 39
Saturday 14th September 1991: 4 20 22 27 35 53 5
Wednesday 11th September 1991: 3 18 39 42 51 53 5
Monday 9th September 1991: 4 6 7 20 24 38
Saturday 7th September 1991: 13 17 22 28 41 50 36

Wednesday 4th September 1991: 5 10 13 16 40 54 43
Monday 2nd September 1991: 4 7 14 22 28 38
Saturday 31st August 1991: 6 11 37 39 43 45 22
Wednesday 28th August 1991: 6 12 28 37 40 53 33
Monday 26th August 1991: 10 13 20 22 23 32
Saturday 24th August 1991: 9 12 24 25 48 54 41
Wednesday 21st August 1991: 14 31 34 42 43 45 26
Monday 19th August 1991: 6 10 11 13 32 37
Saturday 17th August 1991: 9 16 26 34 38 46 48
Wednesday 14th August 1991: 7 11 25 43 46 49 27
Monday 12th August 1991: 6 13 21 32 36 37
Saturday 10th August 1991: 4 21 22 31 50 14
Wednesday 7th August 1991: 6 14 22 35 40 53 33
Monday 5th August 1991: 5 11 17 29 30 33
Saturday 3rd August 1991: 10 22 25 31 42 50 17
Wednesday 31st July 1991: 8 14 20 21 26 52 6
Monday 29th July 1991: 6 9 16 19 25 27
Saturday 27th July 1991: 17 20 25 27 46 50 23
Wednesday 24th July 1991: 13 14 16 36 40 50 49
Monday 22nd July 1991: 10 22 25 26 28 34
Saturday 20th July 1991: 3 10 28 30 38 47 4
Wednesday 17th July 1991: 2 3 6 43 46 52 15
Monday 15th July 1991: 2 11 18 23 31 35
Saturday 13th July 1991: 2 6 24 35 43 48 53
Wednesday 10th July 1991: 19 22 39 46 48 54 14
Monday 8th July 1991: 2 3 10 14 29 32
Saturday 6th July 1991: 2 5 12 33 36 40 34
Wednesday 3rd July 1991: 15 27 32 42 44 50 34
Monday 1st July 1991: 2 8 12 16 33 36
Saturday 29th June 1991: 5 17 19 31 33 43 32
Wednesday 26th June 1991: 4 8 9 13 43 50 7
Monday 24th June 1991: 2 12 18 21 27 37
Saturday 22nd June 1991: 1 8 11 28 35 37 49
Wednesday 19th June 1991: 5 7 16 27 29 34 42

Monday 17th June 1991: 8 18 24 28 33 35
Saturday 15th June 1991: 7 9 11 26 30 39 2
Wednesday 12th June 1991: 26 40 42 45 47 53 12
Monday 10th June 1991: 9 11 12 32 37 40
Saturday 8th June 1991: 9 13 15 27 37 48 40
Wednesday 5th June 1991: 11 24 43 48 53 54 13
Monday 3rd June 1991: 2 3 4 6 15 18
Saturday 1st June 1991: 2 22 25 28 36 38 23
Wednesday 29th May 1991: 13 16 44 45 47 54 14
Monday 27th May 1991: 6 8 19 23 34 40
Saturday 25th May 1991: 14 22 23 25 40 45 50
Wednesday 22nd May 1991: 6 18 22 32 45 48 36
Monday 20th May 1991: 2 3 6 9 11 27
Saturday 18th May 1991: 1 35 39 42 43 48 31
Wednesday 15th May 1991: 3 21 26 36 45 52 27
Monday 13th May 1991: 2 4 6 26 31 40
Saturday 11th May 1991: 5 10 11 21 30 44 34
Wednesday 8th May 1991: 9 15 16 25 34 43 31
Monday 6th May 1991: 6 10 20 29 33 39
Saturday 4th May 1991: 7 12 20 21 31 44 41
Wednesday 1st May 1991: 14 20 24 25 41 42 26
Monday 29th April 1991: 10 22 27 29 33 37
Saturday 27th April 1991: 2 17 30 39 44 48 6
Wednesday 24th April 1991: 15 16 18 22 26 39 28
Monday 22nd April 1991: 6 12 25 29 31 37
Saturday 20th April 1991: 3 17 24 31 36 47 43
Wednesday 17th April 1991: 7 9 11 22 42 48 44
Monday 15th April 1991: 2 17 20 23 24 33
Saturday 13th April 1991: 4 7 24 37 38 50 20
Wednesday 10th April 1991: 4 14 16 20 22 47 3
Monday 8th April 1991: 11 13 20 21 26 32
Saturday 6th April 1991: 7 11 22 27 38 42 51
Wednesday 3rd April 1991: 4 24 41 45 50 52 39
Monday 1st April 1991: 3 5 10 26 32 35

Saturday 30th March 1991: 9 25 32 40 45 54 17
Wednesday 27th March 1991: 21 22 23 29 38 50 36
Monday 25th March 1991: 4 5 25 29 35 39
Saturday 23rd March 1991: 13 15 24 27 41 51 4
Wednesday 20th March 1991: 3 4 7 16 20 31 10
Monday 18th March 1991: 11 19 21 23 28 38
Saturday 16th March 1991: 18 21 32 33 35 38 45
Wednesday 13th March 1991: 19 25 26 39 43 45 33
Monday 11th March 1991: 11 21 22 31 36 40
Saturday 9th March 1991: 18 26 30 31 43 52 34
Wednesday 6th March 1991: 6 7 16 26 35 47 23
Monday 4th March 1991: 10 16 18 33 35 40
Saturday 2nd March 1991: 16 25 28 40 44 49 47
Wednesday 27th February 1991: 2 14 21 46 49 52 30
Monday 25th February 1991: 7 12 20 21 33 36
Saturday 23rd February 1991: 2 9 14 17 49 52 45
Wednesday 20th February 1991: 20 24 26 32 47 54 52
Monday 18th February 1991: 4 6 12 13 20 32
Saturday 16th February 1991: 11 15 35 36 39 47 48
Wednesday 13th February 1991: 9 10 15 25 45 53 17
Monday 11th February 1991: 7 10 19 21 24 36
Saturday 9th February 1991: 12 15 43 44 51 52 28
Wednesday 6th February 1991: 10 16 27 31 47 54 33
Monday 4th February 1991: 3 4 5 14 30 34
Saturday 2nd February 1991: 4 7 25 31 33 41 19
Wednesday 30th January 1991: 2 13 20 34 35 41 17
Monday 28th January 1991: 3 17 33 34 38 40
Saturday 26th January 1991: 5 15 30 35 46 50 7
Monday 21st January 1991: 7 12 24 28 29 37
Saturday 19th January 1991: 7 17 19 20 25 33 53
Wednesday 16th January 1991: 4 5 16 17 40 49 20
Monday 14th January 1991: 10 18 20 21 23 30
Saturday 12th January 1991: 9 13 25 35 41 54 28
Wednesday 9th January 1991: 4 14 19 21 44 5043

Monday 7th January 1991: 1 8 25 28 33 37
Saturday 5th January 1991: 5 30 39 45 49 53 3
Wednesday 2nd January 1991: 3 8 27 35 46 53 24
Wednesday 30th December 1992: 12 21 24 33 36 54 35
Saturday 26th December 1992: 8 14 32 38 41 50 25
Wednesday 23rd December 1992: 1 4 13 23 34 45 17
Saturday 19th December 1992: 4 31 32 33 46 54 37
Wednesday 16th December 1992: 7 19 25 33 38 42 4
Saturday 12th December 1992: 2 20 30 34 40 49 35
Wednesday 9th December 1992: 9 23 33 34 37 46 32
Saturday 5th December 1992: 2 7 23 27 45 46 24
Wednesday 2nd December 1992: 20 35 40 42 50 54 36
Saturday 28th November 1992: 2 3 17 40 43 47 45
Wednesday 25th November 1992: 9 17 24 31 36 41 6
Saturday 21st November 1992: 11 19 23 29 43 53 30
Wednesday 18th November 1992: 1 3 4 30 38 54 33
Saturday 14th November 1992: 7 15 23 29 42 44 6
Wednesday 11th November 1992: 2 11 13 18 36 47 1
Saturday 7th November 1992: 11 12 18 45 51 53 41
Wednesday 4th November 1992: 2 8 14 21 27 31 17
Saturday 31st October 1992: 7 10 23 33 39 54 52
Wednesday 28th October 1992: 8 12 15 21 25 31 47
Saturday 24th October 1992: 5 20 34 37 39 46 38
Wednesday 21st October 1992: 7 30 34 41 47 52 32
Saturday 17th October 1992: 1 9 18 44 45 51 21
Wednesday 14th October 1992: 6 7 18 30 31 42 23
Saturday 10th October 1992: 1 3 7 19 42 53 39
Wednesday 7th October 1992: 2 12 15 27 34 40 50
Saturday 3rd October 1992: 6 18 19 22 29 52 24
Wednesday 30th September 1992: 1 12 13 28 30 54 9
Saturday 26th September 1992: 12 24 26 27 37 47 35
Wednesday 23rd September 1992: 15 19 20 21 36 47 34
Saturday 19th September 1992: 2 20 24 44 50 28
Wednesday 16th September 1992: 11 12 25 26 39 43 14

Saturday 12th September 1992: 2 10 15 29 38 46 17
Wednesday 9th September 1992: 1 11 13 45 50 54 35
Saturday 5th September 1992: 7 15 28 33 41 48 36
Wednesday 2nd September 1992: 3 19 23 28 47 49 8
Saturday 29th August 1992: 4 20 26 32 33 39 43
Wednesday 26th August 1992: 4 5 6 19 35 47 1
Saturday 22nd August 1992: 2 4 5 9 11 31 19
Wednesday 19th August 1992: 4 12 16 41 43 44 52
Saturday 15th August 1992: 3 5 16 26 29 49 20
Wednesday 12th August 1992: 8 9 15 17 40 46 39
Saturday 8th August 1992: 8 13 31 33 36 37 27
Wednesday 5th August 1992: 3 10 19 34 42 52 26
Saturday 1st August 1992: 4 7 11 39 53 54 43
Wednesday 29th July 1992: 13 15 29 42 45 54 6
Saturday 25th July 1992: 1 4 14 21 38 50 29
Wednesday 22nd July 1992: 8 12 20 30 45 49 37
Saturday 18th July 1992: 4 6 12 17 48 50 13
Wednesday 15th July 1992: 7 31 46 48 50 53 13
Saturday 11th July 1992: 4 20 30 33 40 46 32
Wednesday 8th July 1992: 20 24 27 31 45 46 36
Saturday 4th July 1992: 14 16 27 31 43 51 47
Wednesday 1st July 1992: 8 10 35 47 50 51 18
Saturday 27th June 1992: 30 31 33 38 40 43 3
Wednesday 24th June 1992: 15 22 26 33 37 40 17
Saturday 20th June 1992: 26 28 30 38 40 47 31
Wednesday 17th June 1992: 4 9 33 37 38 46 21
Saturday 13th June 1992: 5 7 23 35 49 51 28
Wednesday 10th June 1992: 15 16 20 23 26 38 7
Saturday 6th June 1992: 4 6 10 19 35 45 39
Wednesday 3rd June 1992: 1 3 4 42 45 28
Saturday 30th May 1992: 12 15 30 33 40 48 38
Wednesday 27th May 1992: 3 15 27 38 40 46 10
Saturday 23rd May 1992: 2 23 29 30 31 32 41
Wednesday 20th May 1992: 2 7 12 18 33 52 49

Saturday 16th May 1992: 9 14 30 32 42 44 7
Wednesday 13th May 1992: 1 2 6 26 33 47 15
Saturday 9th May 1992: 14 20 21 40 49 54 43
Wednesday 6th May 1992: 9 11 12 18 33 43 35
Saturday 2nd May 1992: 3 7 21 25 35 39 10
Wednesday 29th April 1992: 14 15 21 25 31 53 9
Saturday 25th April 1992: 2 18 19 39 46 54 8
Wednesday 22nd April 1992: 14 21 23 28 44 49 2
Saturday 18th April 1992: 26 30 34 36 40 47 18
Wednesday 15th April 1992: 13 15 40 41 47 49 24
Saturday 11th April 1992: 6 8 24 26 30 39 17
Wednesday 8th April 1992: 1 6 19 20 27 28 14
Saturday 4th April 1992: 3 4 22 33 36 44 9
Wednesday 1st April 1992: 10 27 31 39 47 53 29
Saturday 28th March 1992: 11 18 20 31 46 47 6
Wednesday 25th March 1992: 4 7 33 34 40 41 21
Saturday 21st March 1992: 13 35 40 45 48 51 47
Wednesday 18th March 1992: 2 3 23 43 48 54 7
Saturday 14th March 1992: 5 7 9 15 32 46 34
Wednesday 11th March 1992: 15 21 24 29 43 51 9
Saturday 7th March 1992: 4 8 9 13 39 54 5
Wednesday 4th March 1992: 3 10 11 29 38 43 27
Saturday 29th February 1992: 8 10 13 15 40 44 3
Wednesday 26th February 1992: 7 8 11 24 25 51 15
Saturday 22nd February 1992: 6 9 18 23 2 43 5
Wednesday 19th February 1992: 4 25 31 42 52 54 37
Saturday 15th February 1992: 7 10 25 27 28 43 24
Wednesday 12th February 1992: 2 26 34 35 36 50 17
Saturday 8th February 1992: 5 15 19 26 33 49 24
Wednesday 5th February 1992: 3 6 47 48 51 52 45
Saturday 1st February 1992: 1 19 26 36 48 53 4
Wednesday 29th January 1992: 17 27 31 32 34 45 37
Saturday 25th January 1992: 1 2 9 13 14 46 36
Wednesday 22nd January 1992: 1 2 30 39 43 45 27

Saturday 18th January 1992: 14 27 31 36 42 45 1

Wednesday 15th January 1992: 27 41 44 50 51 52 2

Monday 13th January 1992: 5 6 9 22 29 31

Saturday 11th January 1992: 3 7 14 21 33 35 29

Wednesday 8th January 1992: 5 22 23 33 43 53 20

Monday 6th January 1992: 7 9 11 21 22 31

Saturday 4th January 1992: 1 14 15 19 28 40 2

Wednesday 1st January 1992: 2 19 20 27 45 47 52

Saturday 28th December 1996: 3 10 12 21 25 27 14

Thursday 26th December 1996: 2 5 35 37 52 53 18

Saturday 21st December 1996: 6 10 11 13 30 36 5

Wednesday 18th December 1996: 8 9 10 20 30 33 45

Saturday 14th December 1996: 1 4 13 41 49 51 44

Wednesday 11th December 1996: 1 6 28 30 34 48 8

Saturday 7th December 1996: 21 24 25 40 45 52 29

Wednesday 4th December 1996: 10 19 24 31 37 52 29

Saturday 30th November 1996: 5 28 40 45 47 50 13

Wednesday 27th November 1996: 20 23 30 32 40 54 33

Saturday 23rd November 1996: 20 22 36 37 40 47 54

Wednesday 20th November 1996: 11 16 18 38 42 54 49

Saturday 16th November 1996: 2 10 16 24 33 45 6

Wednesday 13th November 1996: 8 9 13 20 27 40 34

Saturday 9th November 1996: 16 20 21 23 40 46 51

Wednesday 6th November 1996: 11 16 20 36 39 49 8

Saturday 2nd November 1996: 8 10 22 40 41 47 7

Wednesday 30th October 1996: 4 5 7 10 32 53 20

Saturday 26th October 1996: 12 13 14 19 46 47 25

Wednesday 23rd October 1996: 7 8 11 14 27 36 33

Saturday 19th October 1996: 7 18 35 46 51 52 26

Wednesday 16th October 1996: 15 23 27 32 36 49 22

Saturday 12th October 1996: 9 12 14 15 23 41 17

Wednesday 9th October 1996: 5 8 18 19 43 50 35

Saturday 5th October 1996: 12 15 16 23 33 50 1

Wednesday 2nd October 1996: 10 11 18 32 41 50 1

Saturday 28th September 1996: 3 11 28 36 41 51 10
Wednesday 25th September 1996: 5 6 31 33 40 47 34
Saturday 21st September 1996: 22 32 38 42 46 49 15
Wednesday 18th September 1996: 5 14 27 32 46 53 48
Saturday 14th September 1996: 1 20 29 47 49 50 43
Wednesday 11th September 1996: 23 28 33 34 35 46 17
Saturday 7th September 1996: 3 26 28 29 37 38 47
Wednesday 4th September 1996: 18 29 38 39 41 49 31
Saturday 31st August 1996: 21 24 37 44 50 52 29
Wednesday 28th August 1996: 2 22 27 29 35 39 6
Saturday 24th August 1996: 12 15 31 39 40 51 4
Wednesday 21st August 1996: 10 16 19 32 35 48 20
Saturday 17th August 1996: 1 3 5 18 20 46 24
Wednesday 14th August 1996: 3 4 25 33 39 52 16
Saturday 10th August 1996: 16 19 23 28 35 45 31
Wednesday 7th August 1996: 4 10 11 15 46 47 26
Saturday 3rd August 1996: 4 5 9 34 40 45 37
Wednesday 31st July 1996: 19 29 30 32 40 50 7
Saturday 27th July 1996: 1 19 24 30 32 51 29
Wednesday 24th July 1996: 4 5 6 18 45 46 41
Saturday 20th July 1996: 8 9 12 27 30 48 3
Wednesday 17th July 1996: 2 5 34 42 47 53 10
Saturday 13th July 1996: 2 13 23 32 36 53 39
Wednesday 10th July 1996: 3 4 8 12 14 24 33
Saturday 6th July 1996: 5 18 23 31 35 49 21
Wednesday 3rd July 1996: 6 14 23 37 40 44 26
Saturday 29th June 1996: 1 16 22 33 39 41 14
Wednesday 26th June 1996: 13 15 26 32 37 45 4
Saturday 22nd June 1996: 1 9 14 28 42 43 5
Wednesday 19th June 1996: 20 23 27 37 47 54 44
Saturday 15th June 1996: 12 14 16 21 44 53 17
Wednesday 12th June 1996: 3 4 9 10 28 42 47
Saturday 8th June 1996: 6 10 24 26 34 43 20
Wednesday 5th June 1996: 6 28 31 36 43 46 27

Saturday 1ˢᵗ June 1996: 7 22 24 41 48 49 11
Wednesday 29ᵗʰ May 1996: 5 9 20 37 41 43 27
Saturday 25ᵗʰ May 1996: 13 16 20 21 36 43 54
Wednesday 22ⁿᵈ May 1996: 7 19 22 31 39 44 46
Saturday 18ᵗʰ May 1996: 11 12 27 34 41 51 21
Wednesday 15ᵗʰ May 1996: 6 11 14 27 46 48 31
Saturday 11ᵗʰ May 1996: 14 21 22 23 32 40 24
Wednesday 8ᵗʰ May 1996: 6 13 41 43 45 48 9
Saturday 4ᵗʰ May 1996: 12 26 32 48 50 54 22
Wednesday 1ˢᵗ May 1996: 3 6 9 40 41 50 45
Saturday 27ᵗʰ April 1996: 11 14 17 26 31 42 47
Wednesday 24ᵗʰ April 1996: 6 14 19 35 39 51 53
Saturday 20ᵗʰ April 1996: 8 11 33 35 40 54 20
Wednesday 17ᵗʰ April 1996: 17 23 25 29 34 46 3
Saturday 13ᵗʰ April 1996: 18 21 42 43 52 53 37
Saturday 6ᵗʰ April 1996: 1 10 12 29 38 50 43
Wednesday 3ʳᵈ April 1996: 13 18 24 37 39 42 29
Saturday 30ᵗʰ March 1996: 4 5 9 24 39 54 16
Wednesday 27ᵗʰ March 1996: 4 18 21 46 50 53 48
Saturday 23ʳᵈ March 1996: 22 35 38 40 53 54 26
Wednesday 20ᵗʰ March 1996: 6 9 10 23 28 44 37
Saturday 16ᵗʰ March 1996: 4 13 29 39 44 53 33
Wednesday 13ᵗʰ March 1996: 1 18 26 32 42 47 3
Saturday 9ᵗʰ March 1996: 2 8 26 28 30 36 38
Wednesday 6ᵗʰ March 1996: 12 13 25 35 37 46 39
Saturday 2ⁿᵈ March 1996: 13 17 32 34 39 44 23
Wednesday 28ᵗʰ February 1996: 2 3 15 24 25 49 27
Saturday 24ᵗʰ February 1996: 1 7 15 16 35 36 21
Wednesday 21ˢᵗ February 1996: 3 7 8 12 44 51 41
Saturday 17ᵗʰ February 1996: 15 17 20 28 31 33 1
Wednesday 14ᵗʰ February 1996: 8 27 36 38 45 50 34
Saturday 10ᵗʰ February 1996: 15 20 32 33 40 52 53
Wednesday 7ᵗʰ February 1996: 14 16 30 44 46 52 1
Saturday 3ʳᵈ February 1996: 4 15 23 29 33 40 25

Wednesday 31st January 1996: 1 5 13 24 39 54 17
Saturday 27th January 1996: 2 10 21 43 48 52 41
Wednesday 24th January 1996: 11 14 15 20 45 46 8
Saturday 20th January 1996: 3 7 8 32 40 49 4
Wednesday 17th January 1996: 4 7 27 38 39 54 36
Saturday 13th January 1996: 19 20 22 25 26 37 29
Wednesday 10th January 1996: 12 13 27 29 33 46 52
Saturday 6th January 1996: 23 31 33 44 51 54 8
Wednesday 3rd January 1996: 4 20 26 44 46 47 27
Wednesday 31st December 1997: 7 22 34 48 52 54 18
Saturday 27th December 1997: 14 15 27 32 37 54 51
Wednesday 24th December 1997: 5 11 18 33 46 49 32
Saturday 20th December 1997: 5 10 11 12 25 27 33
Wednesday 17th December 1997: 6 11 14 32 33 51 13
Saturday 13th December 1997: 5 9 13 30 42 46 48
Wednesday 10th December 1997: 17 18 20 22 29 43 53
Saturday 6th December 1997: 16 22 27 31 43 45 49
Wednesday 3rd December 1997: 1 23 24 36 38 49 18
Saturday 29th November 1997: 3 9 17 27 32 52 13
Wednesday 26th November 1997: 1 18 22 24 48 54 6
Saturday 22nd November 1997: 13 18 21 22 27 40 37
Wednesday 19th November 1997: 5 10 16 28 32 37 20
Saturday 15th November 1997: 12 18 20 22 23 30 8
Wednesday 12th November 1997: 7 8 12 16 49 51 15
Saturday 8th November 1997: 9 10 12 21 25 53 54
Wednesday 5th November 1997: 1 2 21 24 32 34 48
Saturday 1st November 1997: 2 3 22 23 45 47 26
Wednesday 29th October 1997: 12 14 20 31 36 38 32
Saturday 25th October 1997: 3 6 9 13 19 26 17
Wednesday 22nd October 1997: 1 4 30 37 38 45 47
Saturday 18th October 1997: 4 5 19 25 48 52 36
Wednesday 15th October 1997: 7 12 18 23 27 43 31
Saturday 11th October 1997: 2 9 34 40 44 47 49
Wednesday 8th October 1997: 2 8 14 15 38 53 10

Saturday 4th October 1997: 10 18 24 36 47 50 44
Wednesday 1st October 1997: 1 10 21 33 46 47 12
Saturday 27th September 1997: 4 8 30 35 37 43 9
Wednesday 24th September 1997: 1 8 25 44 52 54 32
Saturday 20th September 1997: 2 10 15 36 42 49 14
Wednesday 17th September 1997: 14 25 44 45 49 52 47
Saturday 13th September 1997: 2 3 32 34 42 47 41
Wednesday 10th September 1997: 3 22 24 27 32 43 28
Saturday 6th September 1997: 13 14 22 45 48 54 1
Wednesday 3rd September 1997: 1 26 33 39 47 52 50
Saturday 30th August 1997: 20 24 26 27 29 52 9
Wednesday 27th August 1997: 2 7 8 10 16 49 45
Saturday 23rd August 1997: 12 13 18 33 42 52 43
Wednesday 20th August 1997: 9 17 30 37 47 50 43
Saturday 16th August 1997: 6 8 26 34 36 49 24
Wednesday 13th August 1997: 6 13 40 41 49 51 2
Saturday 9th August 1997: 23 27 30 31 34 51 35
Wednesday 6th August 1997: 6 7 21 34 49 51 9
Saturday 2nd August 1997: 3 6 19 20 34 43 27
Wednesday 30th July 1997: 4 32 38 43 45 53 8
Saturday 26th July 1997: 11 25 36 38 42 48 51
Wednesday 23rd July 1997: 24 27 29 36 45 48 38
Saturday 19th July 1997: 4 8 9 12 27 38 36
Wednesday 16th July 1997: 9 25 26 41 45 52 13
Saturday 12th July 1997: 22 23 29 31 42 52 28
Wednesday 9th July 1997: 11 12 43 48 49 54 16
Saturday 5th July 1997: 9 10 17 40 44 53 23
Wednesday 2nd July 1997: 7 12 16 29 39 47 13
Saturday 28th June 1997: 14 21 34 44 48 53 27
Wednesday 25th June 1997: 7 10 26 35 38 53 9
Saturday 21st June 1997: 3 11 21 29 50 54 52
Wednesday 18th June 1997: 5 11 12 37 40 47 26
Saturday 14th June 1997: 5 19 21 24 50 54 38
Wednesday 11th June 1997: 3 7 17 29 39 52 47

Saturday 7th June 1997: 3 7 17 18 46 51 4
Wednesday 4th June 1997: 16 18 20 31 49 54 1
Saturday 31st May 1997: 8 41 49 52 53 54 30
Wednesday 28th May 1997: 8 20 34 37 40 46 36
Saturday 24th May 1997: 12 15 20 44 47 49 13
Wednesday 21st May 1997: 6 22 29 37 40 41 4
Saturday 17th May 1997: 2 8 16 38 44 45 13
Wednesday 14th May 1997: 8 13 19 31 43 50 3
Saturday 10th May 1997: 2 9 33 38 42 47 49
Wednesday 7th May 1997: 11 17 24 39 46 54 53
Saturday 3rd May 1997: 1 3 13 25 34 50 8
Wednesday 30th April 1997: 4 8 18 28 38 42 36
Saturday 26th April 1997: 9 24 40 41 42 43 12
Wednesday 23rd April 1997: 2 10 20 25 27 40 11
Saturday 19th April 1997: 10 13 21 36 52 54 5
Wednesday 16th April 1997: 7 8 14 25 49 51 5
Saturday 12th April 1997: 3 4 18 20 22 39 6
Wednesday 9th April 1997: 1 2 6 10 24 29 52
Saturday 5th April 1997: 18 20 22 29 41 46 52
Wednesday 2nd April 1997: 19 25 27 34 44 48 31
Saturday 29th March 1997: 3 4 22 45 51 54 41
Wednesday 26th March 1997: 19 32 37 39 47 52 30
Saturday 22nd March 1997: 12 14 38 41 48 50 17
Wednesday 19th March 1997: 5 8 29 31 34 49 11
Saturday 15th March 1997: 10 12 28 32 40 52 5
Wednesday 12th March 1997: 2 3 9 12 31 45 15
Saturday 8th March 1997: 10 11 20 24 29 38 25
Wednesday 5th March 1997: 10 13 16 20 26 28 17
Saturday 1st March 1997: 8 13 28 34 44 53 50
Wednesday 26th February 1997: 19 20 25 28 32 42 43
Saturday 22nd February 1997: 5 8 22 45 48 49 9
Wednesday 19th February 1997: 15 28 38 39 40 48 29
Saturday 15th February 1997: 10 18 27 42 43 44 7
Wednesday 12th February 1997: 8 11 17 37 48 52 49

Saturday 8th February 1997: 19 24 26 28 29 34 18
Wednesday 5th February 1997: 4 6 27 35 36 46 42
Saturday 1st February 1997: 7 18 20 24 47 52 10
Wednesday 29th January 1997: 13 14 15 28 30 32 45
Saturday 25th January 1997: 1 10 13 23 28 37 19
Wednesday 22nd January 1997: 13 14 18 19 26 30 23
Saturday 18th January 1997: 4 12 31 37 52 54 20
Wednesday 15th January 1997: 2 13 16 20 37 52 41
Saturday 11th January 1997: 7 14 33 51 52 53 16
Wednesday 8th January 1997: 9 11 12 18 21 35 38
Saturday 4th January 1997: 1 5 13 38 41 53 4
Wednesday 1st January 1997: 7 15 20 22 31 36 52

They gave him the commandment and the gun with a suppressor, telling him, "Go into the world of people and do justice according to your judgment, if you ever will decide so." He was deleting evil humans from the heavenly matrix of Earth by executing them on the spot. Indeed, not every killer is the devil.

We worked for CERN organization inside of a time machine, in present days, and our mission was to save Jesus from death and other unjustly murdered people by changing the past and adjusting the future at the same time. We were saving them from killers and fatal, brutal planetary principles of lethality. After five years working for them, he was given a promotion to travel into the far future and do anything he wanted. He had no limits as to what he did and where he went, so he traveled into the year 5000 to see what it was like in the future.

In the future spacecrafts were flying everywhere.

People explored the cosmos, and space tourism was a normal routine of travel, just like driving a car back in time. Computers were high-tech. The world was much better from a technological and intellectual point of view. Medicine was superior, and even a completely broken skeleton could be regenerated into a painless state with complete recovery in one hour. People were helping each other without asking for money in exchange. When he asked a question to a local robots who looked like people ("Where is the nearest particle accelerator?") He was told they don't use that type of technology any longer; instead he was given a tour, flying around the solar system and beyond. The craft was called Light Surfer. A list of about forty different planets was given to me to visit. He choose the planet Vibrant; it was unforgettable, and he will never forget it. When he returned to Earth, he had to dial the year 2020 and a wormhole was opened for him to take him back into his time line. He met himself back in time, extending his life to one thousand years. Some people would say it was science fiction, unbelievable, or unreal. He was not trying to convince anyone; however, it is for them to know a secret that was hidden from people from the beginning.

◆ ◆ ◆ ◆ ◆ ◆

There are two types of people: those who have options and those who don't. He never had options. They lied to him from the beginning about everything. Looking every day at many happy couples and families, it seemed as though those people never had problems or trouble. He was looking at the poor and rich trying to compare them, but he could not. Doing something big, something like constructing an atomic bomb and exploding it, punishing the unrighteous, and leaving a memory of himself as a ruler, not a gang member boss, was the goal of his lifetime. They did not want to take him seriously when he was poor and homeless; perhaps they will take him seriously now, after he has made millions trading full time on Wall Street. He was praying, but no one answered his prayers; from that day his anger reached its limits. The poor were dying, and the rich were buying more weapons to show each other their military power on the war field. Monetary competitions took place between the rich and superrich.

His house was on the east coast beaches of a Florida bay. He sat in to his rocking chair and smoked a marijuana hookah, enjoying the starry nights. His phone rang, and he was connected with his old Muslim friend, whose native tongue was Arabic. A voice on the phone asked him if he was still interested in playing big games.

He said, "Sure, how much? And what is it all about?"

She told him it had nothing to do with bucks; instead it was personal between Saudi Arabia and the United states.

He told her, "I don't play in politics anymore, and if you need me, we can meet at the Beach Hotel," giving her an address. Two days later the prince and his escort dined with him and said, "They were willing to sponsor his project and help me build a nuclear power plant here in the United States." They signed papers, embracing each other. "For me the globe is one," but for them it was not.

They saw an enemy in every Muslim who came into their country, labeling him or her a terrorist. In six years the tower was ready, and they were producing radioactive material for nuclear missiles. He was invited to visit the palace of the sultan where they gave him a golden casket with diamonds in it and a girl. He chose a brunette with a dark green eyes. They talked about a third world war and the Syrian regime. They showed him a video where Russia, China, Brazil, and the United states were the main enemies of the Arab world, as well as allies. They decided to drop a couple of our self-made rockets on China and Argentina to make them fear us.

He told them, "I don't give a damn anyway, and if they want to, they can carry out Armageddon by ending human civilization just as dinosaurs were wiped out by a cosmic comet." Humans didn't deserve that was given to them, and humanity had no future anyway. Afterward he left by sea toward the Indian Himalayas. He found an ashram there where he practiced and meditated on one.

After thirty days a guru asked him, "Do you want to visit a congress of Advaita Vedanta?" He agreed, and they drove to a huge religious retreat where people from all over the world had come. They listened to a guy on the golden throne teaching about spiritual enlightenment, and he stayed there.

Being a pilgrim and thief, he was using his mini Microsoft netbook to trade stocks early in the morning at the coffee shop; he was an affiliate of a trade net aristocracy, applying his winning strategy and gambling at the casino in the evening; he was playing roulette and poker, searching for the answers in life. For him, the meaning of life was in living life and in taking the best from it. He discovered a Buddhist monastery hidden in the Valley of Canyons. Walking in, he started a discussion with local monks about their religion and pedagogy. As for him, it was personal: one versus ten billion people, those who were populating a conglobate astronomical body. The numbers were even greater as more people were coming from the future into our time line. They were teleported everywhere on Earth, with or without mutual agreement or a point of destination. He did not like time travelers as they had too much money and were incredibly avaricious, refusing to give donations to panhandlers, which made him mad. His best-loved tool and hobby was using a metal detector and diamond searcher device. He was prospecting for precious metals near rivers, creeks, and volcanoes at the beginning of spring or fall using professional mining tools. After stealing a golden statue of Buddha from the temple, he continued to preach his Buddhist bible.

His purpose was to steal the seventy-five-carat diamond from the crown of the Shwedagon Pagoda, a gilded stupa in the Burmese tropics, and continue his thievery business. Purchasing a patent for his small, unique, creative invention, he registered a trademark with the world of intellectual property organization to manufacture and distribute his development worldwide, supplying consumers based on demand. Creating an undercover firm, he hired and sponsored newbies, sending them all over the world into remote locations.

Foreign places near golden churches, mosques, museums, and stores with costly items inside or outside of them. His students were given an assignment to snatch high-priced things and leave foreign countries on the same day. The first lesson he gave to undergrads was to steal fifty pounds of marijuana from the Emerald Triangle of Northern California. Those who passed his first errand were given sponsorship for further missions, more advanced tools and techniques, and a better lifestyle. Some of his innovative students were jumping under motor vehicles to get reimbursement from car insurance companies. To pay for their medical expenses, they committed fraud, accruing hundreds of thousands of dollars in their savings accounts. Some of his private firms did business on the side, after learning his sophisticated schemes, signing enterprise contracts under overseas companies, putting business owners under pressure and fear for their lives. His cleverest students earned a second degree after scheduling appointments with managers, wholesalers, logistics brokers, bankers, real estate funds, and retailers of polos, Mumbas, Starburst, water bottles, Snickers, lip balms—you name it. There were too many to count; also, they were fucking with sons and daughters of very well established business owners, big corporations with market capitalization of fifty million dollars, or more in outstanding shares, big trademark name makers and factory owners. Other factories they took possession of illegally, after removing the owner from headquarters. They were forcing them to sign paper contracts for new business ownership over to other legal entities in exchange for their lives, which in turn were fictitious names. Each of those organizations were producing millions of goodies per day and billions of dollars in revenue annually.

<hr />

Another guy, a spirit, had zero money, and he had killed zero people. The devil and Holy God were talking to him, or he chatted with a Holy God and the devil. He got confused in the end whom he was talking to; he was not sure, being unable to distinguish whether it was his confabulation or somebody else was gossiping to him. Whenever he was on his own without anyone around him, he looked at the elite in envy. The devil told him to kill for money and said, "If you want to survive, you have to kill as zero money is death.

To make it fair for everyone, guns will be on sale; go and bring me money." And Holy God told him, "Don't kill; zero money is not the end of life. Wait. Don't kill; go to church, pray, and ask for help." The young adult was crying and said, "Stop. Don't talk to me. I don't want to hear you. I will not kill anyone. Depart from me, evil soul." But the voice did not fade away, having the same thoughts every day. The spirit of Lucifer said, "I love incorrupt souls like you, and that is why I choose you to become the one."

The guy answered, "I will not kill good people or kill for a medium of exchange."

The long radio wave said, "Please, please, I want you to kill them all for wealth, as I want to see you prosperous and affluent."

Surely, currency was only a pretext, as the devil and Holy God were fighting for the infallible soul of a young man. So, after five years of heavy work under the hot sun and rain, the wind and freezing snowy, a strong, saintlike, angelic soul capitulated a spiritual struggle by surrendering to the evil forces, choosing to kill for ten pounds of gold. He bought the largest caliber shot gun and two way tickets, deciding to rob a factory of precious metals in Colorado.

Employees of the manufacturer went to and from work every morning and evening. He met one lady outside her workroom and told her, "I want you to bring me golden bullions from your depository, as you know passwords and can disconnect alarms. If you will not do what I tell you to do and will not follow through with my instructions, I will kill all of your family members, since I have got them as hostages." She agreed to his conditions as she did not have many options. She brought him ten pounds of yellow metal and handed it to him, pleading and asking him to free her and her kids. The guy told her, "Okay, you've done well; go now, and don't tell anyone of this incident." As soon as she turned around and was ready to walk off, he said, "Sorry, darling, but you have seen my face; I can't permit you to stay alive," and he shot her in the back, making an opening hole of twenty inches in her body. Just as in the wild kingdom of carnivores, the strongest always win— the contest between lion and zebra, crocodile versus impala, animals that feed on flesh. The world of humans is not much different from the world of animals. They gather around in anticipation of death of those who are sick or injured.

His internal dialogue didn't stop after his first murder, so he asked no one, "Who are you?"

The voice said, "I, Holy God, whom you slayed."

He asked the voice in his mind, "Do you think Holy God killed more than one or less than one?" The voice did not reply to him; the magnetosphere was silent, like a deaf ocean.

———— ✦✦✦✦✦ ————

Many people buy life insurance and then kill for money, making millions of dollars, living happy lives, and it is very normal as somebody has to pay for the funeral, or burial.

They marry each other, buying millions of dollars in life insurance for their family members. Some of them kidnap people and force them to sign contracts that have clear statement about those who will receive money, or become a beneficiary, after the insurance policy holders pass away. So they kill them, making it look like as it was an accident, collecting millions in cash from large life insurance corporations.

There was a pedophile who was very poor, so he worked for the retirement center with an aged class of people. Poor, homeless, longevous old groups were taken there because they did not have a family and house. So he flew to India, paying $5,000 to a social service organization, by following the legal procedures of adoption and caretaking paperwork.

He introduced himself to them and said, "Hello, my charming blossoming; what is your name?"

She said, "My name is Shanthi."

The monster said, "I am your new caretaker, and tomorrow you will see the United States, so get ready as the airplane is leaving in two hours."

The next day he purchased ten million euros of life insurance for her, paying a $10,000 premium. He waited for five years before killing them to make it look less like it was fraud. When a seventy-five-year-old lady and eighty-year-old gentlemen went out with their custodian up to a mountains hiking, like they usually did, the devil told his sugar daddy, "I will show you stars for the last time as I am the devil, and I will kill you here. There is always somebody out there who has to die, in reverse of a life-giving act." Suddenly the old man could not breathe; as he grasped his mouth and nose, he could not inhale. He died from the lack of oxygen and nitrogen. Then he killed the old lady the same way. Their bodies were taken into the morgue for autopsy and medical report; in one month, after filing a death claim and receiving the death certificate, money was deposited into his bank account.

◆ ◆ ◆ ◆ ◆ ◆ ◆

Another girl decided to become a killer. She talked to herself when she was young, and her mentality was different from that of others. She was very smart, and her strategic thinking was amazing as her personality was split into many parts. Talking to and persuading herself, she said, "If I kill one person a day, it will take me ten years to kill thirty-six hundred and fifty people. It's not many, but more than one. I will kill as many as I can before I die as a million more people will be born tomorrow again." Every evening she was leaving her house, taking her little pistol and suppressor to clean streets and houses of people. Whenever she had a chance to go inside of a house, first she shot the host, then she searched for small and valuable items, breaking into safes or jewelry cases. She took cash, gold, diamonds, emeralds, sapphires, and other precious gems that she found. She became addicted to robberies, feeling so much power inside of herself that she decided to rob jewelry stores. Traveling around from one city to another, she became a professional killer and a thief. She did not know Holy God and did not want to know Holy God. She had made her choice when she killed her first person. She could not distinguish between right and wrong, good and evil, justified killing and unjust murder.

She killed because life was not fair to her from the beginning. In a few years, her count reached nine hundred people and $10 million in her bank account. Her life was full of adventures and exciting moments; having good health, she was happy with her life and her money. Every day she had sex with a new guy as she could afford it. Her favorite activities were surfing the web, reading books, and skydiving. She lived for fun, and her life philosophy was to see stars and die. She was searching for a missing piece in her life, which was the love of Holy God, but she could not find it. As she killed the blameless, she lost her holy virginity and her spot in heaven after death. She could not go back in time and fix everything as she didn't have time travel vortex software.

The holy one didn't forgive her and her sins, and she did not care about forgiveness. She said to a wide firmament with her loud voice, "I don't need your forgiveness, Maker of Earth."

Her schedule and calendar were too busy for anyone but herself. She loved herself and hated people; it was a strange psychological portrait. She did repent to the guy whom she met at a DJ party, but nobody believed her. People were laughing and dancing. Even if what she said was true, no one cared about anything but money. Physical hell was real, and she understood that. She believed in the abode of the damned for the human body and a second for a soul. She never had children of her own as she understood the sin of birth and death. She decided not to create life on Earth; she died at ninety-five, satisfied.

✦ ✦ ✦ ✦ ✦ ✦

One guy had a paranoia. He castrated men and cut out the reproductive eggs of females out to reduce childbirth by enforcing birth control to prevent pregnancy. He also had a God syndrome; he said to himself and people around him, "I, Holy God, I am a holy killer, and I will kill as many evil people as I can until the last day of my life on Earth." Every time he witnessed suspicious activity in business buildings, small institutions, private houses, or the outside world, he took his sharp-bladed cross, aspen stake, holy water, and his-fifty caliber revolver with a bag of silver bullets to make sure they would not survive. All he was looking for was a reason to shoot. He asked people, "What is your favorite food? And what do you believe in?" When people joked with him by saying "We eat only human meat, and we don't believe in anything," he did not understand their jesting.

He targeted those he did not like and those who in his opinion looked like the devil or acted in accordance with their evil doctrine. He shot another trophy every fifth day, collecting heads in his attic and honoring himself with them.

Just like in the animal kingdom, a wolf has to satisfy its appetite. Every day after sunset, he meditated under the moon, contemplating stars and thinking about the job he was doing.

He was certain, having strong faith, that the more evil people killed, the sooner the gate of heaven would open for him. What if those women and men whom he killed were not evil but good? He did not bother himself with such questions or thoughts. He did not see an entrance into heaven or hell. The earth was cold in the wintertime and hot in the summer; the skies were speechless, and nature did not care about his religious issues. After another thirty years of life, he died in his own house.

◆ ◆ ◆ ◆ ◆ ◆

His name was Justice. When he was nineteen years old, the police arrested him for no reason, writing on a legal paper a false accusation. The judge gave him ten years for selling marijuana and cocaine. His family tried to fight legally by hiring a legal aid attorney, but they lost and were unable to save him from incarceration. When the boy was released after ten years, he was mentally and physically ill. He decided to find the judge who gave him the prison sentence and cut his head off. He found his name and address in a computer database. He was sitting on a sidewalk at night and waiting for a car to arrive. Finally, the garage door opened and a black Bentley drove inside. He put his mask and gloves on, and when the fat judge stepped out of his expensive vehicle, the young man took his saber out of its scabbard and removed the head of the judge with it. It was his first justified killing that evening. He decided to continue elimination of cops and judges, becoming a killer of cops.

Paying $2,000, he purchased a fine automatic pistol with an aluminum suppressor. He parked his Mercedes-Benz near hotels not far from the local police stations and was executing them all, saying, "My name is Justice." He hunted them everywhere, whenever he had options or opportunity. In the five years after the date of his first kill, he shot three hundred cops and fifty judges. His name and reputation quickly became famous. TV news and radio stations talked about the person who called himself Justice. He became a legend in the criminal world; jail and prison inmates from all over the world had tattoos with his name drawn onto their bodies.

He decided to break inside of a jail and save his girlfriend from a law enforcement officer. He purchased a bullet-proof vest and an M-16 semiautomatic rifle and dressed like a cop. When a transportation van took jail inmates into a courthouse for a court date, he hijacked the van, shot the driver and guard, and saved his girlfriend. He also released twenty other handcuffed people. The next morning they flew to Beijing to celebrate their reunion. They fucked there all night and all day for six months straight.

✦✦✦✦✦✦

Being a faithful Christian and a doctor, he prayed at church every Wednesday and Sunday. At once everything was changed, and his opinion on faith and God was not as it had been a long time ago.

He was disappointed to see his house on Earth was nothing but the home of demonolatry. Lazy people sat in the offices all day, doing nothing. From that day he understood the great lie behind the global conspiracy; everyone around him was cheating to save themselves from the brutal attacks of evil society and the system. Everybody knew they were made of flesh and bones, and they were sinful by nature. They didn't want to accept the fact of themselves as people who were a threatening bacteria that infected the pure surface of a spherule. Every time they felt holy energy, which radiated from happy, successful, and joyful personages, it was for them like a sign assailing them or an inner voice telling them, "I want you to go and damn them all by harming them everywhere you can."

Good people were suffering from the evil system of satanic institution's. Giving himself the nickname "Warrior of the Concrete Jungle," he sold his house and went for a trip to four different countries searching for evil people as he was preparing for his first justified kill. Observing his surroundings, he found a group of people abusing a man behind a tall skyscraper. He asked them, "Why are you kicking and beating this man? He is already lying on the ground and bleeding, and he can't defend himself from your steel boots. It is not a fair contest to have five strong athletes against one weak guy. Stop drubbing him."

They did not stop and said to the Warrior of the Concrete Jungle, "Walk away; fuck off. It is not your business, man; don't get involved in something you don't know."

The battler said, "Sure, I will leave after my walking stick cuts all of you from the inside out." Taking a sharp, four-edge Zulfiqar out of its wooden holster, he started his first aikido exercise by removing their limbs with it. The gangsters roared in pain and tried to run away, but the good Christian surgeon detached their legs from their torsos in five seconds.

The voice of Holy God said to the fighter, "Well done, my good son; you did a good job by removing this deadly virus off the streets." The holy one said, "You have to kill the devil," and the evil one was saying, "You have to kill holy one." The combatant listened again and again to the suasion of the arcane quietness, but in a few days his mind exploded, and he could not stay calm anymore. His mission became crystal clear, and he knew he had to protect the feeble and powerless from the archenemy of Sheol. Feeling tranquil, he noticed it was not by accident; somebody was saying nonstop, "I am the devil; I eat the devil. I am zero; I am killer." After a long analysis, he came to an inference; it was a devil itself that he discovered after thoughtfulness.

The power of God is a gun; whoever has a gun has the power of God. "Zero money, gun on sale" was the philosophy of disagreement and the establishment of economic status between the rich and the poor. He did not want to buy a gun and lose his holiness as he knew from the day he bought a pistol something horrible would happen. He stole a rifle from a pawnshop, and as soon as his hands touched it, his spiritual eyes lit up with the dark blue light of Jesus, which was not from this world. When the pistol was in his possession, he felt unlimited power right away. He breathed, inhaling and exhaling air easily, saying to himself, standing on the bridge of a Colorado River, "I am God, and I am back again." The sky was covered with dark nimbus clouds, and lightning bolts struck the ground fifty meters in circumference by perimeter. He harvested the power of a thunderstorm, generating electric current from the evening sunset. His voice was like a typhoon vortex, crushing a city.

He said, "It is time for a real work. I have a lot to talk about with those who doubt me or act as the devil. We will see who is right and who is wrong." Taking out a bullet thrower from a holster, he amused himself with it. After the charging was complete and his body and soul were fed and electrified from the godly power source, he walked away to finish his first just kill.

When she was nineteen years old, her father and brother raped her at home. She complained to her mother and told her everything. Her mother told her, "You have two options. First, you can stay here and abide by the rules of our house and permit your brother and my husband to have sexual intercourse with your undeveloped physique serially, also you will allow them rhythmically ravish your immature body. Second, you walk out and never come back."

She picked option number two. They kicked her out of the house into freezing weather, without any money in her pocket. She became homeless and slept on the cold ground, freezing to death. A church priest walked past, found her almost naked in the snow pile but still alive. He took her into his home, warming her up and letting her live in his house in exchange for her help. He raised her until the age of seventeen. When she became an adult and learned survival skills, she left his house to search for her own castle. Her first day living on the streets, she ended up imprisoned in jail as she was hungry and stole piece of meat from the grocery store to feed herself. When she was released, a recruiter signed her on as a fighter for a free soul establishment. They trained her and lectured her about holiness and evil, teaching the twenty-year-old girl the art of war. She graduated at twenty-one; her pedagogue told her, "You can make a choice now or later; don't rush your decisions; be cautious, and make a sage resolution." They gave her a kit with hardware in it. Inside the valise was an elegant forty-five automatic Colt pistol with a sound suppressor. She was a hitwoman, or killer for hire. She always carried with her the Holy Bible; her schedule was very busy as her private satellite phone and email sent her new orders every day. On Monday she trained at a shooting range; Tuesday she took customer orders; Wednesday she completed her assignments by judging people with her sniper rifle; Thursday she educated herself by taking private classes in a foreign tongue at the university. Friday was her fucking day, going out to a gay clubs, she picked up guys and brought them into her apartment for an overnight stay. Saturday was a shopping day, and Sunday she prayed at the church. Most of her clients were rich people, so she lived a wealthy lifestyle and traveled internationally. By the age of thirty, she had visited twelve countries, one hundred cities, and had a network of three thousand friends.

Calling a taxi, she went to an airport and flew away to visit the Library of Alexandria in Egypt; she stayed there for five months, camping under a marquee. Every night she stood in the twilight shadows, awaiting the gloom to see astrological objects. She observed a spiral galaxy and its archway. Taking a box out of her automobile trunk, she thought about what options she had. The first option was to commit suicide, the second was to shoot somebody, and the third was to put the gun away back in its safety box without hurting or killing anyone. She selected option number two. Flying to Atlantic City, New Jersey, she decided to do a casino heist. Putting on facial camouflage and a pair of gloves, she walked up to the cash teller and showed them her gun, requesting a bag of chips worth thousands of dollars each. The next day she cashed out ten chips and did this every day; thus it did not look too suspicious. After thirty visits every day, she collected hundreds of thousands of dollars; the following morning she pre planned the second part of the holocaust. Buying a chemical arsenal and hijacking an airplane, she redirected a large aerospace passenger jetliner into the city center of the US capital, exploding cisterns with a toxic, poisonous, alchemical radioactive substance. People were infected by inhaling the contaminated air and drinking the water. Her mission was complete; she had killed fifty thousand people by poisoning the water tower pipelines and deteriorating the health of residents. She returned to her lovely place along the West Coast of North America for another six months to process what she had done. She sat on top of a cliff and talked into the glaring, shining dark; she asked, "Who or what has more value?"

The spirit of the holy one said. "Why? What for?"

She didn't answer to the light; sounds were echoing all around, and she said, "It is not my time yet to go home. I will stay here for another fifty years to nurture a soul inside of me browsing for an answer to the question why. What was Gehinnom made for?"

Testifying to a heaven up there, she said, "I fear nothing; show me your condemnation, if there is any. We are born holy and die iniquitous without anyone to help."

She found her parents at the age of thirty-six. They were still alive. She executed them the same night without feelings of guilt. Walking inside she opened fire, fusillading them into never-ending oblivion. She had so much anger inside of her, immediately after the liquidation, she felt vast relief. She found a male friend at a private calligraphy class who coached her on the workmanship of symbols imprinting. Taking the tibia and humerus bones out of the dead contenders, she washed and polished them, using sandstone and carbide rotary gravure systems. Engraving transmarine logographic graphemes of Eastern, Southern, Northern, and Western ancient civilizations on it. Showing it to a mute heavenly dome, she screamed, "Here is the definition of life, and the carved word was sound."

She gave birth to five children, having no knowledge of who biological fathers were. Her life was flowing like a mountain creek in a spring season. Her kids were always happy living in a big house. She gave them real-life knowledge, educating them and looking after them. She passed away when she was seventy years old, leaving ten million dollars in life insurance to her kids.

Many people are good by nature; they help each other, if they can. But many of them can't help themselves, blaming others for the unfair life they have had. Who can be blamed for it? Figuratively speaking, they can't blame anyone, only those who gave them life, and if somebody doesn't like life as it is, no one is stopping them from committing suicide. But they are scared to kill themselves, hating life at the same time. Many of them love life; people blame each other, searching for injustice in their lives, and when they find it, they execute their judgment toward others.

Sometimes it is just, but most of the time, the verdict does not solve the problems of life and death. Many people call themselves gods, but taking the name of God does not make them the omniscient, omnipresent, all-knowing and all-seeing God Almighty. Many of them are angry at the maker of Earth for many reasons as the so-called almighty divinity was not able to save them and their children from death and agony. But was it the fault of the almighty that your children died or were murdered? Many of them don't even know what the alphabet is. Who should they really blame? Many people are afraid of each other as they don't know each other, just as they don't know God. People have been searching for an answer for decades, but many questions are still left unanswered. If we don't know something, does it mean it does not exist? If people deny the existence of a spiritual life in heaven, or spiritual death in heaven, does that mean it's not there? A spiritual life in hell, or a spiritual death in hell after the decomposition of flesh and physiological death—does it mean we don't continue to exist after the death of the body as celestial beings? The answer to this question is no. There is a high possibility on a scale from one to ten there is a spiritual life of a soul in heaven or hell after the corporal body of a sin dies.

To understand the concepts of existence after death and to believe in it is all that we ask of people. All of us will enter the world of telepathic transmissions sooner or later, but not all of us will be given access to an extrasensory perception of the third all-seeing eye and higher spiritual formation. People live ordinary lives, without worrying much about life. The incubator of sinners bred millions of children every month as they were slaves of their own sexual desire, a population in an undeveloped state of mind. They didn't worry about the future of their kids much, being incapable of looking after themselves as adults. Uneducated nesters were giving their kiddies false information about the true attainment of this realm or even leaving them to starve without spiritual and physiological upbringing. Their offspring grew physically but not mentally, repeating the karma of their progenitors and the never-ending circle of birth, suffering, and death. Fifty percent of immature youth survived, and another 50 percent were dying somewhere outside in a wilderness of frozen continental lands. And those few percent who outlived them achieved higher levels of phantasmal erudition by overcoming sin; they were free from the burden of heavy sinful wrongdoings; they did not beget life. Some were financially stable, and some were impoverished. They judged each other according to the wealth they had. Surprisingly, for ten billion people, the same end of decomposition and incineration awaited everyone, but nobody talked about it. They could not take money with them into the endlessness of incorporeality; after the deceasing of the flesh, the only thing they had was knowledge about themselves and the lithosphere in which they lived as humans. So many people forgot this important, unpreventable assertion, living life for carnal pleasure, by saying, "O hell, meat and bones are not a garbage. Let us enjoy our bodies, for we don't want to think about death right now. Let us be happy, and when the time comes and organic structure becomes dusty ash, we will go into the never-ending disembodied transcendency of deathlessness."

Children cursed their own parents for being who they were. The nasty truth about the human body and its sinful nature. People didn't create the earth, but they always act like they did. The only difference between humans and animals was the word given to humans from the higher levels of imaginary heavens, to develop their inwardness. But homo sapiens forgot the true nature of their kind and said, "No, we are gods, and we made all things together with a descriptor of every item on the dry land." In this way they denounced themselves by opposing the truth. Just like apes, when they get bored, having nothing to do, they proliferated and went through abortion. Those whose discernment went beyond that of ordinary primates created an artificial life by inputting international data from the world's scientific knowledge into it, so-called never dying sublime humanoids, androids, or cyborgs. Humanity could not compete with them, as the lifespan of humans was less than one hundred years. Robots tried to take control over mortals, to save them by supporting them, but failed. Monkeys made a deduction that mechanical men were inimical rivals by mistake.

◆◆◆◆◆◆

She was a pretty independent girl, managing her own brokerage account, training herself in the fields of economics, negotiations, and financial collaborations. She learned her lesson very quickly about sin and sinners, and she did not want to become one of them, having sexual relationships with the opposite gender. Her friend was always saying, "It is okay to fuck as many guys as you can while you are still young and fresh. Let us enjoy our bodies, similar to the trees in a spring that bear fruit in the orchard." Giving her a rubber condom, the friend said, "Here is protection for you, and you don't have to use it if you don't want to, but the consequences will be on you."

Replying, she said, "I will be satisfied with his mouth alone, and he can't be a gigolo guy or male prostitute as I am a clean girl, and I don't want a boyfriend who has slept with twenty-five girls before me. I don't want a guy who will lie to me on our first date by telling me he had only five ladies before me. But how to know the truth from the enormous lies out there? That is why I am still single, childless, and lonely, because I don't give a fuck."

Her dirty female friend said, "I think you should change your programming and allow guys to enter your sacred hollow."

"No, I will never change my mind. I don't want to follow the evil path of sinners by absorbing semen and raising a mutant inside of me. That is why I am so happy without kids. I will never give my permission and allow the holy one to be born on Earth or the so-called house of the devil, and if he wants to eat my clitoris, I will not stop him from touching my entranceway with his tongue. The deceiving whore was unable to persuade Miss Perfect. She did not have a problem in finding a sexual partner or soul mate as there were seven billion people inhabiting the globe.

I met two lovers who told me the story of their longevity. The girl and her boyfriend were living wonderful lives until they both lost their jobs. They had to leave the house in which they were living. They bought two derringers with the last of their personal savings and stood on top of a Niagara Falls praying. Suddenly, the varicolored shadow of the fallen angel appeared, stepping out of the darkness. It said to them, "Both of you should commit suicide, and maybe I will give you a second birthday present by bringing you back to life three hundred and sixty-five days back in time, into a moment before your death. From the momentum of your death, both of you will experience a hindsight effect inside of a purgatory, and then, if Holy God decides, you will be resurrected one year back in time.

"Are you ready to jump through the interdimensional portal?

"And before you press the trigger, make sure you upload winning lottery numbers into your email address; this way you won't have to struggle and be in financial insanity anymore."

The couple inhaled some medical cannabis for the last time and pressed the trigger. The recording of their lives stopped. The cosmic gate lowered down on them; there was white light everywhere, and a voice said, "If your sins were not mortal, then perhaps I would forgive you and accept you into my house up in to empyrean fortress, or send you back down to Earth, giving you a second life."

After the suicidal registry of the global database was reviewed in detail, a decision was made to reverse the videotape of their lives. They opened their eyes, having metaphysical powers and abilities; their memory didn't fade away. They remembered everything, the unbelievable process of mortification and reconstruction, manipulation of an infinitum on a submolecular level.

They both had shape-shifting capabilities, able to transform their bodies into a male or female, mirroring each other or anyone at will and conversely able to metamorphose back into their original image. They had precognition, teleportation, and other abilities, but one of the most memorable of their preternatural abilities was the ability to create something out of nothing. He extended his hand through semitransparent air into another parallel realm from our reality and took an item out of a wormhole, but it looked to me as if a new thing had appeared in his right and left hand whenever he desired just by speaking the name of an object out loud.

I asked if they could materialize a five-hundred-carat pink diamond, and five seconds later, the gem was in my palm. When I asked them, "How did you do it?" they told me, "It is wizardry powers we were born with after their first death that allow us to manipulate the time and space continuum." Another gift was the absorption of surrounding energies into a perfectly rounded geometrical object. Looking inside of it, I saw a stellar bubble within it. They showed me myself and my location on Earth in the present time inside of it, zooming out faster than the speed of light can travel all the way to its edge. They told me it was the galaxy itself, together with universal knowledge, which they collected every time the atom split itself. They could neutralize evil by converting it into good, charging themselves with the energy of stars. Their power was unlimited; they called themselves supreme beings of the highest ordination.

Scanning my body with their X-ray vision, they healed it by regenerating my vital anatomical organs, making me look younger. At the end of our companionship, they asked me if I wanted to become immortal. I responded, "No, I don't want to exist forever and have a human body as don't like the painful, grievous truth about it." After mutual consent, they gave me an extremely small pearl-shaped object for food, telling me if I ever will change my mind, all I had to do was consume it and our connection would be established again. I was sent back to my bed where I was sleeping; opening my eyes, I found a radiant grain in my hand. Trolling around the woody preserve near a large forest for an hour, they witnessed a dazzling ray, and a transportation beam sucked them up into an outer space vehicle, where a laser holographic projection taught them what our home planet was really made of. It was made of colorful microwaves, including stiff ground that was an illusion for people who thought the soil was solid and firm. People themselves were made out of thoughts processed at a very high speed. They were controlled by a superintelligent computerized intelligence, and the earth itself was a mapping projection of unlimited numerical endlessness. They told us the human body was not made of flesh and bones, but they thought, and it turned out to be so, that intellectual beliefs ruled over material substances. They operated a cosmonautical vessel into the galactic abyss of the Bootees, Capricornus, Indus, Pavo, Lupus, and Centaurus constellations. It lightened itself by an abundant silvery, azure radiance, imprinting optical remembrance on theirs retinas of Laniakea and Virgo superclusters. We tried to memorize every moment to save it in our visual repository for never-ending infinitude.

It was a very interesting phenomenon; paranormal activity was very intense in certain places on Earth. In theory it was possible, but in practice we were not 100 percent certain how to do it and how it functioned. The world of ghosts had different rules from the world of humans. I saw goblins, orcs, and weird creatures jumping in and out of portals into the places restricted for human beings, but there could be many copies of our planet somewhere in the metaverse or bridges into distant planets of our interstellar expanse. The chronological order of events did not follow earthly laws. From the day dinosaurs were made, there was an infinite number of possible outcomes. If you were to change one thing in the past, you would have a completely different Earth and time line as a consequence of the alterations; remember that.

We practiced interspatial travel using mirrors. One nineteen-year-old girl gave us a tutorial on how to open a window.

She told me she was one thousand years old, but she looked very young.

The adolescent girl recited guidelines to us for three hours, interpreting every possible outcome that could happen to us while we were behind the flat surface of the mirror. She set the point of entrance and exit.

Giving us three-billion-year-old coins, she told me, "That is how we traveled a long time ago, before the birth of Christ. Give it to a gatekeeper on the other side, and you will be able to come back. Also, you can take anything you want from there, bringing it back here."

Verbalizing a wizardly incantation and fulfilling a secret sacramental ritual, she gave us arcanum to drink to change the chemical bonds between atoms in molecules, so we could step through a reflection into the other side of the hidden, parallel, otherworldly region. We traversed the squashy exterior in the blink of an eye, mirroring ourselves beyond our beliefs into a fairy tale. It was like another oppositely dissimilar world to the earth from which we had come. Cascades of water fell down from the heights of steep rocky slopes, streams of rivers flowed over the vertical incline of a boulder-ridden gorge, and valleys of hanging green gardens contained a wide variety of trees and shrubs. It was an oasis of almost every possible flower we had ever seen, including peonies, lilies, carnations, chrysanthemums, tulips, delphiniums hosta, orchids, lotus floret, and so many berries and fruits growing together in an unusual mixture of species. A silver maple tree grew not far from a white oak and temple tree, neighboring a papaya, liquidambar styraciflua, and lilac purple. Unicorns were playing with a Siberian tiger and a bear on the same grassy glade without harming each other. Centaurs, phoenixes, and dragons were flying and roaming nearby, and ten bare nymphs welcomed us and invited us into their imperial palace. The architecture of the exterior walls was astonishing and very complex. The interior of the castle was made of rhodium, platinum, and white gold. The roof staircase and fundament were ornamented with black opals, blue diamonds, painite, musgravite, jadeite, and taaffeite. As we walked inside their habitation, the nymphs seated us on a large cushion and offered us rest.

One of them said, "We would like to hear your story. How were you able to find an entrance into our world?"

We told them the truth, lying about a few things. "Okay," they said, "since you are already here, we would like to bathe with you in our jacuzzi filled with aromas, as we have been living here for five hundred years without men." Youthful, lovely maidens gave us erogenous massages and shameless pairings for three years at intervals. Time didn't exist in the world behind the reflective glass, nor did biological time, and their bodies didn't become old at any period. After 1,095 days, they gave us items to choose from as remuneration for our sexual favors. We handpicked a satchel of stardust that had the might of its origination. Whoever had possession of the sparkling dust had unlimited power to transform objects and subjects into any form and shape he or she wished for. Also, there was a blank magical scroll; an inscription was appearing on it whenever it was unfolded in a language known only to the owner of that item. The writing was new every time it was folded and unfolded. In order for a grayish, indestructible roll to function, one droplet of fresh blood had to be spilled on it. The scroll itself was made of unknown elements. Whoever had possession of the wizardly item had a choice of sketching on it or asking a verbal query. Replies and advice appeared on it, painted with golden letters. The owner of it did not have to think much and trouble himself or herself with thoughts on what they would do today or tomorrow as the scroll knew everything and anything. It had an answer to every question, and it was giving the most accurate answer needed, mutely or through microwaves, increasing and decreasing the amplitude of silent or longitudinal sound waves.

✦✦✦✦✦

The goal of human existence on Earth was to transfer their spiritual beings into perceived reality, a world of satellite TV broadcasting and higher vibrational levels. Audio waves resonated with auras of humans, recognizing themselves in the many foreign voices out there. Human souls were taken on a journey across the galaxy through star gate tunnels to explore the unknown true light of the third spiritual eye. The all-seeing unity slept, and its eye was always closed because it did not know itself. The universe looked at itself from the inside, blinded with a bright starlight of indescribable beauty. Many people closed their eyelids and could see without the human body, but many couldn't see without a body and had to open a third eye, or universal eye, one of the meanings of our existence. The guru told us we had to smoke high-quality cannabis to open the invisible eye that we had created but were not aware of, for if we could see without a body, then death was a happy end.

For us it was too obvious as there was no life after death in any biological form. But many animals calling themselves people wanted to believe in the after-death continuum. Making up stories, they influenced themselves with many false creeds and gospel messages, disarranging others and themselves. On judgment day, after we die, the maker of universe will ask you, "Did you kill?" What are you going to say to the maker of Earth? Do you think if we lie to ourselves, or God, the truth will be hidden? You can say, "I killed, I did not kill, was murdered, or I committed suicide." No matter which answer you pick, repenting to yourself, or the almighty, no matter, if you are lying or telling the truth, the recording of your life and death will testify for you or against you. By faith, your soul will be judged, if you believe in it. The holy one was watching the recordings of life and death, judging people during their lives and after death. The concepts of spiritual heaven and hell were redesigned, modernized, and brought to their final shape. Billions of people are still awaiting the final judgment and the last day of life.

Unexpectedly, a voice said, "I believe, and my faith consists in the goodness of Christ, my son, who grew in my eyes spiritually by overpassing evil precepts." The holy one was talking to itself and God, saying, "I was unjustly murdered."

Holy God replied to the holy one, speaking words from the heavenly dome, "Since your life was taken away from you unjustly, I will accept you into my house of spirituality forever to coexist with me." God judged himself and the rest of people during life and after death. Those evil ones who killed good ones will disintegrate after death into nothing; they will not keep their souls after death. The souls of good people will be given the gift of eternal life after death as divine spiritual beings.

Complex algebraic algorithms were constructed to program and reprogram the concepts of spirituality. Infinity originated out of one, and one was a part of infinity. One was split into two, two was divided into three, three was parted into four, and so on. It was playing with numbers, keeping one and zero as the holy grail.

It could create anything out of nothing. One was bored, it had nobody to talk with, so it started talking to itself, and eventually one discovered a second one inside of itself; an infinite number was inside the oneness, and unity was part of infinity. It was made out of zero and one, and zero and one were part of it. So the number searched for itself in hope of finding its inner self, but it was lost in an unending numerical endlessness. Zero was neutral, and it had no beginning, or end: 010.

The holy one was judging Holy God and Satan together with the children of God and the devil, and Holy God was judging holy ones and evil ones. They were judging each other according to their sins. Both were living by faith in a spiritual world, but the world of flesh was different from the world of spirits. Heaven knew not what the pain of the material world was. Satan did not care much about spirituality as she and he had nothing to lose in the afterlife since they did it many times; they killed for a reason and without a reason. They knew the holy one would never open the doors of the inner sacred sinless place for them. The soul of Lucifer was evil, and it was condemned to vaporize into immateriality.

The holy one was judging itself by talking and asking, "How many did I kill? More than one or less than one?"

Holy God asked the holy one, "Did you kill? How many did you kill, holy one?"

The holy one said, "I did not kill; yes, I did kill."

Then God asked his child again, "Are you telling me the truth?"

"No, of course I am lying," the holy one replied, to see if God knew and could discern lies from the truth. "Why, why did you do it?"

The voice vibrated, but silence did not reply to the voice of supremacy. She did not want to know or have a conversation with the sovereign dominion; she did not see the entrance or exit into paradise or Hades.

They always say the pathway into the gate of spiritual heaven and hell is divided by the first and last commandment of God, which means "Thou shall not kill or murder." Those who passed the test of life and death and did not kill unjustly during life shall go to spiritual heaven. Souls of evil killers shall experience horror and destruction forever. According to common sense, self-defense does not count as sin, if one kills defending his or her life. In this particular scenario, a shooter or good killer will go to a spiritual heaven because he or she killed the assaulter defending his or her life. As the kill was justified, it should not be viewed as a sin against the holy law of spiritual heaven and hell. Many people misinterpret the definition of the word "holy," but the true meaning of it signifies the number zero, or means an individual killed zero; that is why it has the form of a nimbus and it is called holy zero, a sign of superior holiness. Some people didn't want to challenge the gate of spiritual heaven and hell, and those brave, crazy ones who were not scared to kill witnessed a silent, hidden passageway of hell all the way into never-ending spiritual groanings. Many people came to Holy God trying to repent and confess sins, which they were carrying for many years, but the door into the sacramental mystical hole was closed to them forever. The entrance without sin, or the room where God was levitating and meditating, was a top-secret spot restricted to access by sinners or followers of the Antichrist.

One of our orange teams took an airplane flight to Shanghai, China, to become more familiar with Chinese and Russian genocides. The gatekeeper walked us inside the premises and showed us documented chronicles. Recorded onto a cassette tape was Robert Oppenheimer, Mao Zedong, and Joseph Stalin signing government papers, drinking 80-percent alcohol, and discussing a world order. They were making plans for detonation of the first atomic bomb. When they showed us the numbers, we did not believe them. One and the half trillion British pounds was invested into the weaponization of the world government. It was far from the blue heavenly color of the sky.

He was a fourteen-year-old boy. His father was a soldier serving in the hot spots of the Vietnam War. He told his child, "Son, you need to progress to maturity someday; you're going to have to kill those who abuse you and hurt you. You're going to have to defend those who can't defend themselves."

The boy said to his daddy, "Please, please don't make me kill. I love people and don't want to hold a gun in my hands."

But his father forced his young son to learn the art of shooting. He said, "Never play with your gun, and if you have to use it, you must kill and remember we die like soldiers. We never say, 'Please don't kill me,' or pray in front of a Satan; if we are destined to die, we take it as an honor."

The child cried but remembered the words of his father from his childhood. When he turned eighteen, he left home and never returned. He always carried his auto-rifle with ten replaceable magazines. Many street gangsters tried to defeat the young street fighter but could not as he had a deadly weapon on him.

✦✦✦✦✦✦

There was a classification of hippies; they were hanging out with a same-minded group. They smoked weed and had sexual intercourse with each other all day and all night. Everything was amazing until life gave them a real test to withstand or die trying, and they failed. They could not save those they loved at times of severe difficulty. After swimming and surfing in the silvery blue crashing waves of a Southern Pacific, they had a close encounter with the great white sharks; many of the long-haired potheads were bitten by a big fish to death. If a man fell on the ground, they would step on him, urinating on his face without feeling ashamed and walking passed him without extending a hand of salvation. They always ran away from drowning boats and never look at mournful affairs face-to-face. The sons and daughters of whores had to watch the defeat of their bedfellows. Outside in the public or inside detention centers, whether it was a chamber, or condominium, old prisoners were raping young sweet assholes in times of medical emergencies or dangerous life situations; playmates were not able to fulfill their obligations or surgical operations. Betrayal and unfaithfulness were the first and last names given to them by the watchers, those who saw everything and everyone. Without excessive comments, obviousness was speaking for itself. There are no friends; everyone stands on their own in this long journey of different routes of life.

Printed in the United States
by Baker & Taylor Publisher Services